JUST ONE **NIGHT**

USA TODAY BESTSELLING AUTHOR
CHARITY FERRELL

Just One Night

Copyright © 2018 Charity Ferrell

All rights reserved.

www.charityferrell.com

Cover Designer: Mayhem Cover Creations

Editor: Jovana Shirley, Unforeseen Editing, www.unforeseenediting.com

PROLOGUE

Willow

"WHAT THE FUCK HAVE I DONE?"

I've never had a one-night stand, but I'm positive those aren't the first words you want to hear the morning after.

I twist in the warm yet unfamiliar sheets and can taste last night's whiskey in my mouth.

I lick my lips—*wrong move*—and regret it when the flavor of him hits my tongue.

Him.

The man pacing in front of me with his head tipped down while wearing only boxer briefs that show off his bulge.

I've lost count of the number of times the word *fuck* has fallen from his mouth.

I don't know what to say.

Don't know what to do.

"How the fuck could I have done this?" he continues.

My heart rams into my rib cage, just as hell-bent on escaping this situation as I am.

I'm stupid.

So damn stupid.

I drag the sheet up until it hits my chin, and he runs a hand through his thick bedhead hair, tugging at the roots the same way I did last night when he went down on me. He doesn't know I am awake and can hear him, but that doesn't make the wound any less severe.

His head rises when I jump out of bed and start scrambling for my clothes. The sheet drops from my body at the same time I frantically pull my dress over my head.

I have to get out of here.

Our eyes meet as I yank my panties up my legs. Apology and torture spill across his clenching jaw. The tears are coming, warning me to look away so that he won't see my humiliation, but I can't. I stare and silently beg him to change the outcome of this morning. The string to our stare down is cut by the sound of my name, a mere whisper falling from his loose lips.

I dart out of the bedroom, snag my purse I drunkenly threw over the arm of the couch, and rush toward the front door, not even bothering to search for my heels.

I refuse to glance back, but I hear him. No, I *feel* him behind me.

"Willow, please," he pleads to my back with a strained voice while I fight with the lock.

I slam my fist against it. *When did they start making these things so damn difficult?*

"Don't cry." He blows out a stressed breath. "Just give me a fucking minute, okay?"

Relief hits me when the lock finally cooperates, and I slam the glass door in his face at the same time he repeats my name. I nearly trip on my feet when I jump down the porch steps.

I pause when I make it to the last one.

One more.

Against my will, I turn around for one last glance.

He's staring at me in agony with the door handle gripped in his hand. For a split second, I'm stupid enough to think he'll fix this. Stupid enough to believe he'll say something, do something to make this right.

But he doesn't.

He drops the handle, spreads both palms against the glass, and bows his head.

That's my cue to get the hell out of here.

Fuck him.

Fuck whiskey.

Fuck my stupid decisions.

This is what I get for sleeping with a man mourning his dead wife.

CHAPTER ONE

Willow

THREE MONTHS LATER

I SHOULD'VE NEVER ANSWERED his call.

"Have you been smoking crack?" I screech into the phone. "I'm telling Stella to break up with you. I can't have my best friend screwing a dude who does crack." I'm deleting him from my Contacts as soon as the call ends. I can't associate myself with someone this batshit crazy.

Hudson sucks in what sounds like an irritated breath. "No, Willow, I'm not smoking crack. It'll be the icing on the cake if you show. She misses you."

"You know I can't come back there." My throat tightens, the memory of that night crashing through my mind like a horror movie that keeps you up late at night. Hell, he does keep me up at night.

"It's not like you're fucking blacklisted. You've chosen not to come back. I emailed you your flight information. See you in a few days."

The line goes dead.

Asswad.

I grip my phone, ready to call him back and tell him to shove that ticket up his ass, but I can't.

I can't because he's proposing to my boss/best friend at her surprise birthday party. Stella deserves this—deserves love, happiness, and her best friend in attendance for one of the most important nights of her life. So, I'll put my hate of the small town aside and risk seeing him—the jackass whose bed I fled from after our very drunken and very regrettable one-night stand.

He'll be in attendance, given it's his brother doing the proposing, which means I have to put my big-girl panties on, keep them on, and refrain from smashing a wine glass over his head.

All while keeping the biggest secret of my life.

While staying sober.

This will be interesting.

SOME PEOPLE BELIEVE in soul mates.

I believe in champagne and cupcakes.

The problem tonight is that I can only binge on one of the above, and it's not the one I prefer.

I get a whiff of Stella's signature rose perfume before she cages me in for a hug. I squeeze her tight, a silent sorry that I've been a sucky friend, and we're both nearly gasping for breath by the time we release each other.

Damn, I've missed my best friend and how I could always confide in her without judgment. That's changed now. My secret will destroy her relationship.

"I can't believe you came," she cries out with a red-lipped smile. "How did Hudson convince you? Buy you a mini pony? Promise to kick Dallas in the balls?"

I laugh. "Two horses actually. And I didn't consider the second option, so thanks for the idea. I'll add it to my list of demands next time."

I snag her manicured hand to admire the glistening princess cut diamond sitting beautifully on her finger. It's perfection and so Stella—nothing too exuberant or obnoxious but still flashy.

"I have to give it to the corn-fed, small-town boy," I go on. "He did a kick-ass job in the ring department."

She stares down at her finger, her smile now nearly taking over her entire face. "He did, didn't he?"

Hudson threw her a great party. He invited the few family members she talks to, his family, and everyone on the cast and crew of her show. There's food galore, confetti sprinkled all over the white-tableclothed tables, and a *Happy Birthday* banner hangs in front of the empty DJ booth.

Stella is not only my boss, but also childhood star turned Hollywood's princess. I'm her assistant. That's how I met Mr. Wrong One-Night Stand. We worked together for years until he quit to move back home, and Hudson took his job.

Hudson couldn't give Stella mansions or fancy cars, but he did shower her with enough love and happiness to make up for it. She moved from LA to Blue Beech, Iowa, after convincing a producer to shoot her new show here. I tried to resign, but she wasn't having it and agreed to let me do all my work from my apartment in LA.

Her hands rest on her hips over the black designer dress. "Are you staying with us tonight? I just put a new smart TV in the guest room, and we know how much you like your classic movies."

I grimace. "That's a giant *hell no*. The last thing you need around on the night of your engagement is Willow, the giant contraceptive. I'm crashing at Lauren's."

Lauren is Hudson's and Mr. Wrong's sister.

She groans. "Fine, I'll settle for that because you showed up. That's a big deal, and you did it for me."

I crack a smile. "I also came for the cake." That comment results in her pushing my shoulder.

Her face turns serious. "Have you seen him?"

The mention of him gives me a nasty taste in my mouth. "Who?" She crosses her arms at my response, and I scoff, my heart racing, "Oh, you mean the bed evacuator? Nope."

That's a lie. He was on my radar as soon as I walked in—for precautionary reasons, of course. I saw his back first, the one I assaulted so much, I ruined my manicure, and worry snaked through me. I cowardly fled the scene when he spun around and saw me.

"Hopefully, he's ducking underneath tables, so we don't have to face each other," I say.

She smirks. "We both know Dallas is not a man who ducks underneath tables."

"Looks like I'd better start then."

"Don't you think it'd be a good idea if you talked? Cleared the air?"

"I need to talk to him like I need anal bleaching. Both of them would be a pain in the ass and are never happening."

She laughs, snagging a bubbly glass of champagne from a waiter walking by, and thrusts it toward me. "Here's some liquid courage. Just don't drink too much that you land in his bed again."

I swat the drink away. "Not happening, and no, thank you."

She stills and studies me. "Since when do you turn down champagne? Alcohol is always mandatory in these situations."

"I'm trying out a new diet."

"You might want to wipe the icing off the side of your mouth if you want to keep up with that lie."

I scrub away the remnants of my sugar binge and lick my finger. Thou shall not waste buttercream frosting. "It's this new craze diet where sugar is the main source of nutrition and alcohol is bad. *Very bad.* It's called the good decision-making diet." I start fake picking lint from my dress, so she doesn't see the untruth in my eyes. The black dress is ugly and shapeless, and I bought it specifically for tonight to hide my body and secrets.

"So, you're not drinking because he's here?"

Shit. That would've been a more believable excuse than a damn diet. I nod, feeling bad for lying to her, but I can't break the news here. It'd ruin her night.

"Does that mean, the chances of letting him rip off your panties for round two is likely?" She sets the glass down on the table behind her and bounces in her heels, like me banging Dallas again would cure world hunger.

"Calm down, matchmaker. Studies show that alcohol gives you shifty eyes." I point to my hair. "Shifty eyes don't look good on redheads."

"Bullshit. You can't deny you had a connection. Neither one of you is the casual banging type. Talk. Maybe there's a spark that'll lead to a firework."

More like a wildfire breakout.

"The only *connection* we have is that he stuck his penis inside me once. That's it. Nothing more. Now, it's time to move on."

She pushes my shoulder when I go back to my fake lint-picking. "Okay, what the hell is going on with you?"

"Nothing," I blurt out, shifting my neck from side to side like I'm sore. "Jet lag is a bitch."

"Liar."

I wave off her accusation. "It's your engagement party. Tonight is all about you."

"If that's the case, then I want answers."

I chew on the edge of my lip while her dark eyes study me. I get the opportunity to look away when music starts to blare through the room. I glance at the DJ booth and then to the makeshift dance floor in front of it and almost gag at his first song choice.

Boyz II Men? Really, dude?

Looks like we're getting served cheese with these cupcakes.

The sight of Hudson hurrying over to us relieves me. He

wraps his arms around Stella from behind and squeezes her hips, his mouth going straight to her ear.

"Dance with me," he attempts to whisper, although I'm sure everyone in the state heard him.

Stella melts at his touch, like it's the first time they've ever had physical contact, and my heart hurts. This is what real love is. This is something I'll never have. She groans, and I know my best friend well enough to know she's going to turn him down to continue our conversation.

"Go dance with your *fiancé*," I insist. "We'll talk later."

A smile accompanies her next groan. "*Fine*, but you're not leaving this town until you spill the tea."

"I wouldn't imagine it any other way."

Hudson kisses her cheek, snags her hand in his, and sweeps her toward the dance floor. The crowd cheers, and people jump up from their seats to join them.

I release a deep breath, happy I dodged that conversation, and decide to reward myself with another cupcake. I grab a chocolate one with strawberry icing and huddle myself into a corner at the farthest end of the room. Shame sinks through me when I do another once-over of the party to search for the man who screwed me in more ways than one.

One more glance. That's it.

One more view of the man who gave me the best night of my life and the worst morning.

My throat tightens when I spot him sitting at a crowded table in the middle of the room with the entire Barnes family. His daughter, Maven, has his full attention as she grins wildly and dramatically throws her hands up in the air while telling him a story. His head tilts back in laughter, causing my knees to weaken. That's the smile I longed for that morning.

God, he looks sexy.

More delicious than these cupcakes.

Too bad he isn't as sweet.

Dallas Barnes is tall, dark, and handsome but also scarred,

rough, and broken down by burdens. He's the man of your dreams who has been through hell and hasn't risen above it yet.

Tingles sweep up my neck as flashes of our night together come crashing through me harder than this sugar rush. I drink him in like the glass of champagne I can't have while he runs his strong hand over the stubble of his dominant jaw. The same hand that ignited nerves in my body I never knew existed. His hair, the same color as the whiskey we threw back, is freshly cut on the sides and grown out on top.

I rub at the sudden ache in my neck while begging my mind to forget, to stop feeling *something* every time I see him. Hell, every time I think about him. It's always hate laced with desire.

We were two lonely and heartbroken souls who connected over a night of drinking our pains away. When the alcohol proved not to be potent enough to heal, we tried to fuck it away.

Fucking and feelings do not go together like macaroni and cheese.

I used him. He used me. I thought I was okay with that until reality smacked me in the face when he kissed me for the first time. That was the moment I turned greedy and wanted more than just a quick fuck. The problem is, he didn't.

As if he senses me watching him, his deep-set charcoal eyes move in my direction, and my back stiffens. I hold in a breath when he scoots out his chair, gives Maven a quick peck on the top of her head, and walks toward me.

Oh, shit.

Shit. Shit. Shit.

The first few buttons are undone on his chambray shirt, exposing the top of his broad chest, and the sleeves are tight around his muscular arms. He's not fit from spending seven days a week at the gym. No, he's naturally buff, and the manual labor he does now only amplifies it.

Was driving me crazy his goal tonight? No doubt Hudson told him I'd be here.

I move my gaze from one side of the room to the other,

desperately searching for the nearest exit, as he gets closer. I'm his chosen target. I bite my lip at the realization that I'll have to walk past him to leave. The determination on his face assures me that I'm not going anywhere until he gets what he wants.

I shove the remainder of the cupcake in my mouth and silently give myself a pep talk to make it through this conversation without plowing my heel into his balls. I stupidly run my hands over my dress after swallowing down the last bite and then cringe at the pink frosting smear.

Real smooth.

So much for appearing cool and collected.

This hot-mess look won't make him regret kicking you out of his bed.

I tense when he reaches me, and he shoves his hands into the pockets of his jeans, staring at me with affliction. The thread around his shirt buttons stretches when he leans back on his heels and waits for my response.

"Willow." He releases my name like an announcement, and the familiar scent of him drifts up my nostrils, a mix of regret and whiskey with small notes of cedar.

It's comforting at first since I've always felt a sense of security when he is around, but then I remember what he did.

I settle my hand against the wall to keep me from falling on my ass. "Dallas," I reply with a sneer. "Fancy seeing you here."

"It's my brother's engagement."

My mouth slams shut, and my gaze drops to the floor at my stupidity. "Oh, yeah … right."

Silence passes.

I don't look at him when I lift my head back up. Instead, I avert my attention to the people dancing, laughing, and having a good time in the room, wishing it were me.

Hell, three months ago, that would've been me. I cast a glance to his mom and dad. *Do they know what we did? That he screwed my brains out one night?*

He clears his throat to gain my attention again. I give in and focus on his broad-jawed face. He's staring at me in gentleness, almost pity, which surprises me.

"How long are you in town for?" he asks.

"Two days." My initial plan was to fly in and out within the same day, but Hudson begged me to stay longer for Stella.

"Get breakfast with me in the morning."

His question startles me. The breakfast offer is a little too late. That should've happened on our morning after.

"I'm not much of a breakfast person."

He scratches his cheek. "Grab coffee?"

"I don't drink coffee." This is the truth. Never been a coffee fan. Never will be.

"What the hell do you do in the morning then?"

"Sleep." *Get sick. Roll around in my sheets, wishing I could turn back time.*

He pulls his free hand from his pocket and slides closer into my space.

Way too close.

His steadfast eyes meet mine. "*Please.* I want to make shit right. My brother is marrying your best friend. I'm the best man. You'll no doubt be the maid of honor. We need to be civil and stop dancing around each other if we don't want everyone to know something happened between us."

There's the answer I was looking for. I wince, unsure if he's more worried about our tension ruining the wedding or that people will find out about our one-night stand.

I wave my hand through the air, careful not to hit him in the face. "Consider that night forgotten. I already have."

"Don't bullshit me. We've known each other long enough for you to be honest with me."

I hold up my hand in anger, the need to spew out something terrible snapping at me. I want to strike him with pain that consumes him like he did me. "In case you've forgotten, *you* kicked me out of your bed. What do you want from me? A friendly hug? A casual conversation with fake smiles? Not going to happen, so quit wasting both of our time. You stay out of my way. I'll stay out of yours. Agreed?"

"I didn't kick you out of my bed," he hisses. "You ran out my front door faster than a speeding bullet."

I forget we're not alone and edge closer until my chest hits his. "You jumped out of bed like *you* were dodging a speeding bullet." I grit my teeth to gain control of myself. "That was before you said that what we did was a mistake, *over and over again*, like your lips were a broken record."

His face burns like I didn't just hit him with the verbal truth, but also a physical one. He lets out a hard sigh, giving me a small sampling of the whiskey and frosting lingering on his lips. Tightness forms in my throat, and I clutch at my stomach. Just like his cologne preference, I'm sure the taste of him hasn't changed.

"I'm sorry. I overreacted," he replies. "I tried calling to apologize, but you wouldn't take my calls."

"Nor will I ever."

"Fuck, Willow, how many times do I have to say this until you forgive me? I was in a dark place and was out of line." His voice lowers even more, and I barely make out his next words. "I didn't regret that it was *you* in my bed. I was pissed at myself for even letting it happen, for putting you in that situation."

His answer doesn't make me feel any better.

I slide against the wall to move away from him. "It's done. I'm over it."

"Twenty minutes and a pastry," he pleads. "Give me that, and I promise I'll never bring it up again."

I take a deep breath. This is Dallas Barnes. A man I worked alongside for five years. A man whose job was to protect Stella and me. Tragedy changes a man. Loss changes a man. This isn't the Dallas I knew. This is a new man, a man who lost himself when he lost his wife.

I sink my teeth into the inside of my cheek. "I'm sorry, but I can't. I'll be civil for Stella's sake, but I won't spend a minute longer with you than I have to." This is for the best. I want him to hate me. I want him to want nothing to do with me in case he ever finds out what I'm keeping from him.

The anger in my words shocks him, and he runs his hand over his face.

"Daddy!"

He stumbles back at the sound of his daughter's voice. She's barreling our way, and her brown pigtails soar through the air. She runs right into his leg with a *humph* and giggles when he catches her.

"Come dance with me!"

Affection fills his face when he peeks down at her with a smile and twirls a pigtail around his finger. "Give me a second, sweetie. I'm talking with Willow, and then I'm all yours."

"But this is my favorite song ever." She pouts.

I force a laugh, seeing my perfect escape plan. Dancing seems to be my savior tonight. "You can't deny a dance with a girl that adorable," I say, shooing them away. "Go. I need to make a call anyway."

Maven jumps up and down, clapping her hands in excitement, and Dallas stares at me with concern before leaning forward.

"I never had any intention to hurt you," he whispers.

But you did, I mouth back.

Damn, did he.

"Daddy!" Maven whines. "The song is going to be over!"

He gives me a nod before walking away.

I don't let the tears fall until I see his back.

The fuck?

I'm not this overly sensitive chick.

These hormones are messing with my hard-ass persona.

I brush them away, sniffling, and dash toward the exit. I need to get out of here and away from these people. I need silence, a moment to sulk about how I made a stupid decision for the millionth time.

I'm almost out the door when I nearly trip on my feet. My arm is grabbed, and I'm pulled down a dimly lit hallway. I attempt to swat the connection away, but it doesn't work, and I'm not released until we land in a small utility room.

"What in the flying fuck is going on with you?" Stella demands, crossing her arms. "And don't you dare try to feed me some new diet bullshit. Diets don't make you cry."

"Nothing," I stutter out, wiping my warm cheeks in an attempt to rid myself of the evidence.

"Bullshit." She pauses, waiting for me to let out my secret, but I stand my ground. "I'll keep us in here all night." She narrows her smoky eyes my way. "Do you want to be blamed for keeping a girl away from her engagement party?"

Guilt trips. Stella excels at giving them.

"I'll tell you later. I promise."

She shrugs, pops a squat on the carpeted floor, and stretches out her legs.

I let out a dramatic breath. "*Fine.* But you have to promise, it won't leave this room."

"All of your secrets are safe with me. Always have been."

"This is bigger than hacking into Brett's phone or when I pissed myself after we drank too many Skinnygirl margaritas."

"You could've killed Brett, and I wouldn't blab."

"Promise me."

"Jesus, Willow, *did* you kill the bastard?"

My heart thunders in my chest. I'm on the verge of passing out, so I sit down across from her. I can't take these words back. The secret won't be mine any longer, and she'll be thrown into a difficult position.

"Someone you care about will get hurt if I tell you."

Her voice fills with worry as she hunches forward. "Is it about Hudson?" She relaxes when I shake my head. "Then, what is it?"

"I'm pregnant." The words feel heavy when they fall from my lips for the first time.

She silently stares at me, stunned at my response, and then her face brightens with fake excitement. "That's great! Congratulations." She's won an Emmy, but even she can't fake enthusiasm about this. "I didn't know you were back with Brett."

Brett. My asshole of an ex who's out on bail and awaiting trial after driving drunk and hitting a family of four.

"We're not. I haven't seen him since we broke up."

"Then, who's the father?"

I wait for her to come up with the answer, so I don't have to give it to her.

Her mouth drops open, a gasp escaping her. "Holy shit. Dallas is the father?"

"Yep, and I don't know what to do."

"I take it, you haven't shared the news with him?"

"Nope."

Her gaze lands on me in expectation. "But you're going to before you leave, right?"

"Not exactly. I was, uh … thinking about, say, never?"

"What?" she screeches. "Have you lost your mind?"

"It's for the best."

"You can't do that." She leans forward to take my hand in hers. "Don't see this as me being unsupportive, but that's fucked up. And that's coming from a girl who faked a relationship with a douche bag for months."

"It's for the best. I'm going to raise this baby on my own."

"Why?" She shakes her head, rolls her eyes, and sighs at the same time. "And I suppose you want me to keep quiet?"

My voice cracks. "Yes. *Please.*"

"If I do what you're asking, I'll be hurting Dallas. I'll be hurting the man I love. It'll ruin my relationship with everyone in their family if they ever find out." Her eyes start to water.

This is the first time I've ever doubted my trust in her.

"What they don't know won't hurt them. If the truth does come out, I'll tell them you had no idea."

Stella turns around at the same time my attention goes to the door when it opens. Hudson is staring at us with a bloodthirsty expression on his face.

"Excuse me for interrupting," he huffs out. "I was searching for my bride-to-be."

Did he hear our conversation? The look on his face confirms he heard *something*, but how much?

"I wasn't eavesdropping … at least, not at first," he goes on. "Some words of advice: when you have a conversation about fucking someone's life up, you might want to lower your voices."

My heart thuds in my chest. "Hudson, please," I beg. "Please don't tell him."

He moves into the room, closing the door behind himself, and thrusts his finger my way. "Don't you fucking dare ask me to keep this from my brother." His piercing stare goes to Stella. "And please tell me you weren't going to agree to it."

Stella's eyes swell as she throws her arms out toward me. "She's my best friend!"

"And he's your soon-to-be brother-in-law who deserves to know!" he yells. "That'll be my niece or nephew. Did you even wonder how keeping this to yourself would hurt me and my family?"

Talk about a fucking loud mouth.

"Keep your voice down," I hiss in warning.

His face hardens, almost appearing sinister, and sweat builds along his forehead. "I swear on everything that I will hate you if you do this. You don't pull shit like this on a man, especially one who is as good of a father as Dallas. He's not some piece-of-shit, deadbeat dad."

I squeeze my eyes shut in an attempt to not only stop the tears, but to also block out the view of Hudson's disgust. "It has nothing to do with him. It's what's best for me."

"Bullshit. It's you being selfish."

"Hudson," Stella snaps. "Enough!" She pulls herself up from the floor and helps me to my feet. She doesn't release my hand until I'm stable. "What are you so afraid of, Willow? What's the worst that could happen?"

Fear does the Macarena in my stomach. I can't tell them the truth. "Everything," I release. "He's a grieving widower who regrets touching me."

Stella's face softens. "This secret will add to his hurt when he finds out later."

"That's *if* he finds out." I peek over at Hudson, the anger still manifested everywhere on his body.

He locks eyes with me and shakes his head. "Un-fucking-believable. You fucking do this to him, Willow, and I will never speak to you again." His glare goes to Stella. "Good memories of our engagement night, huh?" He turns his back on us and slams his hand against the wall before opening the door and storming out.

"He's going to tell him, isn't he?" I ask.

"I'm sorry," Stella replies. "I shouldn't have pushed you, but you have to tell Dallas before Hudson does. Maybe this baby will bring some joy into his darkness."

"I'll tell him. Just give me a few days, okay?"

She nods. "As much time as you need. I can't say the same for Hudson though. You know how close they are."

"Fuck!" I scream, grabbing the ends of my hair and pulling it.

"That's what put you in this situation." She smiles when I flip her off.

"I need another fucking cupcake."

CHAPTER TWO

Dallas

I OPEN the fridge with more force than necessary and snag a beer. My brain pounds when I pop the cap off, take a long yet unsatisfying drink, and set it aside for something stronger.

Nothing will be potent enough for me tonight.

But that won't stop me from trying.

Maven is at my parents', so I have no responsibilities tonight.

To say surviving the party was a challenge is an understatement. I wasn't sure I'd be able to make it through and good thing I didn't have to do it sober. I should be glad my brother found happiness, but I'm an asshole living in a dark hole, avoiding the sunlight. I'm only happy I managed not to stand up and object to him asking Stella to marry him.

Marriage isn't the answer, I wanted to scream out. *Don't let yourself get wrapped up in someone so much, you don't know who you are when they're gone.*

I pat myself on the back for keeping my mouth shut. The glass bottle feels chilly when it grazes the bare skin of my neck.

Then, I saw Willow. Hudson gave me a heads-up that she was coming, and even if I had tried to argue about it, nothing would've changed. She's Stella's best friend … and the only other woman I've slept with since Lucy died. Hell, the only woman I've slept with other than Lucy.

I decided I was going to talk to Willow and make things right between us. The problem was, I wasn't expecting my chest to ache at the sight of her walking in … or my hands to grow sweaty as I wondered how her skin felt underneath that black dress.

Is it still as soft as it was that night?

Does she still smell like strawberries?

Taste as sweet?

My plan to make shit right went out the window. All I thought about was asking her to come home with me and let me make up for my asshole behavior. I haven't touched anyone in months, haven't had the desire to, but seeing Willow made my heart race and my dick stir. Hell, it was a full-time job stopping myself from staring at her every three seconds.

I asked her to breakfast, and she looked at me like I was scum beneath her shoes. I had done a shitty thing, but I've tried to man up to it on more than one occasion, and she keeps shooting me down. So, I'm still a lonely asshole who only gets turned on at the thought of his dead wife and a woman who hates him.

I reach up to the tallest cabinet above the fridge and pull out the bottle of Jameson, my good friend who doesn't judge me when we hang out too much. I owe this motherfucker thousands of dollars in therapy. The liquid burns but feels almost euphoric, seeping down my throat.

Lately, all I've done is pretend—pretend that I'm okay in front of my family. I put on a brave face and make it through the day for my daughter … and then I go to bed, wanting nothing more than to rip myself out of my skin.

I flinch when I hear my front door slam and take the bottle with me to investigate. I stumble back at the sight of the last person I expected to show up at my door tonight.

"Yikes, what the hell are you doing here?" I ask. "Stella decide to leave your ass already?"

Hudson snatches the bottle from my hand with a snarl. "We need to talk."

I put my hands in the air. "If it's about me cornering Willow, I only did it, so we'd be civil during your wedding festivities."

He lifts the bottle to his lips and takes a sip. "I, uh ..." He takes another. "I have a feeling the two of you are going to have to learn to be civil long after my wedding."

His response doesn't make sense, but I'm blaming it on the alcohol. "I won't be an asshole again, okay? I tried to apologize, but the chick wasn't having it." Not that I blame her. I pulled the biggest dick move out of all dick moves ... because all I was thinking with was my dick.

"Willow is pregnant." He grinds the words out, the air in the living room shifting to something I don't recognize.

I blankly stare at him. "Okay?" My heart sinks that she's found someone else. No wonder she wanted nothing to do with me. She's found a man who isn't a broken asshole. Good for her. I would've only ruined her.

"Willow. Is. Pregnant," he stresses.

I'm not catching his drift. What does he want me to do? Throw her a baby shower? "I'll be sure to buy her a gift."

The coffee table shakes when he pounds his fist against it. "Willow is pregnant with your goddamn baby, you fucking dumbass. I thought you'd be smart enough to put two and two together."

Good thing he grabbed the bottle from me. This would've been the moment it crashed on to my hardwood floor. "You're fucking with me."

His straight face answers my question. He can't give a DNA test with his eyes, but I believe him.

"Why would you assume it's mine? We slept together once."

"I overheard her telling Stella."

I digest his news and swallow a few times before grabbing

my keys. A picture cracks when I throw them across the room as I realize I'm in no condition to drive.

"I need a ride."

"The fuck you do. In case you forgot, I got engaged tonight. I've already missed a few good hours because I couldn't think of pussy when I knew I was keeping this from you."

"How very noble of you," I mutter, wincing when he slaps the back of my head. "Stella's vagina doesn't have a curfew. Take me to Lauren's."

"Hell no. Stella will bite my dick off the next time I ask for a blow job."

"Take me to Lauren's, or I'll walk."

"Get in my fucking truck."

CHAPTER THREE

Willow

BANG! Bang! Bang!

I'm having a nightmare where a psychopath is pounding on the door of Lauren's apartment. I'll be murdered, and my skin will be worn as a coat. I don't realize I'm awake until I hear the familiar, masculine voice.

"Willow!" he screams on the other side of the door.

Bang! Bang!

"I know you're in there! Open up!"

My heart races, and I slap my hand over my mouth, not sure if it's because I don't want to make a peep or I'm close to puking.

"Lauren!"

Bang! Bang!

"One of you had better open this door before I break it down!"

Oh, shit.

Shitty-shit-shit!

I should've known Hudson couldn't keep his fat mouth shut. He probably went and tattled as soon as he got the chance.

I rub my eyes when the lights turn on. Lauren comes

rushing into the living room, tying a purple robe around her waist in frustration.

"I hope blood doesn't make you queasy," she bites out, stomping her feet.

I raise a brow.

"Because I'm about to castrate my brother."

If only she had done that sooner.

I pull myself into a sitting position, resting my back on the couch, and shrug like the shitshow about to happen isn't my fault.

Curse words fly out of her mouth with every step she takes while he continues his tantrum on the other side of the door.

"Jesus, fuck, Dallas!" she yells, swinging the door open. "You'd better be getting a bedroom ready at your place for when I get evicted."

He bursts into the living room without paying her a glance. His sharp eyes cut straight to me, demanding answers, and his pain-stricken face confirms what I was afraid of. He's as terrified as I am.

"Is it true?" he blurts out.

Lauren slams the door and storms into the living room. "Is what true?"

His attention doesn't leave my face. "Are you pregnant?"

I have no words. I'm frozen in place—unable to move, unable to talk, unsure of where to go with this.

"I'm confused as to why that's any of your business and why you felt the need to show up here like someone is about to blow the place up," Lauren replies for me.

He doesn't answer her. His attention stays fixed on me, as if Lauren weren't even in the room.

"Answer me," he demands.

I clear my throat, about to cave in and tell him but chicken out and nod instead.

The anguish on his face amplifies. "Is it mine?"

This is the moment.

This is where I have to decide not only my future, but also my baby's.

"Wait … what?" Lauren screeches.

CHAPTER FOUR

Dallas

MY HEAD SPINS like I've been beating it against a wall all day.

Not one rational thought has climbed through my brain since Hudson broke the news. He'd been thrown into a tough spot. He either had to betray the woman he loved or his blood.

He chose me. He chose the truth. Instead of fucking his fiancée senseless the night of his engagement, he came over and spilled her best friend's secret. I would've never forgiven him had he kept it from me. Pure ice sinks through my veins as I just think about it.

Lauren is behind me, firing off question after question, but my attention is pinned on Willow. Her green eyes, filled with confliction and scorn, narrow my way.

I take a calming breath as an attempt to help us both relax. "Is the baby mine?" I ask again.

All eye contact shatters when her gaze drops to her lap, and she fidgets with her hands. Sure fucking sign of lying. I stupidly pull out the pregnancy test I forced Hudson to buy at the pharmacy before coming here from my pocket. I can't decipher if the gasp coming from her is from surprise or anger.

The snarl of her upper lip answers my uncertainty.

"You brought a freaking pregnancy test?" she shrieks. "Have you lost your fucking mind?"

A reaction. Finally, I get *something* from her.

Hudson warned me she'd go Muhammad Ali on my ass when she saw the test, but as I mentioned before, my brain isn't functioning at its finest.

I stumble forward when Lauren pushes my back to gain my attention.

She signals between Willow and me. "Why would you assume the baby is yours if she's pregnant?" Her hand flies to her mouth. "Holy mother of God, you two are banging?"

"No!" Willow yells, as if the thought horrifies her.

That puts a damper on a man's ego.

I grit my teeth. This isn't a conversation I want to conduct in front of my baby sister. "Lauren, some privacy, please."

She scrunches up her nose. "In case you've failed to notice, this is my apartment. Where do you expect me to go at three in the morning?"

"Your bedroom."

She rolls her eyes. "Whatever. You suck."

"And be sure to put on earplugs," I call out to her as she heads down the hallway.

She twists around on her heels with a smirk. "And miss this conversation?"

I give her a look, one that tells her I'm not fucking around, but that only grants me another eye roll. Her bedroom door slams shut, and I know she's not going for her earplugs.

The air is heavy.

I'm staring at Willow.

She's staring at me.

A scarlet flush rides up her high cheekbones.

I've never had a staring contest last so long.

Willow has the face of an angel with light freckles scattered along her nose and cheeks. Her personality-matching fire-red hair is pulled back into a ponytail with loose strands flying in every direction. I've never had one negative thought about her until tonight. She has a huge heart and bends over backward to help others, often putting them before herself. She smiles as if she's never been hurt, but I know she has from the many times I saw her dip out of rooms with tears in her eyes after an argument with her ex-boyfriend. She acts hard but is a softie.

She's also cautious with letting people in. This is going to be a challenge.

"Put that pregnancy test away before I shove it up your ass." Her cold tone startles me.

It takes me a few attempts before I manage to push it back into my pocket. She flinches when I move in closer and drop to my knees in front of her. Pain coats my throat as I clear it.

"If you're pregnant," I say, blowing out a breath. It takes me a second to continue. "If you're pregnant and I'm the father, we need to come up with a plan."

There.

That's me stepping up and being a man even though I want nothing more than to throw myself out the window. No matter how broken I am, no matter what hell I'm going through, I could never turn my back on my child.

Willow shakes her head, swatting her hand through the air, as if dismissing what I said. "Dallas, don't worry about this, okay? You're going through a lot. I can do this on my own."

"If there's one certainty I have for you, it's that, that's not fucking happening, do you hear me?"

She sighs, rubbing her forehead. "*Fuck.*" An annoyed laugh leaves her full pink lips. "You storm over here at the ass crack of dawn after one of the most exhausting days of my life and demand I make a plan?" She snorts. "That's not what's happening right now, *do you hear me?*" She lies back down on the couch and pulls the blanket up her body. "I'm going to sleep, and you can go back to doing whatever it is you were doing … as long as it's not drunkenly waking up the entire building while waving pregnancy tests through the air."

Fuck. She has a point.

Lauren interrupts us by walking back into the living room and holds both hands in the air. "Don't get pissed at me, but, Willow, take my bed. I can't have a pregnant chick crashing on my couch."

A slight smile hits Willow's lips. "I appreciate the offer, but I'll be fine." The smile collapses when her attention goes to me. "As long as it's quiet."

That's Willow—accommodating everyone else and always putting herself last in line.

"You sure?" Lauren asks, and Willow nods. "Okay, let me know if you change your mind or need anything." She tells us good night and goes back to her bedroom.

"What are you doing?" Willow asks when I grab a blanket and pillow from a closet.

I throw them on the floor next to the couch. "You're exhausted. I'm exhausted. Let's get some rest and talk in the morning."

"You have a bed *at your home.* Go sleep in it."

I squat down and fluff the pillow. "I'm crashing here. End of discussion. I can't risk you sneaking out on me in the middle of the night and flying thousands of miles away before talking. We'll be having a conversation about this tomorrow."

She sends me one last glare before shifting on her side and giving me a view of her back. I switch off the light and make myself as comfortable as I can, resting my arms behind my head and staring at the ceiling.

A baby.

A baby with another woman.

I fight every day to hold Maven and myself together. How am I going to do this?

It'll be a struggle, but I'll figure it out.

I made Lucy a promise to be a good man, and I plan on keeping it.

CHAPTER FIVE

Dallas

THREE MONTHS AGO

THE GOOD PEOPLE of Blue Beech visit the Down Home Pub for three reasons:

#1: To forget.

#2: To feel alive.

#3: A live band is playing, and they don't have shit else to do.

I'm number one.

It's a hole in the wall, the only bar in the county, and it has been here longer than I've been alive. It's not fancy, and it doesn't carry top-shelf shit, but I feel more comfortable here than any upscale club in LA.

I've been a regular since my twenty-first birthday, but in the past ten months, I've become almost a part-time resident the two days a week I don't have Maven. My parents demand they get plenty of time with their only grandchild. I tend to come during the week when the people who don't like conversation are here.

It's a full house tonight, which is why I didn't want to come. I hate crowds. Hate the flashes of pity men give me after sucking down another shot of cheap whiskey. Hate the women who take turns coming over with the belief that food and attention will heal me.

A fucking casserole isn't going to restore this empty soul of mine.

I walked into the bar to find Lauren and Willow sitting at a table in the back. Lauren ordered a round for everyone and did her best to get us to get up and socialize, but neither one of us was having it. Willow eventually convinced her to bail on us and have fun on the dance floor.

Thank fuck.

My sister goes overboard when she tries to pep me up and give me a good time.

How Willow ended up here is a mystery to me. Pubs aren't her thing. She sips champagne, does yoga, eats chocolate with fancy-ass names. She flew in for Stella's crew party, so the only reason I can come up with is, she's trying to stay away from Stella and Hudson's lovefest.

I lean back in my chair, balancing the neck of my beer bottle between two fingers, and stare at her as she gives the bar a once-over. The pendant light above us shines over her head like a halo when she starts peeling paint off the table. Her weariness surprises me. I've always thought of her as a chameleon— someone who adapts to any situation she's thrown into.

I set my beer bottle down and wipe my sweaty palms against my jeans. "What's Tinder?" *Really? This is what I say to break the ice? It's all I could think of.*

My question surprises her, and she lifts her gaze to me. "Tinder?" She scrunches up her face like she didn't hear me correctly.

"Yeah, what is it? Lauren has been up my ass all week, insisting I join it."

She laughs, a smile cracking at the side of her lips. "Really? You've never heard of Tinder?"

"Trust me, I wouldn't be sitting here, feeling like an idiot, if I had." I grab my beer and take a long draw, finishing it off. "Looks like I'm the only one lost on the Tinder subject."

"It's a dating app." She pauses. "Let me correct myself. It's a booty-call app. Swipe right; swipe left. Let's bang; let's not."

"A booty-call app." I snort. "It's sad when your sister cares more about you getting laid than you do."

"I seem to have the same problem with everyone *but me* worrying about my vagina getting the business." She laughs again, the sound of it putting me at an unfamiliar ease— something I haven't felt in a long time.

I want to hear that laugh again. A woman this beautiful doesn't deserve to be sitting in the back of a run-down pub with sadness in her eyes.

"Hudson told me about the bullshit your boyfriend pulled," I say.

Her ruby-red lips frown, and she runs a nervous hand down her dress. I pinch the bridge of my nose, regretting my words. Bringing up her douche-bag ex isn't going to get me another laugh.

"Hudson has a big mouth," she mutters. "And *ex*-boyfriend."

"Sorry 'bout that. Hudson told me what your *ex* did."

"What he did was fucked up and the final straw of our relationship."

"Did the kid die?" I pause, the question hitting too close to home. I have a daughter. That could've been Maven. I can't imagine what those parents are going through.

"Fortunately, no. Unfortunately, he has severe brain damage and will never be the same."

Fucking jackass. Shows how one stupid decision can impact the lives of others. I only met her ex a handful of times, but I instantly knew he'd never be a friend of mine.

"And him?"

"He's out on bail, and his trial has been postponed until he completes physical therapy."

"You shitting me?"

She shakes her head. "The perks of being the son of the town mayor."

"I'm sorry," I whisper.

"It makes me sick that I loved someone who did something that bad."

She snatches the drink Lauren ordered her and downs it. My lips slightly turn up when her face twists into something that resembles disgust.

She sticks out her tongue and points to the glass, like it's poison. "Is your sister trying to kill me? What is this shit?"

"Jameson," I answer, feeling my lips tilt up again—something they haven't done with anyone other than Maven.

She stares at me, blinking.

"Whiskey."

She pushes the glass up the table with both hands. "Well then, that's my first and last time drinking whiskey. I'm more of a wine-slash-champagne-slash-give-me-something-fruity kind of girl."

"Whiskey is stronger on the heart than champagne. You can't go wrong with trying to forget with whiskey. I promise you that."

"In that case, order me another." She pauses to wag her finger at me. "Wait, if it's such a heart-mender, why aren't you drinking it?"

I shrug. "I planned on being good tonight with beer."

She holds her empty glass up. "I planned on champagne. If I'm drinking it, so are you."

I smile for what feels like the first time in months and hold my hand up to tell the bartender, Maliki, we need another round.

"This'd better work," she says when Maliki drops off our drinks. She knocks the whiskey down like a pro, inhales a deep breath, and squints her eyes when it's gone. "Shit, that one was even stronger."

"It'll help. I promise." I tap the table before draining mine. It burns as it goes down.

"Do you miss her?" she asks out of nowhere, as if the question had been on the tip of her tongue all night.

My jaw flexes. I'm surprised at her question. "Every fucking second of the day." My honesty shocks me. I've shut down every conversation my family has tried to have with me about Lucy. "Do you miss him?"

"Every fucking second of the day, and I hate myself for it. I can't stop missing the parts of him that weren't terrible."

Maliki, like he can read my mind, brings us another round. She takes another long drink, and I still in my chair, all of my attention on her while I wait for her to go on.

She scoffs, "This is *not* a conversation I thought I'd be having tonight. No one brings him up, for fear I'll want him back if they mention his name."

I nod, a cloud of grief passing over me. I want to be mad that she's complaining about losing someone she can take back at any second because I don't have that option. I'd be irate, pissed, and ready to spit out fire if anyone else had said that to me.

But not with Willow.

I grip my glass and watch her take another sip of her drink. The strap of her green dress hangs off her shoulder, giving me a glimpse of the light freckles sprinkled along her pale skin. I've never looked at her, *really seen her*, until tonight. Her red hair is pulled into two tight buns at the top of her head, a few spirals of perfect curls falling out of them.

"How about we make a toast?" she asks.

I hold up my glass. "To what are we toasting?"

"To getting wasted. To going numb. To forgetting."

I like the way she thinks. "To drinking the pain away." I tap my glass against hers. "Let's drown our sorrows."

We drink our pain away. We forget our troubles. Hell, we forget everything and everyone around us.

My brain isn't functioning when I ask my next question. It would've never happened if I were sober.

"So, have you tried it out? Had a booty call with this *Tinder?*"

CHAPTER SIX

Willow

I HAVE TO PEE.

The bathroom is across the hall, only steps away, but I can't go. I'm fake sleeping, and I have been for what feels like days. My muscles hurt. My head aches. As soon as Dallas leaves, I'm off Lauren's couch, out of this town, and on my way back to California.

Even though my back is to him, I can sense him watching, his eyes slicing into my skin, hoping to cut answers out of me. He'll end up empty-handed because I have nothing for him. My goal is to exhaust him with silence until he gives up.

What happened last night runs through my mind. I've never seen Dallas so angry and intense.

In an attempt to go back to sleep, I close my eyes, but my plan is ruined when it hits me. I nearly trip over him when I jump off the couch and race down the hall, straight to the bathroom.

Un-fucking-believable.

Why now?

I make it to the toilet just in time as everything I shoved down my throat last night comes up. It's disgusting. I'll never get used to this morning-sickness hell. I flinch when a cold hand moves along my neck to attentively grab my hair and hold it behind my shoulders. He silently kneels next to me and keeps his hand in place until I finish.

"Good ole morning sickness?" His voice is soft and comforting—the complete opposite of what he gave me last night. He must've slept off the asshole.

I flush the toilet and slide away from him, my butt hitting the cold tiles, and I rest my back against the bathtub. He waits until I get comfortable and hands me a bottle of water.

"Thank you," I say, taking a long drink. "It seems morning afters aren't our thing."

"I'd have to agree." He slumps down against the closed door and stares at me, doing what I knew he'd do—wait for answers. His foot brushes against mine when he stretches his legs out. He's in the same clothes as he was last night, his jeans unbuttoned, and his hair is messy.

I cock my head toward the toilet. "You want a go at it now?"

His thick brows squish together. "Huh?"

"I figured it was your turn to puke your guts out. You had to have been wasted off your ass to tell yourself that showing up last night was a sound idea."

He chuckles. "I'll admit, that was a stupid decision. I'd been drinking, but I wasn't wasted, and I'm sure you understand the shock I was feeling."

"No," I reply sarcastically. "I can't relate at all."

He found out I was pregnant. I'd found out I was carrying a physical being in my body by someone I couldn't stand.

He scratches his cheek. "How long were you planning on keeping this from me?" And he jumps right in.

Eighteen years. My entire life if I could've gotten away with it.

"To be honest, I have no idea."

He links his hands together and holds them in front of his mouth, trying to come up with the right words. He blows out a ragged breath. "You don't like me. I get it. And, to be honest, you're not exactly my favorite person right now either for keeping this from me. But I have to get over it, just like you have to get over what happened between us." He points to my stomach. "Because that? *That* changes shit."

"It doesn't change anything. I'm not expecting anything from you. I can do this on my own."

He holds his hand out, looking shocked. "Let me get this straight. I'm an asshole because I had a minor freak-out after we had sex? What does that make you for your secret? You've known you're pregnant for who knows how long, and you didn't think it'd be right to let me in on that tidbit of information?"

"You have a halfway good point," I mutter.

Okay, it's a full good point, but I won't give someone credit when I don't like them.

He clicks his tongue against the roof of his mouth. "Make yourself comfortable, sweetheart. Looks like we're about to have that talk."

I snort. "Not happening. I can still taste puke in my mouth. I'm not doing anything but brushing my teeth and getting in the shower." I narrow my eyes at him. "So, don't make yourself comfortable. We're postponing the talk."

"Okay, *princess.* Tell me when it's convenient for you. This afternoon?"

"Tomorrow."

"You'll be on a flight tomorrow."

"And? Lucky for you, they've invented this thing called a phone. I'll call you when I get home."

"I'd rather do it face-to-face."

"Then, we can FaceTime."

He pulls out his phone. "What time is your flight leaving?"

"Why?"

His eyes are on his phone as he starts typing and scrolling his finger down the screen. "Lucky for me, Hudson booked your flight and sent me the information this morning."

"Fucking snitch," I mutter.

"Looks like I'll be joining you. Hopefully, I can pay off the poor soul who's stuck next to you, and we can talk about it all the way back to California." He gives me a cold smile. "It'll be fun."

If he thinks his behavior is going to make me *work with him*, he has another thing coming.

"You're joking."

"Do I look like I am?" He holds his phone out, so I can see his screen. "Would you look at that? They have seats available."

"Don't you think that's creepy? Following me around? Stalking me?"

"Not stalking you. Asking for answers. This conversation will happen whether you like it or not. I'd prefer not to chase you around the goddamn country, but if that's what it takes, I will."

I cross my arms with a snarl. "Fine, I'll talk to you later."

His dark eyes level on me. "Promise you won't bail."

I force a smile. "I promise."

He hesitates before getting up and taps his knuckles against the door. "I'll be seeing you soon, *Baby Momma*."

"I hate you!" I yell to his back.

"I'M PISSED at the both of you for keeping me in the dark about this," Lauren says, placing her glare on me before switching it to Stella, who ditched Hudson this morning to show up here with muffins and a list of everything she wanted to know about what had happened with me and Dallas last night. "I have so many questions right now."

Lauren hasn't let me do anything since she woke up this morning. She's a nurse, so you'd think she knows that carrying a baby doesn't make you disabled.

"Questions I won't be answering," I mutter. "No one, except for Stella and Hudson, knew about that night. I was hoping it'd stay that way."

"One question, and I'll shut up," Lauren pleads.

"I'm not talking about having sex with your brother," I argue.

Her face pinches. "Gross. Not where I was going with this, creep."

I lean back in the barstool. "You'd better make it a good one because that's all you're getting."

She settles her elbows on the counter and eagerly stares at me from across the island. "How did it happen?"

I wag my finger at her. "I'm blaming it on you."

She takes a step back and shoves her finger into her chest. "Me? I might get messy drunk sometimes, but I don't recall telling you to take your panties off and give my brother the business."

I frown. "Fine. Let's blame it on the whiskey and lack of entertainment in this town's only bar."

Her mouth drops, satisfaction twinkling in her eyes as she puts two and two together. "The night at the pub?"

I stubbornly nod.

"Holy shit. I am to blame."

Stella scoots in closer. "They're the last two people I imagined screwing."

"Screwed," I correct. "A one-time thing."

"Have you decided what you're going to do?" Stella asks. "You do know, Dallas isn't going to let you freeze him out."

"No." I was so hell-bent on keeping this a secret, I never thought about what would happen if the truth came out. "We're talking later."

Stella perks up. "Like, a date?"

Lauren cracks a smile. "Survey says they've surpassed dating. She's carrying his baby."

I flip her off, and my throat tightens while I prepare myself to ask her a question I've been trying to avoid. I stare at Lauren. "So, you're not mad at me?"

Dallas's family's reaction is another reason I wanted to keep this private. They loved his wife, Lucy, like she was their own, maybe even more than Dallas. He'd started dating her before he even knew his dick could get hard, and I'm some random one-night stand crawling in to replace her.

"Why would I be mad?" Lauren questions. "As long as you're not screwing the same man as me, I couldn't care less, and inbreeding isn't my thing." She skips around the counter to wrap me in a hug. "It's no secret that I loved Lucy, but I understand the circumstances. I want my brother to be happy. He *needs* to move on." She pulls away and settles her hands on her hips. "Now, my answer would be different had you kept this from him."

She's acting cool but also letting me know where her loyalty stands. If she has to pick a side, it won't be mine. If she thinks I'm the one Dallas needs to move on with, she's out of her mind, but like so many other times, I choose to keep my mouth shut.

CHAPTER SEVEN

Dallas

"NOW, there's a sight for sore eyes."

Hudson's voice sends a rumble through my skull. I had too many drinks and bombs thrown at me last night. The way he sluggishly climbs up the stairs and collapses into the red rocking chair next to me tells me he didn't get much sleep either. Hopefully, for a better reason than mine.

"You're on my shit list," he grumbles.

I point to his rib cage that's exposed by his cutoff T-shirt. "Those scratches of anger or pleasure?"

He holds up his arm and inspects the skin with an amused, almost boyish smile. "Pleasure. Most definitely pleasure."

I never thought I'd see him happy again after his ex dumped him for his best friend while he was stationed overseas, but Stella came along and changed everything.

"Then, I beg to differ that I'm on your shit list. Had you slept on the couch, I'd feel sorry for you, but from those marks, I'm positive you didn't. End of discussion." I hand him the extra cup of coffee I poured while waiting for him to show up, certain he'd make an appearance this morning.

"Not end of discussion. Stella ran off at the ass crack of

dawn to gossip at Lauren's because you knocked up her best friend."

"Fine, I owe you one. I'll mow your grass. Work one of your shifts."

"You going to tell me what went down?"

I snort. "I see Stella isn't the only gossip enthusiast in your home."

He scratches his unshaved cheek. "She's rubbing off on me."

I drum my fingers against the wooden arm of my chair. "Willow didn't deny she was pregnant, so I'd say that confirms it."

The words *I'm pregnant* never left her mouth, but she would've been hell-bent on denying it if it weren't true. She's spent years working with Stella's publicist, making up stories to clean up gossip about Stella. She would've had a good-ass comeback if it weren't true. Hell, I'm surprised she didn't have an excuse already laid out, waiting for when shit hit the fan.

"And?" he pushes.

"There's a possibility I'm the father."

"A possibility? She seemed pretty damn sure about it last night."

She still does.

"What if it's not mine though?"

"You and I both know, Willow isn't like that or a liar. Stella swears Willow hasn't slept with anyone but you in months." He chuckles. "Trust me, from the look on her face, she wishes it were someone else's."

I scrub my hand over my face, hoping it'll help clear my head. "That's what I'm afraid of."

He laughs. "Get prepared, brother. This is happening whether you like it or not."

"We're talking today, figuring shit out."

"The first shit should be, figuring out the living situation.

That was my biggest struggle with Stella. Blue Beech was out of her comfort zone, and LA was out of mine."

LA was once my home. I didn't mind leaving Blue Beech years ago when Lucy asked, but that's no longer an option. Maven needs to be here with my family. *I* need the support from them. Willow, on the other hand, is stubborn. I can't picture her packing up her life and moving away from the chaos of the city life.

"Stella changed," I argue, trying to convince myself that it could work.

"She did, but that doesn't stop Willow from begging her to move back every time they talk."

"Fuck," I hiss. I'm going to have my work cut out for me.

Hudson slaps my shoulder and gets up. "Good luck. Let me know if you need anything, but try to wait a few hours, okay? I have a beautiful fiancée waiting at home for me, hopefully wearing nothing but her engagement ring."

"WHAT DO YOU MEAN, she's not here?" I ask, standing in Lauren's doorway and feeling a sense of déjà vu from last night. It seems like I've done nothing but chase Willow around since Hudson broke the news.

"I mean, she's not here," Lauren repeats, shuffling backward to let me in.

"Goddamn it," I mutter, rushing into her apartment like a madman.

My first pit stop is her bathroom to pull back the shower curtain. All clear. Next is Lauren's closet. Then, underneath her bed. No sign of Willow.

"She promised," I repeat over and over again while checking the linen closet. "She fucking promised."

Lauren meets me in the living room with an apologetic face.

"I'm guessing she called a cab and bailed while I was in the shower."

I collapse on her couch and drop my head back. Lucy never fought me like this. Our relationship was always easy. She was mine. I was hers. No power struggles existed.

"Maybe she went for a walk?" I ask.

The couch dents when Lauren sits down next to me. "Her bags are gone, and I doubt she's taking a walk with them."

I slowly lift my head, and she bends forward to snag her phone from the coffee table.

She sucks in a breath a few seconds later and ends the call. "Straight to voice mail."

"Same with me. That's why I came over."

Willow promised.

Promised we'd talk.

Promised she'd stay.

She's nothing but a goddamn liar.

I'm not letting her run.

I won't let her shut me out.

CHAPTER EIGHT

Willow

I'M A RUNNER.

Not one who runs 5Ks for fun.

A runner from situations I don't want to face.

I shut my phone off when it rings for what seems like the hundredth time and slip it into my bag. I'm not ready for this—for the reality of what's about to become my life. I don't want to engage in conversations about childbirth, epidurals, and midwives. And definitely nothing about moving.

Call me selfish, but I refuse to move thousands of miles for a man in love with another woman. A man who'll *always* be in love with that woman. A man who, even though he irritates me to no limit, made me feel beautiful and wanted one night.

He gave me an intimacy I'd never had. All I'd gotten in the past was a boyfriend who lied and cheated like it was his job. The more time I spend with Dallas the more those memories of how he made me feel that night will pop up.

I check the time on my watch and relax in my seat, my shoulders drooping. It never fails that I choose the worst in the penis pool. Millions of men in this world, and somehow, I manage to always pick the screwed up ones who see me as nothing more than a disposable fuck.

"Did you think it'd be that easy?"

I tense at the sound of his sharp voice. It's as if a knife has been jabbed into my throat. I'm terrified to face him. I can sense his eyes tearing into my back, feeling the pain as if they were breaking flesh.

I should've taken the Greyhound or hitchhiked. I probably shouldn't have headed straight to the most obvious place—the fucking airport.

"You had enough balls to run away. Don't be a coward now. Turn around and look me in the eyes," he demands. "Tell me you're not only selfish, but a liar as well."

His bossiness and cruel words set a match to my already shitty mood.

How dare he judge me. How dare he act like he understands what I'm going through.

"Willow." My name sounds like a threat, assuring me he's not leaving until I give in.

I pull myself up from my chair with a dramatic moan and jerk my purse over my shoulder. The airport is no LAX, but there are plenty of people around with curious eyes.

Dallas's face is challenging, like he's ready to close a business deal. He did nice, and I took advantage of it. Now, he's giving me something else.

I made a promise and broke it. He has every right to be pissed.

I'm ashamed it takes me a minute to square up my shoulders, to show him I'm not someone who can be scolded like a child.

"We're not doing this here," is all I say.

He sweeps his arm out. "After you, your highness."

Since I'm not that familiar with the airport, I head to the women's restroom, uncertain if he'll follow me.

He does.

"This is a better place to do it?" he questions, locking the door behind us and leaning back against it when I nod. "Suit yourself."

I throw my arms down to my sides with a huff. "What do you want from me, Dallas?"

"What do I want from you?" He lets out a mocking laugh. "I want you to act like a responsible adult. It might be hard for you to realize, but this isn't only about you."

"I know."

"So, why run?"

"I'm scared!"

"And I'm assuring you, there's no reason to be." He comes closer as a long breath releases from his broad chest. "I know your trust in me is shit." He signals between the two of us. "I'm not asking you to marry me or be with me or, hell, even like me. I'm sure we can both agree that a relationship is out of the question. You can think I'm a shit person all you want, but I'm not a shit dad, and you fucking know it."

He's hitting me with all the truths. You'd think someone would break entirely when the love of their life died. Lucy's death shattered Dallas, but she left scattered pieces, so he'd be able to take care of Maven. She knew their daughter would be Dallas's savior when she was gone.

He goes to grab my bag. "Come on. Lauren has a twelve-hour shift. We'll talk, and then you can have her apartment to yourself for the night."

I hold my hand out to stop him. "I'm getting on that plane."

His lips press into a white slash, and he tiredly rubs his face.

"Scooby is waiting for me."

He blinks. "I'm sorry, *who* is waiting for you?"

"Scooby."

He folds his arms across his chest and kicks his legs out. "You two hanging out in the Mystery Machine with Velma?"

"Scooby is my cat, smart-ass," I snap, jutting my chin out.

"Why you named your cat Scooby is a conversation for another time, but we'll be having some serious talks about the name of our child. I won't have a Shaggy Barnes running around."

My hand falls to my chest at the sound of a knock on the door. Dallas holds a finger to his mouth. The knocking stops, and I open my mouth to tell him that I'll see him later when it starts back up again. The person on the other side must really need to go because the knocks get louder and faster.

"Out of order!" Dallas finally yells. "Go somewhere else."

The knocking subsides, and I narrow my eyes his way. "You do know, this is the women's restroom? They're probably going to security."

I shrug. He can't badger me if he's in jail.

"Then, let's make this quick."

"My mom is watching Scooby for me. I told her I'd be back by tomorrow. I also need to tell her about the whole becoming-a-grandma thing."

Family—Dallas's weakness.

I realize I chose the right words when his face falls into an apology.

"Why didn't you tell me that?"

I wrinkle my nose. "If you haven't figured it out by now, I'm not the most open person."

"That makes two of us. What a pair." He gives me a gentle smile. "Go home, Willow. Tell your mom, but keep in contact."

My shoulders slump. "I will."

"Promise me." I open my mouth to do what he asked, but he stops me, scowling. "Actually, don't bother. Promises don't mean shit to you." He unlocks the door. "If you don't answer my calls, the next time you see me will be when I'm standing on your mom's doorstep, introducing myself."

"I DON'T KNOW why you won't let me keep him," my mom whines while running her fingers through Scooby's thick white hair.

A few strands stick to her hand because he sheds like no other. We have the whole let-me-keep-Scooby talk every time she cat-sits.

I flew into LA, got my car from my apartment, and then drove to my mom's house. She lives in the same house I grew up in, in a small suburb three hours out of LA. The ride gave me time to figure out how I was going to break the news to her.

"Mom, you bought him *for me* as a present."

After Stella moved away, he was a birthday gift to keep me company, but I think she used me as an excuse to buy herself an animal.

"You're out of town so much, and you don't give him the attention he deserves," she goes on.

She's right. I'm not much of a cat person, but I couldn't ask her to return him to the animal shelter. Scooby came from a good place. I only wish she'd chosen something that needed less upkeep—like, say, a goldfish.

"You seem to enjoy spending time with your grandcat," I reply. "I'm doing you a favor by traveling so frequently."

She lifts her chin. "When are you going to move home, find a good man, and settle down? Stella is doing it. Maybe you should follow her example."

Here we go again.

This is why the majority of my visits with her are when she's Scooby-sitting.

"Men and I aren't on the same page right now." *I have a feeling we'll never be.*

"If you'd quit looking in all the wrong places, they'd be. Come to church with me tomorrow, honey. They expanded, and traffic is booming! God-loving young men are scouring the place for a good wife to start a family with."

I can't stop myself from scowling. "Men scouring the place

for a wife? Not my type, Mom. That sounds not only desperate, but also scary." I'm sure those men wouldn't approve of me carrying someone else's baby out of wedlock.

I drag my phone from my pocket when it beeps. I turned it back on when my plane landed but have yet to reply to the seventy-eight text messages from every citizen in Blue Beech.

Dallas: You make it to your mom's okay?

I set my phone to the side, ignoring it, and then pluck it back up. His threat wasn't empty, and the last thing I need is him showing up here.

Me: Just got here. Talking to her.

Dallas: You break the news yet?

Me: I need to loosen her up with a glass of wine first.

Dallas: Good luck.

Me: I should be the one telling you good luck. She'll probably take it better than your parents.

Dallas: I haven't told them yet. I'm waiting for you to be here. Consider your mom practice.

Me: Not happening.

He's eating bath salts if he thinks I'll be attending that shitshow. Dallas's family is as traditional as it gets. They're nice people, don't get me wrong, but super old school.

Dallas: We'll talk about it.

We'll talk about it?

The hell kind of answer is that?

I toss my phone onto the pillow next to me on the couch. "How about we go to dinner at La Vista tonight?"

MY PLAN of liquoring my mom up, so I could spill the beans wasn't as bright as I'd thought it was an hour ago.

She wisps her hair, the same color as mine, away from her eyes to better stare at me. She's been eyeballing me since our drink order was placed five minutes ago. I'm doing my best to avoid direct eye contact with her, scared she'll read my mind.

The restaurant is packed. It always is on Saturday nights, given it's the nicest place in our suburb. A few of my mom's friends stopped to talk to us while we waited for our table, their eyes scrutinizing and judging me for the wrongs my ex-boyfriend did to a young kid who was the star of his little league baseball team.

"I take it, you have something to tell me," she says.

A knot ties in my belly. "Huh?"

"You've been nervous since you got home today. You then bring me to La Vista and order a glass of wine for me before the waiter even got the chance to introduce himself. You bring me here whenever you have news you don't want to break to me."

Come to think of it, she's right. I brought her here when I decided to move to LA, when I got back with Brett, and then when I told her I'd officially broken things off with him.

I lower my head in shame and blurt out my confession, "I'm pregnant."

She takes a long drink of wine before giving me a response. Her brows pull in as she carefully chooses her words. "This isn't some April Fool's Day joke, is it?"

"It's June."

I'm trying to read her, but I can't pinpoint what's going on in her mind. She's not happy, but she's not unhappy.

"How do you feel about this?"

My heart thrashes in my chest, and my chin quivers. "Like an idiot." An idiot for not using protection. Go figure, my ovaries are the .01 percent that gets pregnant while taking the pill.

"Do I know the father?"

"It's not Brett's."

A rush of relief releases from her lips. "Thank Jesus."

"It's Dallas Barnes."

"Stella's old bodyguard?"

I nod. "And Hudson's older brother."

Mortification floods her face. "Isn't he ..." She grabs the glass of red wine and chugs the remainder of it down, her emerald eyes wide. "Isn't he married?"

Oh, fuck. She's afraid I'm a homewreckin' ho.

"His wife passed away almost a year ago."

She nods slowly, digesting my answer, the familiarity of it flashing across her face like a burn. "You didn't tell me you two were dating."

I can't distinguish if she's asking a question or giving a warning. My mother knows the nightmare of never getting over your first love—a memory that bites at every inch of your body until your last breath.

"We're not dating," I answer. "It was a one-time thing. Too much whiskey, not enough thinking."

I take a sip of water, a breath of courage, and proceed to tell her everything minus the details of the actual baby-making, and I am unable to stop the tears from falling from my eyes ... and hers.

She stretches her arm across the table to grab my hand in hers. "If Dallas wants to be in the picture, give him a chance." Her voice is soft, caressing, a vocal hug. "He's a father, a single one at that, who knows the responsibility of taking care of a child."

"I'm strong, Mom." My throat is dry, causing my words to come out raspy. "I can do this on my own."

"Honey, I'm not denying you can, but I know from firsthand experience, it isn't easy, doing it alone. No mother can replace the void of a father. We can both agree on that."

A knife slashes through my heart. The reality of what I did smacks me in the face, like I've been unconscious this entire time.

I was that child, the one without a father. It was by choice for the first fifteen years. He didn't decide he was ready to be a dad until he was diagnosed with stage five colon cancer. My mother welcomed him with open arms. I didn't.

He passed away at the young age of forty-one when I was sixteen. My mother forgave him at his deathbed. I didn't. I couldn't. The bitterness was still wrapped in my heart. I couldn't forget all the times I'd been a jealous-filled child when I watched my friends have fathers.

Everyone has choices in their life. He chose to leave. You can't take that shit back when you find out your time is limited, and you have no one to help you through it.

She drops my hand and sits back in her chair, the wine now relaxing her. "Your father always wanted grandchildren."

I want to tell her that I don't care what he wanted. My mom has gone through hell since he left her … both times.

"I doubt that dream included a love child," I mutter.

"A grandchild is a grandchild. A blessing. No matter what the situation."

CHAPTER NINE

Willow

DALLAS: **You break the news yet?**

The text was sent two hours ago. My phone stayed in my purse throughout dinner, and when we got home, we spent the rest of the night bingeing on popcorn and Matthew McConaughey movies.

Me: Sure did.

I change into my pajamas and slide into bed. My mom kept my room how it was when I moved out. The same sponge-painted yellow walls and pictures of me at different school events on the dresser. I zero in on the prom picture of Brett and me and tell myself to toss it and any others with him into the trash tomorrow.

The phone rings, and I freeze up and stare at the screen for a few seconds when his name flashes across it. We've talked on the phone before, for business, so why am I terrified of answering?

I inhale a breath of courage before accepting the call. "Hello?"

"How'd she take it?" Dallas asks.

Hello to you, too.

I chew on my nails. "Not bad. I did crush her hopes on if I'd decided to move home and find a husband though."

"You dream crusher, you."

I smile.

"Did she ask about me? About who the dad is?"

"She knows who you are."

A brief silence passes.

He met my mom at Stella's Christmas dinner one year. I brought her as my plus-one after Brett went missing for forty-eight hours on a drinking binge. He and Lucy were there, and Mom talked about how their relationship was beautiful on our way back to my apartment.

"She's happy I at least got knocked up by a decent man."

"Good." He pauses for a few seconds. "I need to ask for a favor."

"If it's being present and accounted for when you tell your parents, that's gonna be a hard no."

"Let me correct myself. I need to ask you for *favors*."

"You're really pushing it, you know that?"

"Come to Blue Beech."

"I was just in Blue Beech, remember? Hudson having a big mouth, three a.m. wake-up call—all of that jazz."

"Damn, Ms. Difficult, *stay* in Blue Beech. Give it a try. A trial run, if you will."

"Didn't we have this talk in the bathroom?" I ask, exasperated. *No way in hell is that happening.* "We decided we're not moving in together, getting married, or any of that forced nonsense."

"Whoa, whoa. Pump your brakes, sweetheart. I promise, this is *not* a marriage proposal. It's a moving proposal, so we can do this as a team."

"Why can't we do it as a team in LA?"

It's his turn to let out an exasperated breath. "I have a daughter here who adores her friends and family. My business is here. Hell, *your* job is here. Any other points I need to throw out? You belong here, Willow."

I grow quiet, and he lets out an irritated groan.

"Fine, I'll come to you if I have to, but prepare to explain the reason to my family. I won't be pushed away from this, and I am not a man you can play games with. I'm a man who will fight for what he wants and the people he loves. You might not have given birth to our baby yet, but that doesn't mean I don't care for it."

He has a point. Maven has already lost her mom. It'd be greedy of me to ask Dallas to move her away from her home and the family she has left.

"Where am I supposed to stay? On the streets?"

"You can stay at my place. I have a guest room."

"Not a chance in hell."

"Stella's?"

"Shack up with the lovebirds? Again, not happening."

"We'll find you a rental then."

I yawn. This conversation is getting too dangerous, sounding too final. "Let me sleep on it. I'll talk to you tomorrow."

I'M READING another article of what having a baby does to your vagina when the doorbell rings. My mom left for church an hour ago, so yelling for her to answer it isn't an option. I throw the covers off me before slipping out of bed with a groan. It rings again as I trek down the stairs.

I'm cranky. Heartburn and headache made an appearance and decided to stay all night. Heartburn was the consequence of overeating pasta, and the headache was from the regret of possibly agreeing to move to Blue Beech.

I swing the front door open, and my temples throb at the sight of the world's biggest asshole standing on the porch with white roses in his hand like he's picking me up for prom.

"Nuh-uh, not today, Satan!" I yell before slamming the door in his face and locking it.

Someone must've spotted me at La Vista last night and told him I was in town.

Brett bangs on the other side. "Willow! At least talk to me!"

"Fuck you!" I yell back. "Go give those to one of the fifty women you fucked behind my back."

"I have a key," he warns. "Don't you make me use it!"

"I have a baseball bat. Don't you make me use it!"

He knocks a few more times. "I'll be back. Don't think I won't. Every fucking day until I break you down."

"That's what they make restraining orders for!"

He knocks again. "I'll be back."

And then silence. Not surprising. Brett is one of the laziest men I know. He doesn't like to work for anything, but he'll try to sweet-talk me like he did every time I took him back in the past. Dealing with him is the last thing on my to-do list. Actually, not even on the list. He's lazy but also irritating when he's not getting his way. I'm guessing the woman he was cheating on me with got a glimpse of the real him and bailed. That means, he's ready to run back to me.

Maybe I do need to get out of California, get some fresh air, and clear my head. I lean back against the front door as frustration builds in my head. I'm mentally cursing myself when I head back to my room.

I snatch my phone from the nightstand, nearly ripping it from my charger, and hit Dallas's name, praying to God I don't regret this tomorrow.

Me: Blue Beech. A trial run. That's me compromising.

My phone beeps seconds later.

Dallas: Thank you. You have no idea how much I appreciate this.

I exit from his name and hit Stella's.

Me: Hello, new neighbor!

Stella: YES! Team Stella for the win! You're staying with me, BTW.

Me: Not happening, BTW.

Stella: Why? Don't tell me you're crashing at Dallas's? How romantic.

Me: Are you nuts? I'm renting a place.

Staying with Dallas is not an option.

What would he tell his daughter? That I'm homeless and then— surprise!—I'm carrying your sibling?

CHAPTER TEN

Dallas

"BUT … but Auntie Lauren lets me have it," Maven whines.

I snatch the coffee cup from my six-year-old, who is under the impression she's a grown-up, and replace it with an organic apple juice box. "I'll be having a conversation with Auntie Lauren."

My sister's idea of a well-balanced diet is iced coffee, margaritas, and deli sandwiches from the hospital's vending machine.

She sits down at the table with a un-caffeinated frown at the same time I place a bowl of strawberry oatmeal in front of her. I promised Lucy that Maven would be taken care of, and that means making her eat balanced meals.

My days have gone from traveling the world with Hollywood's elite to packing nutritious lunches, attending dance recitals, and reading the same bedtime stories for months on end.

But I wouldn't trade it for the world.

Time is valuable. Hug your children. Kiss your wife. Make life your bitch because you never know when it's going to turn on you.

I grab my phone and sit down next to Maven.

"What are you doing?" she asks before taking a bite of her oatmeal.

"Texting your aunt."

"Tattletale," she mutters with a frown.

Me: Mom and Dad paid for four years of nursing school, and you don't know that kids shouldn't have coffee? Your license needs to be revoked.

My phone beeps a few minutes later.

Lauren: Relax, old man. Unbeknownst to your caffeine-fiend spawn, I give her decaf. She wants to be my mini me, which I approve of.

My family has been the key to my survival. Lauren stepped up to be a mother figure to Maven when Lucy passed.

Me: That's scary. Is the apartment underneath you still vacant?

The struggling musician who lived underneath her got evicted last month for playing music all day and night. She threw a party in celebration when he left.

Lauren: Depends on why you're asking. If it's for a dude in a band, then no.

Me: Give me your landlord's number.

Lauren: WHY?

Jesus, they might be my backbones, but they are damn nosy.

Me: I need to find a place for Willow.

Lauren: Holy shit! She's moving here? The apartment is open. I can't wait to have a front row seat to your guys' drama!

Me: Send me the damn number.

I grab Maven's backpack, and she gets into my truck at the same time Lauren sends me the number. I wait until I drop Maven off at my parents' before calling Lauren's landlord, Fred. He gives me the good news that the apartment is vacant but is unwilling to put a hold on it for me, so I drive to his office and pay the security deposit.

The apartment comes fully furnished, but I decide to take a

peek at it before Willow moves in. I'll do anything in my power to make sure she's comfortable here.

It's a damn good thing I did.

"I need help," I tell Hudson when he answers my call.

"With what?" he asks.

"Getting Willow's apartment together. I'll also need some input from Stella."

He takes a deep breath, almost sounding surprised. "So, you're really doing this, huh? Moving Willow here?"

"Did you think I wouldn't?"

"No, I thought *she* wouldn't. I'll believe it when I see it."

CHAPTER ELEVEN

Willow

LAUREN POPS the trunk and steps out of her over-the-top pink Mustang when I walk out of the airport. The car is hideous yet has a certain appeal to her.

"You know, I'm confused," she says, helping me with my bags and then throwing her hands on her hips in question, as if I can read her mind as to what she's confused about.

One thing I admire about Lauren is her inability to bullshit. She might just barely be grazing five feet, but she'll ask you straight up instead of gossiping behind your back.

I slam the trunk shut. "Confused about what?"

She doesn't answer my question until we're in the car. "On why you'll screw my brother but refuse to let him pick you up from the airport."

It's a three-hour drive to Blue Beech, and I asked Lauren to pick me up instead of Dallas, so I wouldn't have to spend hours alone with him, answering questions. I have the impression it might not be much different with his sister.

I fix my glare on her. "Haven't you ever had a one-night stand?"

"I live in a town with a population of six hundred. Half of the men were married off before their balls dropped. There's no one to have a one-night stand with." She pauses to give me a side-eye. "I guess I can't speak for everyone."

"Oh, kiss my ass," I grumble, rubbing my eyes.

Sleep hasn't been my friend lately, and I had an early flight. I doubt I'll be able to unwind when I get to Blue Beech either.

"Did he do that, too?" She laughs when I flip her off. "You kinky kids, you."

"I wish you had never found out," I grumble.

"Secrets don't make friends," she sings out, gearing the car in drive.

"They sure can keep them though."

She tips her thumb toward my growing belly. "That, *my friend*, would be a mighty hard secret to keep."

I made a list of lies when my first pregnancy test came out positive. IVF treatment. Secretly adopted a baby. A one-night stand, and I didn't get the guy's name. The last one is technically only a half-lie.

I slump down in my seat. "I can't believe I'm doing this."

"Doing what? Moving to the best place in the world and being surrounded by delightful company? We're going to be neighbors. That, my dear, will be the highlight of your life."

"No, I can't believe I packed up and moved to a town void of takeout sushi but also where I'll be labeled a widower-chasing tramp. Might as well pin a scarlet letter to my chest and call it a day."

"You can't be serious." She peeks over at me, her amused smile fading into concern. "Willow, no one is going to call you a widower-chaser. I mean, not to your face at least." She pauses to give me a cheesy grin. "Although it does have a nice ring to it. Willow the Widower-Chaser."

"That's it. Turn this pink puss car around."

I yelp at the sound of the door locking. "Prepare for a three-hour drive filled with prying questions and nineties hip-hop. I hope you're a Snoop Dogg fan."

"WOW, THIS IS A NICE PLACE."

I drop my bag onto the mahogany wood floor and explore my new apartment. It's an older building with a floor plan similar to Lauren's, except mine is a two bedroom and has more space. Something like this would cost a kidney in LA. My mom told me I was choosing to live in rich-people poverty when I moved there.

A fresh coat of taupe paint covers the walls, and an exposed brick fireplace is at the front of the living room with a flat screen TV mounted above it. The furniture is new, and decorative touches are scattered throughout the living room and kitchen. A red-and-black-checkered throw is thrown over the back of the couch, and succulents are placed on the end tables to each side of it.

"Thank you for talking to your landlord, putting down the deposit, and getting everything in order on such short notice," I say to Lauren, pulling my purse up from the floor by the strap. I rummage through it in search of my wallet. "How much do I owe you?"

Her hand goes up, stopping me. "Put your wallet away. Thank Dallas. This was all him."

I give the apartment another once-over. "What? How?"

Blame it on the loser I dated for nearly a decade, but my mind can't wrap around a man doing this for me. I guess Stella wasn't lying when she said small-town guys were a different breed.

"Ask him. In the meantime, get yourself settled in. I have a double shift in a few hours and need to hit the shower. Text me if you need anything, *neighbor*."

I smile. She made a six-hour round trip to pick me up and then has to pull a double. "Have fun. Thank you for the ride. I owe you one."

"I got you, girl," is all she says before winking and waving good-bye.

I scoop up my bags and take them into the bedroom when I hear the door shut. Just like the rest of the apartment, the bedroom is spacious. Settling my suitcase on the cream-upholstered king-size bed, I start to unpack.

I let my mom watch Scooby for a few weeks, so I could get settled in and check with the landlord if pets were allowed. Only a few bags came with me on the flight, and I'm having my other stuff and car shipped. I have a baby on the way and am not handing an airline my savings to have a few extra bras.

I drop the shirt I'm hanging up at the sound of the doorbell.

"You forget something?" I ask, opening the door. I stumble back when I don't see Lauren.

Dallas is standing in front of me, shoulders broad and square, wearing a red-buffalo-plaid flannel that nearly matches the throw on my couch, dark jeans with holes in both knees that hug his legs, and brown boots. My heart races, and I can't stop myself from running a finger over my lips.

Shit. Pregnancy hormones are making an appearance. They seem to be well acquainted with him.

Dallas has the efficacy to pull off attractiveness with this casual demeanor better than any man wearing an expensive suit. My ex was a hipster wannabe who regularly sported holey jeans, beanies, and flannels. He was a generic version of the real thing—Dallas. He's no wannabe. He's this rugged, down-to-earth man who has no idea how wet he makes my panties.

I smooth down my hair and shyly smile. "Hey," I say in nearly a whisper.

Tension bleeds through the air like an open wound. Our last face-to-face conversation wasn't exactly pretty.

His thick lips curl up. "If it isn't Blue Beech's newest resident."

"*Temporary* resident," I correct, scooting to the side. My back brushes against the wall as I give him enough room to step into the apartment and shut the door.

His scent, a light evergreen that reminds me of a vacation lodge deep in the mountains where you never want to leave, hangs in the air like smoke as he skims the living room. "You getting settled in okay?"

A few inches separate us, and I play with my hands in front of me, nervousness climbing up my spine. We haven't been alone like this since that night with the small exception of the women's restroom at the airport, which has the privacy that's equivalent to one in prison.

"I haven't had a chance to find a place for everything yet, but the apartment is gorgeous. I can't believe you did all of this. Thank you."

He stares over at me, his eyes flashing with victory and satisfaction. "Thank you for moving here."

I draw in a sharp breath when he edges closer into my space, standing in front of me, as if he's geared to tell me a secret. Being too close for comfort seems to be his thing, which I find completely unnecessary. This isn't L.A. *The square footage is out of this world, dude.*

"You have no idea how much I fucking appreciate it."

I shrug off his gratitude and laugh. "I needed a getaway for a while anyway. Nothing like a vacation before delivering a baby."

He chuckles lightly. "Just a vacation, huh?"

I nod.

He runs his boots back and forth over the hardwood floor. "I stopped by to make sure you showed up and weren't planning on bailing again."

I hold out my arms. "I'm here, in the flesh, breathing and everything."

"I also wanted to see what you might be doing tomorrow night."

Like I have big plans here?

"Most likely, unpacking."

"Perfect, you're free. I'm taking Maven to the fair tomorrow. Come with us."

Is he nuts? He wants me to hang out with not only him, but also his daughter?

"The fair?" I scrunch up my face. "Like vomit-inducing, spinning rides and honky-tonks?"

"No." He pauses. "I mean, yes to the rides, no to the honky-tonks. You watch too many movies."

"I work for movie stars. Watching their movies is part of my job."

"I'll pick you up at six."

"I'll have to pass."

"Come on, who doesn't like the fair?"

"I've never been to one."

His lips tilt into a half-smile, and he opens the front door, patting the inside of it. "I'll pick you up at six."

"Wait!"

"Have a good night, Willow."

The door slams shut behind him.

CHAPTER TWELVE

Willow

THREE MONTHS AGO

"WANT TO DANCE?"

Dallas and I both flinch at my question.

Did those words leave my mouth?

This whiskey shit is messing with my insanity. I shouldn't want to dance with Dallas. I definitely shouldn't be feeling this weird pull between us after only a few hours of drinking together.

Lauren stopped by our table earlier to give me a ride back to Stella's, but I wasn't ready to end my time with Dallas. Turned out, neither was he. He offered to walk me back to Hudson's on his way home. Surprisingly, Lauren didn't find it weird and took off.

The place is close to empty, except for the few lone rangers at the end of the bar, and the band left with their armful of groupies. The music has been downgraded to static-infused country songs coming from an old jukebox in the corner of the room.

He stares at me with hooded eyes, and I wave my hand in the air as rejection slaps me in my stupid, drunken face.

"Forget it," I rush out, beating him to the punch. "Of course you don't." This will mortify me when my senses come back in the morning.

He holds his fist to his mouth and lets out a shuddering breath. "I'm not really up for dancing."

He jumps up from his stool, and I avert my eyes to the tabletop.

This is where he bails. Do they have Uber around here?

His tall frame towers over me, and I jump when his strong hand grabs my chin to tilt it up.

Our gaze meets, latching on to each other's in a strong hold, and he lowers his voice. "But I will for you."

His fingertips smooth over my chin as he waits for my answer, and my brain goes fuzzy. Every person and every noise disappears around us.

"Never mind," I stutter out, not sure if my words are even audible. "It's okay. I'm a terrible dancer anyway."

His hand disappears, and he bends down, so his lips are at my ear. "Get up, Willow."

I shudder at the feel of his breath against my skin, goose bumps popping up my neck.

"You've been answering my Tinder questions and listening to me be a miserable bastard all night. I owe you a dance."

"Are … are you sure?"

"Positive. Hell, I need it as much as you."

I take his hand and slide off my barstool. "Lead the way."

His grip is tight. Secure. I keep my eyes downcast, so I don't see the expressions on people's faces when they see him dancing with someone who's not *her.*

Judgmental eyes won't ruin my night.

My heart races when his hand leaves mine, and he swoops his arm around my back, looping it around my waist. His hand settles on the arch right above my ass, and he starts moving us to the beat of the music.

"What song is this?" I ask.

"'Hurt' by Johnny Cash."

He shuts his eyes, holding me closer, and I take in the lyrics. Dallas didn't choose this song, but God, does it fit his life right now.

The jukebox is giving me a warning. *Run! Run! You naive girl. This man will only end up hurting you.*

A sharp pain fills his eyes as he stares down at me. "You have no idea what you brought out of me tonight." He blows out a ragged breath. "What you gave me tonight, Willow. I've never opened up like this to anyone."

Even Lucy? is the question I want to ask, but I bite my tongue. *Me either* are the words I want to say next, but again, I don't, for fear he'll run away.

Almost a decade with Brett, and never did emotions drum through me like this.

Is this what it feels like—falling for someone? Is this why people who've experienced love crave it so much?

Love.

I gulp down a thousand feelings. I'm overthinking this.

I can't fall for a man after one night of conversation and a dance.

"I've never danced with anyone like this," I admit.

Instead of pulling away, he draws in nearer, pressing his mouth to my ear. I shiver as his crisp breath hits my sweaty skin. "Like what?"

"Without grinding my ass against someone while Lil Jon plays in the background."

Proms. Frat parties. Clubs. Those are the only places I've danced with men. Never so slow, so personal, so gentle. Never like *this.*

He chuckles—not only surprising me, but also making me

smile. "I'm taking your virginity of how a real man dances with a woman."

My response is resting my chin on his shoulder and losing myself to the music as he takes me into another world. We stay silent in our moment, but it's a comfortable silence, something that feels necessary right now. I expect him to pull away when the song ends, but he doesn't. We dance into the next one with my arms nestled on his rugged shoulders as we feed something we shouldn't.

"Last call!" a voice yells in the distance, snapping me out of my powerful trance. I'm unsure of how many songs we've danced through. "Five minutes until closing time!"

I attempt to pull away, but Dallas tightens his hold, silently asking me not to let go yet.

"Give me that five minutes," he pleads.

"Of course," I whisper, slipping my hands down his back. "I'll give you however long you need."

He nods his thank-you. Time slows. These five minutes feel like a lifetime. Our embrace grows tighter, our sway to the music slower and the connection sharper.

"Dallas, man, I hate to do this, but I have to shut this shit down," the guy who screamed out the last call warns.

I lose our connection when he retreats a step, my arms splaying down his sides and then falling to mine, and he gives me an apologetic look.

"Sorry," he whispers to me before turning his attention to the bartender. "You're good, man. Enjoy your night."

The bartender, the same man who was making our drinks, gives him a thumbs-up and a smile. "It was good seein' ya!"

His gaze lowers to mine. "You ready to go back to Stella's?"

No! No!

I'm debating on asking the bartender how much he wants for this bar, so we can stay longer.

I force a smile. "I have to be, considering we're getting kicked out."

He grabs my hand, interlacing our fingers, and holds them against his shoulder. "It's beautiful out tonight. How 'bout we take the scenic route? Might be a good idea to show you the beauty of Blue Beech since Hudson says you hate it and refuse to move here with Stella."

I tilt my head to the side. "Hey now, did he tell you to give me a good time in an attempt to change my mind?"

"You know me better than to think I'd take commands from my baby brother. *But*"—I knew that *but* was coming—"that doesn't mean I won't try to convince you Blue Beech is a good place, and you should really consider moving here."

"I'll keep that in mind." *Especially if I can get another night like this.*

He bows his head. "Thank you."

"I didn't make any promises."

"Not thank you for allowing me to show you around. Thank you for making me forget I'm a miserable man missing half of who he is. Thank you for not treating me like a broken fucking object that needs fixing."

I hide my face on his shoulder to conceal my smile. "You've done the same for me." With my mouth pressed against his denim shirt, my face hidden, I take a risk that could go horribly wrong. "You know somewhere I haven't seen in Blue Beech?"

"What's that?"

"The home of Dallas Barnes."

Don't judge me.

I know what I'm doing is wrong, but bad ideas sometimes lead to good things, right?

CHAPTER THIRTEEN

Willow

ONE OF THE biggest things I've learned about Blue Beech so far is real-life county fairs are nothing like the movies.

Dallas texted me this morning to remind me of the time he was picking me up and told me to have an appetite. The impulse to decline spilled through me, but the thought of experiencing something new prevented it.

I mean, who doesn't want to find out what the fair hype is all about?

Dallas parks his truck in a grassy field converted into a parking lot. The amount of cars surprises me. *This many people live here?*

He helps Maven out of the truck before circling to my side. "Thank you for coming," he says when he opens my door. He grabs my hand and assists me out of the lifted truck. "It's all Maven's been talking about today."

I nervously laugh. "Guess it was time to pop my fair cherry." I grimace at my word choice. *No, Willow. No flirting with the widowed asshole.*

He smirks. "Honored to be the one to do it."

I nod, relieved he didn't shut down on me but scared it'll

happen sometime tonight. Like me, Dallas is a pro at freezing people out at the snap of his fingers.

Maven is spinning in circles with her arms out in the air. Her hair is pulled back in two French braids that are finished off with furry pink bands holding each one in place. *Did Dallas braid them for her?*

I swing the strap of my cross-body bag over my shoulder while Dallas scoops Maven up and spins her around one last time. He takes her hand and leads us toward the flashing lights and white tents. When we hit the dusty pathway, I peek down at my feet, wishing I'd chosen different shoes. Everyone is in boots or sneakers while I'm sporting studded black flats that are going to be ruined by the end of the night.

"I want to ride that one!" Maven exclaims, pointing at rides as we make our way through the crowd. "Then, that one. And that one."

"Dinner before rides," Dallas replies, casting a glance my way. "What's your fair poison?"

"My what?" I ask.

He peeks down at Maven with a smile. "This is Willow's first time at the fair," he explains, as if I were the only person who hadn't done such a thing.

Maven giggles, her face lighting up. "Really?"

I nod, and she reaches out to connect her hand with mine. My chest tightens when I squeeze my hand around hers, a sadness sinking through me. We resemble the other families here —mom and dad treating their eager daughter to a night full of games, candy, and fun.

"My absolute favorites are elephant ears and cotton candy!" she says.

"Hey, I've had cotton candy," I argue.

"But have you had *fair* cotton candy?" Dallas counters, causing Maven to burst out into more giggles. "*Blue Beech* cotton candy?"

I glance over at him. "Wasn't aware there was a difference."

His dark brows rise. "Oh, there most definitely is."

We stop at a table underneath a blue tent, and Dallas insists on getting our food. Maven takes the seat next to me, her legs bouncing up and down in excitement.

"Did you know Daddy said I get to ride big-kid rides this year?" she asks with a burst of energy I wish I had every morning. "Last year, I wasn't tall enough, but I've grown *lots and lots*!"

"No way!" I reply before holding my hand up in the air. "I had to wait until I was *this* big before I got to do that."

Her head tilts to the side. "I thought you'd never been to a fair?"

Girl is smart for a six-year-old.

"I've been to Disney."

She bounces in her seat. "Me, too! Mommy and Daddy took me for my birthday. I had lunch with Princess Jasmine!"

I place my hand over my heart and gasp. "Princess Jasmine? That's so cool. Is she your favorite princess?"

She nods repeatedly. "Who's yours?"

"Ariel." I point to my hair. "Have to support my fellow redhead."

"She's my second favorite!" She claps her hands. "Maybe, next time, you can come with Daddy and me and meet Princess Jasmine!"

I nod timidly. "Yeah, maybe."

Our conversation stops when Dallas gets to the table with drinks in his hands and plates lined up his arms, like an experienced waiter. I slide out of my seat to help him set everything down.

"Are you feeding the entire town?" I ask.

"I promised to give you the full fair experience," he says, sitting down across from me. He points to the plates the same way Maven did with the rides. "Tenderloins are Maven's and my favorite. I also grabbed some fried chicken, shish kebabs, and pizza in case you wanted to play it safe. Then, we have some elephant ears and cotton candy. Drinks are an option of a lemon shake-up, water, or soda."

I snag a lemon shake-up. "So many healthy choices."

He chuckles. "We're splurging tonight."

Maven sticks out her tongue. "It's better than broccoli. Daddy makes me eat gross broccoli."

Dallas points his fork at her. "Give a man some credit for adding cheese to it for you."

Maven picks up a shish kebab and waves it through the air. "Not better than cotton candy! Pink is the best!" she sings out.

The nauseating smell of meat smacks me in the face, causing my stomach to churn, and she sets it back down on her plate. I close my hand over my nose and mouth—not only to block out the stench, but also to stop myself from vomiting in front of a crowd of people.

Dallas drops his sandwich. "Everything okay?"

"The meat," I choke out underneath my hand, shaking my head. "None of that."

He gets the hint, grabs it from Maven's plate, and tosses it in the trash. "Sorry, honey," he tells her. "Bad meat."

She nods and moves on to a tenderloin.

I move my hand and take a deep breath, whispering, "Thank you," to him.

His lips tilt up in a smile, a real one, something I haven't seen from him since I've been here. My breathing hitches. My heart skitters.

"Any weird cravings yet?" he asks.

"Cupcakes. Cake. Brownies. Sugar in general."

He laughs, another authentic one, making me happy I came. "I'll remember that."

My lips curve into a smile, meeting his, and I snack on a slice of cheese pizza while Maven takes over the conversation of how excited she is to leave for summer camp in a few days. She shoves her plate forward after the last bite and focuses on Dallas in determination that is too intense for a kid whose age hasn't reached the double digits yet.

"Time for rides, Daddy!" she declares. "And don't you forget, I get to ride the *big-kid* ones. No more kiddy zone for me."

Dallas holds his hand up. "Hold it, youngster. Only the ones you meet the height requirement for, remember?"

"Is she trying to talk you into letting her bungee jump again?"

Hudson's voice catches me off guard, and I turn around to see him and Stella coming our way. The sight of her eases me. Hudson ... not so much. I'm not sure how he feels about me. Stella insists he holds no grudges against me, but I don't believe her.

"I'm not old enough for that *yet*," Maven says.

"Or ever," Dallas corrects. He stares down at Maven, shaking his head. "You, my dear child, are going to give me a heart attack before forty."

"Hey, brother," Hudson cuts in. "Which will be worse—the day she wants to bungee jump or date?"

"Dating," Dallas answers without hesitation. "I will bungee jump at her side before I agree to dating."

"Gross, I don't want to date," Maven chimes in with disgust.

Dallas taps the top of her head. "That's my girl."

"You want to ride roller coasters with me, Uncle Hudson?" Maven asks. "Willow is coming!"

Pregnancy and carnival rides don't go together.

"Oh no," I moan out. "I get motion sickness."

I'm not sure when Dallas is going to break the news that she's going to be a big sister, but I most certainly don't want to be in attendance. Lord knows the questions she'll have.

Maven's smile morphs into a pout. "My mommy did, too, but she was always okay."

I regret looking at Dallas at the mention of Lucy. His body goes still, and I'm confident his heart is beating faster than anyone on a roller coaster here. The lightness of our time together has been extinguished, a whirl of unease stepping through. He scratches his neck, and I notice a vein popping out from it.

"How about I go with you? I love roller coasters!" Stella quickly offers up, lying to the poor girl.

"Thank you," I whisper to her while Maven waits for Dallas's permission.

His eyes are vacant, his face cloaked with pain. He's checked out.

"I'll make sure the two of them stay out of trouble," Hudson says. "You keep introducing Willow to coma-inducing foods and sell Blue Beech to her."

Dallas pinches the bridge of his nose and nods. I grab my lemon shakeup and suck it down without even bothering to argue with Hudson about the "sell Blue Beech to her" comment. The thought of Dallas showing me around makes me queasier than the meat.

Stella grabs Maven's hand, and the three of them take off through the pack of people. I'm struggling to find the right words. I want to console Dallas, but I'm not sure if it's a good idea. It might push him away more.

Isn't that what I wanted when I found out I was pregnant?

Now, I'm thriving for more from him.

For as long as I can remember, I've admired his love for Lucy. His commitment to her, even when half-dressed women threw themselves at him in hopes of seeing Stella.

Seeing their relationship made you believe in love again.

And that's why I can't get close to him.

He'll never give me that.

You don't get love like that twice in a lifetime.

You can't awaken those emotions back out of a broken man.

I need to back off and quit trying to make strides with him that'll only end up stomping on my heart when I'm forced to face the devastation that he's just around me because I got knocked up by him.

I don't realize I'm staring until his hollow eyes meet mine. His Adam's apple bobs while he piles the plates on top of each other and disposes them into the trash.

He fraudulently smiles down at me. "You ready for your Blue Beech pitch?"

I grab a bag of cotton candy. "I'll listen, but I'm not someone easily convinced."

"Oh, Miss Andrews, I can be a very persuasive man." He must've given himself a pep talk on his way to the trash because his excitement meter has risen a few notches.

I shove a handful of cotton candy into my mouth before getting up. We walk in silence, side by side, passing annoyed parents yelling at their children and people spending their paychecks on games that are scamming them.

Everyone stops and stares when we walk past them, like we're the show animals. A few women have pulled out their phones to record us. We appear as platonic as it gets. Hell, maybe more like strangers, considering we're not saying a word to each other.

No story here, people.

Don't twist it into something it's not.

Because it's way more complicated than us having sex.

"How about a game?" Dallas asks, breaking my attention away from the crowd of women pointing our way.

I throw them a dirty grimace and set my eyes back on him.

We've stopped in front of a ring-toss game with giant animals hanging from the roof of the tent.

"The chances of me winning that small stuffed animal is one in a gazillion, and it will cost me a couple of hundred bucks. I'd rather save my money and buy a new handbag." *Or a crib.*

"I like your style." He laughs, shaking his head. "I've blown so much money on those stupid things. Lucy loved them." He tilts his head toward the flashing lights and spinning rides. "Ferris wheel?"

"I see you live on the wild side."

"Risky is my middle name. Be right back."

I combatively stare at him while he jogs over to the ticket booth without waiting to hear my answer.

How do I tell him I'd rather blow my life savings on a game than be stuck in the air with him?

As bad as I want to, I can't. It's hard for me to give him shit when it looks like someone ran over his dog.

So, I wait in line.

He hands the bored attendant our tickets and helps me into the car. It's cramped as we sit across from each other. I blush each time our knees brush in the tight space.

"You make a doctor's appointment yet?" he asks when the wheel starts to move.

I sigh playfully. "This was your plan, huh? Get me hundreds of feet in the air, so I can't bail when you ask me complicated questions?"

He holds his hand up, a smile cracking at his lips. It's not as real as the one he gave me at the beginning of the night, but it's better than the artificial one earlier. "Convenient timing, I swear." He pauses, the smile still flickering at his lips. "Subconscious smart move on my part, considering your history of being a runner."

His jeans rub against my bare leg when I situate myself on the metal seat. Like my flats, shorts weren't the best fashion choice.

"Awkward conversations aren't a favorite pastime of mine," I mutter.

"You mean, making adult decisions aren't?"

"I'm twenty-six." I mentally slap myself. *That's my argument?*

"Last time I checked, twenty-six was an adult."

"I mean, I don't have much experience in making adult decisions that don't only impact my life."

When I graduated from high school, I moved to LA for college and have lived my life without answering to anyone. I travel regularly for my job and don't have to worry about anyone other than my boss controlling what I do. My personal decisions have never impacted anyone else's life before.

"You'd better get over that shit *fast*. We're about to be making some big decisions together," he says.

My chest feels tight. I haven't come to terms with having a long-term relationship with Dallas, and I don't feel like diving into the reality of it now. "I haven't made a doctor's appointment yet. I have no idea where to go, but I'd prefer an office not close, considering the town doctor probably delivered you." *And Maven.*

"That's true."

I throw my arms out. "Exactly!" *Does it make me a sucky person that I don't want the same doctor Lucy had? God, I sound like a jealous brat.*

"Dr. Riley's son recently graduated from med school and moved back to work at the practice. He said he'd see us on the low until you're ready to tell people."

On the low? Like I'm going to be pushing a royal baby out of me?

"You're positive he won't tell anyone?" I ask.

"Positive. I have plenty of dirt to easily blackmail him."

"Good. Blackmail away. I'd rather not have any more attention brought to us."

He chuckles and leans forward to scan the crowd below. "I take it, I wasn't the only one noticing all the prying eyes?"

"Sure weren't."

"Ignore them. Something new will come up, and they'll forget about us."

"Doubt it. You're like the bachelor of Blue Beech, and I'm sure they want you to give a rose to a *local girl.*"

"Other people don't decide whom I spend my time with."

They might not decide, but that doesn't mean they won't talk shit about it.

I point to my stomach. "In other news, I need to find more creative ways to hide this. I'm showing more, and I don't want people to find out."

"We're having a baby, Willow. It's eventually going to come out. You're struggling with the reality of it, and that's why I'm holding back on saying anything, but you'd better come to grips with it soon. I need to tell my daughter and parents before you go into labor."

Dallas isn't a bullshitter.

He shoots it to you straight. Been that way for as long as I've known him, which is something I'm not used to. The guys I date tend to be liars who whisper sweet nothings into your ear and then do the opposite. I've never had a guy ... a *man* like Dallas.

He clears his throat. "And, since I have you hostage, I'd better ask the question that's been bugging me."

Oh God. What now?

"Tell me the truth. Why did you hide this from me?"

I look around. *How long does it take for us to get back to the ground?*

"Willow," he says, practically growling my name. "Give me a clear answer, not something half-assed. I want real. The truth."

I lean in and take a deep breath. *Here goes. He wants it. I'll give it. He's not going to like it.*

"I remember every second of our night together." My pulse races like a freight train is about to hit me. "You made me feel special, like I could have someone other than a cheating scumbag. You made me feel alive." *Am I really going to do this?* I want to sound strong, but my voice cracks. "At least temporarily." I stop to inhale another breath, chickening out.

"What happened that makes you question our night wasn't special?"

His gaze is fixed on me, intense, and he settles his elbow on his knee. His free hand rests on my thigh.

"You called me her."

I thought I had his attention before, but my admission kicked it into overdrive.

His head jerks to the side. "What?"

"You called me her ... *Lucy.*" Tears bite at my eyes, breaking the hold I've been trying to keep. *There. I said it. I gave him the truth.*

His face contorts with a mix of pain and disbelief. "What? No way. You're lying."

"I'm not lying."

I regret it every day. Regret not slapping him in the face or screaming when it happened, but I couldn't blame him. I couldn't blame him because my intention of having sex with him was the same—to forget the person I longed for. I wanted to erase Brett. He tried to erase Lucy.

He scrubs his hand over his face. I've spent the last decade reading a man who lied for years, and Dallas isn't lying about not remembering.

He scoots in closer to clasp my chin in his hand. "Fuck, Willow. I'm sorry. No wonder you hate my fucking guts and can barely stand to look at me. I'm sorry. God, I'm an asshole."

He runs his hand over my cheek while apologizing repeatedly. I draw in the trace of cotton candy and cinnamon on his breath.

The end of our ride is getting closer, and I wish I had a panic button to freeze us in place.

"You're the only woman I've kissed other than Lucy," he says, his lips inches from mine. "The only woman I've touched. The only woman I've ever had in my bed."

I relax into his touch, into his words. *Should this admission turn me on? Should it make me want to straddle him and get a public indecency arrest?*

"And it's not for lack of trying," he goes on. "This will make me sound like an arrogant jerk, but I've had women knocking on my door daily, but I've never given them a second look. Replacing Lucy with a quick fuck wasn't my intention. I could've done that with anyone. I might've said her name, but I swear to you, I knew who I was inside of, and it wasn't her."

I breathe heavily and take in the callous palm roaming over my cheek.

"We were both missing other people that night. We can agree on that."

I nod at the truth. "What do you want from me?" I whisper, my lips nearly hitting his.

"I want you to move here permanently. I want you to raise our baby here. I don't want you to leave."

His eyes soften, and I dart my tongue over my lips without even realizing it.

God, the desperation of wanting to kiss him, of wanting to screw him, of wanting his touch anywhere on my body is all I'm feeling right now.

"What do you want from me, Willow?"

To wrap my hand around your cock again. To feel you inside me one last time. To love me like you loved her.

"I ... I don't know," I answer breathlessly. I can't concentrate on anything but us.

He takes in a sharp breath. "Why can't I stop thinking about you?"

I make my move, unable to stop myself, and crash my lips against his. He tastes more like cotton candy than he smells. He groans while moving his hand from my face to the back of my neck, diving into my hair and drawing me in closer, opening his mouth so that our tongues meet.

His mouth is soft and forbidden. Him only kissing me is going to send me over the edge. He scoots in closer to use his knee to separate my legs more and slides his hand up my thigh, stopping where my shorts end.

"What are you doing to me?" he mutters, taking me deeper into his mouth and inching his hand underneath the fabric, his fingers spreading apart.

I moan and tilt my hips up, permitting him to keep going. His fingers crawl to my middle, right over my panties, and he rubs his thumb across it.

"Fuck," he groans. "You're soaked."

I close my eyes as he moves my panties to the side.

"Okay, who's next in line?" the operator yells.

Dallas's hand disappears in seconds, and his back hits the seat, his breathing labored. "Fuck. I'm sorry. That shouldn't have happened."

I straighten my shorts, rub my hands over my hair to fix it, and curl my arms around my stomach. No doubt I would smack him in the face if we weren't in a public place.

"You're right. It won't happen again," I whisper.

The operator winks at us when the car stops, and we get out.

"It happens all the time, man," he says, smirking. "Figured you wouldn't want to keep up your show in front of everyone."

Oh, hell. He saw us.

I stumble forward, my legs feeling weak, and Dallas rests his hand on the small of my back to stabilize me. We're back to silence, like he didn't have his hand in my shorts only minutes ago, like he wasn't about to get me off in a Ferris wheel car. He guides us straight to Stella, who's waiting on Hudson and Maven to finish up a ride.

Our conversation ends.

Our connection ends.

My hope for him ever touching me again ends.

I can't get attached. I can't let Dallas Barnes in again.

In my head. In my vagina. In my heart.

CHAPTER FOURTEEN

Dallas

MY HOPES of taking Willow to the fair, so she'd change her mind about staying here blew up in my face.

All because me and my dick.

All because my lack of being laid.

And the fact that she looked so delicious, so damn sexy, sitting there, that I couldn't stop myself. I nearly lost it when I felt how wet she was for me. I wanted to prove to her that I wasn't an asshole whose mind was on my dead wife when I slept with her. I fucked up. I'll be the one to blame when she packs up and leaves.

We'd started to break ground, begun building something, and then my dumbass took a wrecking ball to it. My night with her had been incredible. Touching her had been incredible. What I had done that morning was fucked up and is one of my biggest regrets.

I called her Lucy.

Humiliation and stupidity crack my core.

I don't blame her for hating my ass and keeping her distance.

Had the roles been reversed, had a woman called me

another man's name in bed, I would've stepped away … and most likely kicked her out of my bed.

I want to change. To be the man who can rise through the flames stronger than ever, but I can't.

That's why what happened tonight scares the shit out of me.

My goal at the bar had been to drink away the pain, the memories. I hadn't been searching for someone to talk to. Nowhere in my mind was the idea of having a one-night stand. It all took a turn when Willow spoke to me. My attention was all hers as soon as we had our first drink together. I wasn't going to leave that bar unless it was with her.

Tonight has proven it wasn't only a drunken attraction that brought us to my bed.

That fucking terrifies me.

Maven is passed out in the backseat, exhausted from going on every ride multiple times, and Willow hasn't said one word since we got in my truck.

Man, I wish my daughter would wake up and start rambling about random shit like she usually does. I gear my truck into park when we arrive at Willow's apartment and unclip my seat belt to open the door for her, but she's faster than I am.

"Well, uh … good night," is all she says before opening the door and jumping out of the truck like it's on fire. "You don't need to walk me up." She slams the door, races up the steps, and goes inside.

I shut my eyes. "Good night, Willow," I whisper even though she can't hear me.

I wait to pull away until I see the light come through her windows.

I get Maven changed when we get home, tuck her into bed, and start to pick up around the house. If I slack on the housecleaning, my mom comes over and not only plays maid, but detective as well. She checks the fridge to make sure we're consuming all the food groups and goes through my mail and underwear drawer.

I grew out of letting my mom make my bed over a decade ago—the reasons different now than before. I'm not stashing porn and condoms underneath my mattress. It's more her searching for evidence that I'm getting laid or seeing someone. She's resorted to leaving information about online dating and schedules of all the social functions happening in town.

No fucking thank you.

I finish cleaning up the aftermath of Maven's sleepover with her stuffed animals last night. It happens when I go into my bedroom. I tried to hide all the pictures once. Picked them up and shut them away in the attic. Ten minutes later, I returned them.

I like to see Lucy when I'm having a bad day, when I need someone to understand me, when I need to tell her about all the crazy stuff our daughter does. I grab the picture from my nightstand and trace my fingers over her wedding dress, her tan face, her blonde hair, and then her pink lips.

"You always were the best at giving advice," I whisper, setting the frame down to twist my wedding ring. "Tell me what I should do."

I shut my eyes and remember her last words. Lucy knew what I needed before I knew it myself.

"Find someone to love," she demanded.

"That's not … that's not possible," I whispered.

"It is. I promise you, the day will come." I opened my mouth to argue, but she placed her finger against the crack of my lips. "You might not see it now, but it will. Your heart will make the right choice to move on with someone who loves you and Maven. Don't be scared, my love. Give it a chance. Heal and let her help you do it."

I kiss my fingers, press them to her picture, and turn off my lamp.

Sleep doesn't come to me.

CHAPTER FIFTEEN

Dallas

MAVEN GRINS at me with her gap-toothed smile, a clear sign she's up to no good. Two bags are set at her feet, waiting for me to load them into my truck. "Daddy, I need your phone this week. Pretty, pretty please."

"For what?" I ask.

"In case I need anything," she answers in annoyance, as if it were a reasonable request for a six-year-old.

"Nice try. You're not taking my phone to camp."

She huffs and stomps her feet. I've already vetoed her iPad making the trip. *Damn kids and electronics.* They act like it'll kill them to spend a weekend in the wilderness without Wi-Fi.

"What if I get lost in the woods and can't find my way back?"

"I've pointed out the North Star to you several times."

She frowns. "What if I see a big ole mean bear?"

I laugh. "Having a phone will be the last of your worries. If you see a bear, slowly back away, and don't make eye contact." *I thought I wasn't supposed to deal with this shit until her teenage years.*

She crosses her arms and gives me her best pouty face. She knows how to pull at my heartstrings. Her perfected pouty face has landed her a gerbil, a goldfish, and the iPad.

"Don't act like you won't miss me," I tease.

Her pouty face turns into an annoyed one.

"Now, grab your sleeping bag, and let's get going," I instruct.

This will be the longest we've been away from each other since Lucy passed. It was different when she was here. I lived states away, traveled frequently, and only came home a few times a month. I regret having that long-distance relationship. I thought I'd have more time, but it just goes to show you that time is never guaranteed. Live each moment and hug the ones you love because you don't know what can happen tomorrow.

"What are you going to do when I'm gone?" she asks as I strap the seat belt around her.

"Work. Do grown-up stuff."

I shut the door and jump into the driver's seat. The camp is about an hour drive, and I made a playlist for us to enjoy during the trip since we have the no-electronics rule. Maven is going to hate it ... at first because I usually let her listen to her teenybop bullshit, but I want to introduce her to something new today.

"One Direction, Daddy!" she yells as soon as we pull out of the driveway.

"Oh, man, I forgot to tell you."

She scrunches her face up. "Forgot to tell me what?"

"Now that they broke up, their music can't be played anymore. It's banned."

"Since when?"

"Yesterday. It was all over the news." I peek back at her silence to see tears running down her face. *This can't be for real?* "What's wrong, May-Bear?"

"They're gone," she cries out, her pouty face intact.

Jesus Christ. "Let me double-check. It might have changed."

I switch to Maven's favorite station and groan when a One Direction song conveniently comes blasting through my speakers.

So much for Bob Dylan.

My little girl always wins.

KIDS ARE JUMPING out of cars, backpacks strapped to them, and running toward the group of others congregated in front of the clubhouse. Maven has already said her good-byes and taken off with her friends.

I lean back against my truck and slide my hands into the pockets of my jeans. My parents sent us kids to Camp Maganaw, and I never failed to have a blast. My attention goes straight to Bear Claw Cabin. It's been updated with a fresh slab of paint and a new door, but the memories I have in that cabin will always be there. Lucy and I had our first kiss behind Bear Claw after sneaking out one night.

"Dallas, how are you holding up?"

I briefly glance over when Cindy stops at my side and copies my stance. Cindy and I went to high school together, and she was Lucy's hairdresser. She married the quarterback, had a baby, and then divorced the cheating drunk a few years ago.

I move dirt with the toe of my boot. "As good as I can be, I guess."

A breath bursts from her lips. "I get it. It's hard. I never thought I'd be with anyone other than Phil, but I've learned that the best way to heal is by moving on."

I ram my heel into the ground as anger flushes through me. "A divorce and death are not fucking worthy of comparison," I grind out.

I bite my tongue to stop myself from telling her what wants to come out. Cindy was one of the casserole-and-muffin-making chicks who checked up on me daily in the weeks after losing Lucy. I finally had to put a stop to it after the third week.

If she believes finding someone else with help, more power to her, but I won't be the man to do it … and she sure as hell isn't replacing Lucy.

"You know, you're a jackass. I'm sorry if my concern for you and your daughter eating makes you so rattled," she snaps.

"I told you I appreciated the meals, but they weren't necessary. I don't need help feeding my daughter. We both know your *concern* wasn't making sure we had hot meals twice a day."

She slumps back against the truck. "So, it's true then?"

"What's true?"

Her *concern* has switched to annoyance. "You and the new chick in town have something going on?"

My eyes stay pinned to her.

"Stella's friend," she clarifies, annoyed.

"The hell you hear that?" I ask with a scoff.

"We all saw it at the fair—to my surprise, considering, months ago, you made it clear you weren't interested in dating, *period.*"

"I'm not dating anyone." I pause and pinch my lips together. "Not that it's anyone's fucking business."

A rush of red storms her cheeks. "Asshole," she mutters before turning around and stomping to her car.

TWO DAYS HAVE PASSED since the fair fiasco, and communication with Willow has been limited and vague. Phone calls go unanswered. Text messages consists of one word. I've never received so many *K* and *Cool* responses.

That's changing today.

It's our first doctor's appointment. I texted Willow the details after scheduling it and waited for the argument I knew was coming, but surprisingly, she agreed ... with a fucking *K.*

I park my truck and wait until she walks out of her apartment before jumping out and joining her on the sidewalk.

"Nuh-uh," she says. "I'm driving myself."

"No one is driving," I reply. "It's a five-minute walk. I thought we'd enjoy the stroll."

She pinches her lips together, and her shoulder smacks

against mine when she bursts past me and down the sidewalk. "I'll pass."

She pushes when I pull.

I pull when she pushes.

One of us is always resisting when the other comes forward.

I speed-walk to keep up with her. "Come on. The weather is perfect. Let's save the environment and conserve gas, not pollute the air. Walking with me will save the world."

My humanity-saving argument doesn't stop her, and I nearly miss her mocking me, an uneven smile on her lips. I don't hold back my shit-eating grin when she passes her car and keeps walking. I stay a few steps behind and let her believe she's getting her way until it happens.

I rush forward when she trips on her feet, falling forward, her knees almost hitting the concrete while her lips are close to kissing the sidewalk. I stretch my arm out to capture her around the waist, and she yelps as I steady her. Instead of breaking my hold when she's stable, I tighten my grip, my fingers sinking into the cotton of her *Girl Power* T-shirt, and stare down at her.

I wait for her to pull out of my hold and tell me never to touch her again. She does none of that. She stays still, catching her breath, and shakes her head.

"Really?" she mutters. "So damn cliché. I fall, and you catch me."

I can't help but chuckle at the actuality of her words. "Just like in the movies."

I release my hold on her waist but move my hand to her elbow just in case.

"You're nervous," I say.

I run my hand up and down her arm in an attempt to calm her nerves. I don't know what has her riled up more—her almost fall, us touching, or this appointment.

She pulls out of my hold with a grimace and runs her hand down her long hair. "No shit, Sherlock."

"Anything I can do to help?"

"Not come."

"Anything I can do *but* that?"

Her hands start shaking, and I turn so that I'm standing in front of her. She attempts to maneuver around me, but I take a step over. She tries the other side. I do the same thing.

"Breathe. Relax." I inhale and exhale a few times in hopes that she'll follow my lead. She does. "Everything is going to be okay, I promise. If you feel uncomfortable, we'll leave."

We do this for a good five minutes, and she sniffles while calming down. "These damn pregnancy hormones are going to be the end of my sanity."

I smile. "I wish I could say they get better, but from what I've witnessed, they don't." I move out of her way and settle my hand on the arch of her back when she starts walking again.

"Then, I'd be careful not to piss me off."

"That's been my goal since day one."

I've been sucking ass at it though.

She sniffles again. "You need to work harder."

Thought confirmed.

I move my arm up and wrap it around her shoulders, bringing her to my side, hoping she doesn't pull away. This isn't sexual. It's something you do to a friend having a bad day.

"Come on, I can't have you showing up to the doctor in tears. My mom would have my ass if she found out. Give me something I can do to calm you down."

"Punching you might work."

I break our connection to move back in front of her and start walking backward. "If being your punching bag helps, then have at it." I throw my arms out and gesture for her to take a swing.

I'm the one stumbling this time when she pushes me back. "God, you piss me off."

"What? Why? I'm giving you what you want."

I've never had complications like this with a woman. Granted, my experience is limited to one woman, so that doesn't say much in itself. I don't remember learning Lucy's quirks because I grew up with them. They were instilled in me before I knew how to spell my name.

She scowls. "What I want is for you to stop being so damn nice."

"What? Why?" I repeat, confused as fuck.

If I'm an ass, she's pissed. If I'm nice, she's pissed.

"Because you're making it difficult to hate you right now."

"That's a bad thing?"

"Yes!"

I'm doing everything in my power to fix this, to make her feel comfortable, so she doesn't run away again, but it's killing me. I'm very rarely the fun guy. My role has always been the serious and overprotective brother. Hudson was the Marine who thrived on having a good time, and Lauren was the mischievous one I caught sneaking out on too many occasions. I was the big brother who made sure everyone was okay and protected.

I stop us in front of the restored yellow Victorian home. "And we're here." Perfect timing before we get into another argument, and my goal of distracting her has somewhat succeeded.

She assesses the building and glares at me like I'm fucking with her. "This ..." She does another once-over. "This is a house. Where's the office?"

I point to the sign with the doctor's name.

"This isn't some midwives shit, is it? Not to be judgmental, but I'm not having my baby in some old home's bathtub."

"We'll go to a hospital when you give birth, and so will the doctor. Give Dr. Riley a chance. If you hate him, we'll go to the city."

Compromise. Compromise. Fucking compromise. Marriage taught me that compromise is what keeps you going when the tides get rough.

She sighs. "Let's do this then."

CHAPTER SIXTEEN

Willow

THE DOOR CHIMES when we walk in, and the nurse behind the counter jumps up from her chair to greet us. Her smile collapses when she notices Dallas behind me. She has the perfect sun-kissed blonde hair and a summer tan. She reminds me of Lucy. Dallas's type.

She tucks a strand behind her ear. "Dallas … I didn't see you on the books today."

"Hey, Fiona. I'm with Willow Andrews. We have an appointment with Aidan," he explains, keeping his focus on me.

Dallas wasn't lying about there being an office inside. It's not modern, like the one I went to for my first pregnancy test. First professional one. I'd taken fifteen at-home tests and then finally gone to the doctor because I was in denial and determined they were all defective.

A few chairs sit in the waiting room across from the wooden front desk A photo of an older man with his name underneath it is centered on the wall, and a corkboard covered with flyers is hung next to it.

Get your flu shot!
Join the bowling league!
Fire department fundraiser this Friday!

The nurse's red lips dip in surprise as she stares at me in curiosity the same way everyone did at the fair. "I see. Let me collect the paperwork your doctor sent over this morning, and then I'll show you to your exam room."

Dallas tucks his hands into the pockets of his jeans. "Is Rick in today?"

"No, he's out hunting. Won't be back until the weekend. We have a light schedule today, even with Aidan here." She laughs. "Everyone remembers all the trouble he got into when you guys were younger, and they aren't sure if they trust him with needles yet."

I jerk my head to glare at Dallas. *The hell? Is he bringing me to some quack?*

"Aidan knows what he's doing," Dallas says, reassuring me. "We can't all stay the kids who drank behind my parents' barn or nearly lit the town square on fire."

Fiona slaps his shoulder. "I miss those days." She taps it next. "How have you been doing?"

He nods, scraping a hand through his hair, and his face tightens. "Fine."

"You let me know if you need anything, all right?"

"Thanks," he replies flatly.

Well … this sure is fun.

"So, where to?" he asks.

She leads us to a room at the end of the hallway. The door isn't numbered but does say *Dr. Aidan Riley* across the top glass.

I sit on the exam bed while Dallas scoots his chair next to me. I don't realize I'm tapping my feet until he rests his hand on my thigh, causing me to flinch. I surprise myself by not moving it. He might piss me off, but his touch relaxes me. That still doesn't stop me from scowling at him though.

There's a knock on the door, and Dallas moves his hand like a kid caught with it in the cookie jar when the doctor walks in.

The first thing I notice shouldn't be how attractive he is, but he's definitely a looker. Blond hair cut short in almost a frat-boy style but more sophisticated and an oval face with perfect features. I was expecting a dude in overalls. Now, I'm stuck in a room with two men I wouldn't have a problem screwing. My OB-GYN and the off-limits man who knocked me up.

He holds out his hand with a smile. "Willow, pleasure meeting you. I'm Dr. Riley, but call me Aidan, considering my father has the same name, and I'm not an old goat."

I smile back, and his attention goes to Dallas next, worry crossing his features.

"Dallas, you doing okay, man?"

My smile collapses. I feel bad for Dallas. His loss follows him everywhere. He will forever be known as the man who tragically lost his wife too soon. And I'll forever be known as the woman who screwed the heartbroken widowed man and got knocked up.

Dallas's attention stays on me as he answers, "Sure am, Doc."

Aidan sits down on the rolling stool and comes closer. "The doctor who gave you your initial pregnancy test sent over your records. It appears, you're around twelve weeks. Good timing for your first ultrasound."

"Right … right now?" I ask. I knew he'd want to run tests but figured he'd want to ask more questions before diving straight in.

"We can do it another time if you'd like," Aidan replies.

"No." I clear my throat. "Today's fine." I want to see my baby. I peek over at Dallas. "You probably don't want to be in here for this."

He kicks his legs out and makes himself comfortable in the chair. "I'd like to be. That cool?"

Fuck no.

Aidan opens a cabinet and pulls out a cup before handing it to me. "You think about it. Meanwhile, I need a urine sample." He tips his head toward the other side of the room. "Bathroom's right there."

I shut the door behind me and am washing my hands when I hear their conversation.

"Your mom know about this?" Aidan asks.

"No," Dallas answers. "Just Hudson, his girlfriend, and Lauren."

"Is she ..." Aidan pauses. "Are you two ..."

"Are we dating? No. It was a one-time thing."

Aidan chuckles. "Oh, man. Good luck, my friend, and congratulations on the baby."

MY HEAD FLIES UP, nearly colliding with Dallas's, and I'm struggling to keep my breath.

"Twins?" I yell. "Did you ..." My gaze flicks to Dallas, who looks in as much shock as I am. "Did he ... did he say twins?"

"Sure did," Aidan answers with a wide grin. "My first prenatal patient, and we're having twins. *Yes!*"

"Don't take this the wrong way, Doctor, but you're new at this, right? Are you sure you know how to read these correctly? They're probably more ancient than what you worked with in med school."

Aidan is still smiling, not offended. "I read these things for years when I shadowed my father. I clearly see two fetuses." He puts his finger on the screen. "Here's baby one." Then, he moves it over. "And baby number two."

Holy shit. Holy shit.

Dallas is sitting up straight, mouth open, and staring at the screen like he has to memorize it for a test tomorrow.

I can't think straight. I was scared shitless when I thought I was having one baby. Now, I'm having *two?*

Double the responsibility. Double the diaper-changing. Double the expenses. Double the help I'm going to need from Dallas. Double the time we'll be spending together.

"LET'S GET LUNCH."

I stop in my tracks and coldly gape at him. From now on, I'll be placing all of this pregnancy blame on him because it's too much for me to carry two babies in my body along with the responsibility of our choice on my shoulders.

He knocked me up. I'm the one who has to push the babies out, so he can deal with the blame for the pain and fear I'm experiencing. It only makes sense.

"Lunch?" I repeat. "Don't you mean, let's find a safe, pregnancy-approved Xanax? Or let's go to yoga? Or find a stress-management class? Did you hear what Aidan said? I have two babies inside me."

We found out we're having twins, and he wants to get fucking lunch? Surely, I can't be the only one in shock.

Lucky for me, Fiona was on break and unable to witness the panic in me when we left the exam room.

He stares at me with unease. "I heard him loud and clear. Two babies make feeding you even more important."

"Are you not fucking terrified?" I shout.

We're on the sidewalk outside the doctor's office, which isn't too far from the town square where most of the people hang out and gossip. There's a chance someone might hear us, but I don't care right now.

He takes a deep breath. "Nervous? Yes. But it's nothing I can't handle." He takes the step separating us and runs his hands over my arms. "You can do this. *We* can do this. You're going to be a great mother. When the babies come, your instincts will kick in, and you'll have it figured out. Hell, I've seen you do shit for Stella that's more demanding than children. So, yes, I'm nervous and surprised as fuck, but I'm relieved, knowing our twins will have a kick-ass mother. I trust you. I have faith in you. It won't be easy, but we'll make it work."

I scrunch up my face when he snorts. "What's so funny?"

"I bet you're glad you didn't hide this from me now. Admit it. You're going to need my help."

"You're changing all the diapers, by the way. That's your daddy duty."

"Whatever you need, I'll be here." He rubs his hands together. "Now, how 'bout that lunch?"

"Lunch together? Like, in a public place?"

He chuckles. "Yes, together. There's a diner down the street that serves the best sandwiches and pies you've ever had."

I fake a yawn. "Thanks for the invite, but I'm pretty exhausted."

I used to feel comfortable with spending hours with Dallas. We traveled together for weeks straight at times and ate meals together, and it never felt weird. *So, why does it seem like such a big deal now?* We slept with each other, for God's sake.

"Come on." He places his hands together. "*Please.*"

"Fine, but a quick meal, and that's it." It's hard to turn down this man.

He grins in victory. We pass small shops and bakeries before stopping in front of Shirley's Diner. Large windows line the front, and I see the prying eyes before we even step foot inside. My anxiety triples when I follow him to a booth at the front of the diner sitting along the window.

"You okay?" he asks when we sit down.

I lean in and lower my voice. "They're staring at me like I'm from a different planet."

"They're just curious." He rests his hands on the table. "Say the word, and I'll get up from this table and tell them to stop."

"You'd do that?" I grab his arm when he starts to get up and let my fingers linger around his muscle before slowly peeling them away. "No!" I spread my napkin across my lap in an attempt to calm my nerves. "Forget I said anything."

An older, dark-skinned waitress comes to our table. "Dallas, it's nice to see you. I was afraid you'd been cheating on me with a new diner."

Dallas chuckles. "You know I'd never betray you, Shirley. I've just been busy."

She waves off his response with a grin. "You know I'm only giving you a hard time." Her lips form a sincere smile when she glimpses at me. "And I see why you've been busy. What can I get for you, sweetie? Iced tea? Lemonade?"

"Lemonade." I hold the menu up and set it back down. "And whatever today's special is."

"I'll have the same," Dallas tells her.

Shirley grabs our menus. "Coming right up."

"She's nice," I comment when she scurries over to the booth across from ours.

"Blue Beech is filled with nice people," he replies.

"I'm assuming you meant to say nosy people." *How bad will it get when news about my inhabited uterus gets around?*

"Yes, they're nosy, but they'll lend you a helping hand without asking for anything in return, feed you, take care of your pets when you're out of town, and always make sure you're doing okay when something tragic happens. They're only staring because they want to get to know you."

"Or because they're not used to seeing you with someone who's not Lucy."

A hint of a frown hits his lips, and his shoulders stiffen. "You could say that. I've been the town's brooding bachelor for a minute now, who's never been seen with another woman."

"They see you as a traitor. You're finally seen with a woman, and she's an outsider." I stop when I catch my words, my brain scattering to backtrack them. "Not that we're, uh ... more than friends. Just *friends* sharing a meal."

"They're well aware we're more than friends sharing a meal." He relaxes in his seat. "They're really going to find out when you start to show and wear clothes that don't swallow you up."

"I'll tell them I got fat."

"And then lost all the weight, and we suddenly have two babies?"

I shrug. "Sounds legit to me."

Shirley interrupts us and winks while dropping a turkey bacon club and our drinks in front of us. "You two enjoy."

"You ready to come up with a plan yet?" Dallas asks when I take my first bite.

"Nope," I answer after chewing.

He nods, telling me the conversation isn't over but that he'll save it for later. "What's your favorite food?"

I look up from my plate. "What?"

"Your favorite food. We can't sit here in silence, and I figure we'll ask each other questions we never did when we worked together."

I tell him it's a tie between sushi and tacos. His is his mom's carrot cake. We throw questions at each other back and forth while we eat. Having a normal conversation with him feels right. It's comfortable. It doesn't feel like first-date awkwardness because this is definitely not a date.

My dream vacation is staying in one of those tiki huts in Bora Bora. His is Yosemite. Black-and-white movies are my thing. He's not much of a movie buff, but we both agree that anything with Tom Cruise is overrated.

Shirley collects our plates and comes back to set a delicious piece of blueberry pie in front of me.

"Oh no, I didn't order this," I say.

She smiles. "It's on the house, honey. First slice for a newcomer is always free."

"Thank you." I take a bite and groan at the deliciousness. "Shirley is officially my favorite person in this town."

He smiles in amusement. "She's bribing you. The first piece is never free."

"What do you mean?"

"Don't think I'm the only one hoping you stay in Blue Beech."

CHAPTER SEVENTEEN

Willow

"GUESS WHO'S BACK, back again. Willow's back, tell a friend," Stella sings when I slide into the passenger seat of her BMW SUV.

My best friend might've shut the door on the celebrity lifestyle, but that doesn't mean she gave up her love of expensive handbags and foreign cars or that she doesn't stop gifting those cars to her favorite personal assistant.

She's grinning, her eyes pinned on me, and her charcoal-colored hair is pulled back into a high ponytail that shows off her Spanish features.

I buckle my seat belt while groaning. "I'm officially putting my two-weeks' notice in."

It's my first day back at work since moving to Blue Beech, and it feels good being around Stella again. We went from spending endless days side by side to communicating through video conferences and text messages.

Her lips curl into a smile. "You'd miss me too much, but you can bet your ass I'll be giving you maternity leave for as long as you'd like, and then you can bring the cute munchkin to work."

No one knows we're having twins yet, and Dallas promised

to keep it that way until I was ready. I need time to wrap my head around everything in my life being multiplied.

"Paid leave, right?" I ask.

"Duh." She wiggles in her seat before shifting the car into drive. "So … does this mean, you're staying?"

I've lost count of the number of times Stella has asked me to move here—before and after the Dallas situation. I would've been fired for refusing to relocate if I worked for anyone else.

"Undecided. I'm giving it a chance, but I can't make any promises. I still need to come up with my single-mom plan."

We don't leave the parking lot because she puts her car back in park to give me her full attention.

Her face fills with worry. "You're not a single mom, Wills. You have Dallas."

I'm single. I'm going to be a mom. Hence, single mom.

"Not sure that makes a difference," I mutter.

Her hand tenderly brushes against my arm. "If you're worried about that, I can assure you, Dallas will be there for your baby … *for you.* He'll change diapers and wake up when the baby is screaming bloody murder in the middle of the night. He'll help financially. If that's not someone supporting you, I don't know what is."

I snort. She has a point, but I still want to see him as the jackass I thought he was that morning.

"Why are you so uneasy about a man being a *good man?* If I recall correctly, you were jumping my ass when Hudson and I were going through a rough patch. It's your turn to listen."

I hate when my actions come back to bite me in the ass. "Different circumstances."

"How are they *different circumstances?*"

"Hudson had cheating fiancée baggage. He wasn't a single dad who lost his wife. What's Dallas going to do? Have sleepovers with Maven at my apartment? I won't be stepping foot into his house after what happened there."

She rolls her eyes, her understanding moving into aggravation. "Grow up. He was going through a rough time."

"He didn't seem to have a problem with me in his bed when we were screwing—only when it was time to face his mistake."

"He doesn't see you as a mistake."

"You didn't see his reaction. The way he still looks at me."

"I'll pay better attention today."

"*Today?*"

She shrugs casually with a mischievous smile. "We're bringing them lunch."

"We?" I turn around to view the backseat. "Do you have someone shoved in your trunk?"

"You and me. *Us.* We're bringing the guys lunch."

"They're grown men. Can't they feed themselves?"

I've texted Dallas a few times on the phone, but I haven't seen him since the diner. I'm still in the process of getting comfortable with him when we're alone. Hudson and Stella breathing over our shoulders won't make it any easier.

CHAPTER EIGHTEEN

Dallas

I WIPE my hands on a shop towel and toss it to the ground when my stomach growls. "Shirley's for lunch?" I ask Hudson. "I'm fucking starving."

I've been here since five in the morning, finishing up an engine on a tractor for my father's friend who needed it done yesterday. One of our biggest battles of working with agriculture and construction customers is that they're seasonal. They want their equipment done the moment they drop it off, or they're losing money.

Good for our pockets.

Bad for our stress levels.

He shakes his head. "Nah, Stella is bringing me food."

"Ah, yeah. Forgot about your little lunch dates." I smirk. "Cute kids, you. Reminds me of when I was in third grade, trying to convince Lucy to kiss me by bringing her pieces of Mom's pie on the playground."

"Asshole." He throws his towel at me and slides off a stool. "Want to join us? She brings enough to feed an army."

"I'll pass."

He returns to putting all of his tools up, and I snap my fingers to gain his attention.

"And don't forget, we have the auction tomorrow. What time do you want me to pick you up?" I ask.

That gets his full attention. "Shit, I forgot about the auction." He narrows his eyes at me. "Now that you bring it up, I told you I couldn't go."

"Nice try, jackass. I would remember you trying to bail because I wouldn't have let you. They have an excavator going through that I know we can get a kick-ass deal on."

We're in the process of expanding the family business my grandfather started decades ago. Our dad is ready to retire after twenty-five years and wants us to take over.

"I have plans with Stella."

He runs a hand through his hair, which is lighter and longer than mine. All of us Barnes children look alike with a few exceptions. I don't sport as much facial hair as Hudson. I'm convinced he does it to hide his jaw since mine is stronger than his, but he won't admit it. He argues that the few inches he has on my height counts for more than good bone structure.

"Your fiancé will be fine without you for a day."

"She'll be fine … because I'll be with her. Go alone. You're a big boy."

I frown. "It's an eight-hour round trip."

"It'll give you time to reflect."

"Reflection and I aren't a good match. Trust me." I fucking hate being in my head.

He winces, shocked at my response, and I'm positive I've won this discussion. "Ask Willow to tag along."

And I'm wrong.

"She can hardly stand spending twenty minutes around me at a doctor's appointment. I doubt she'll be jumping at the idea of a road trip."

He shrugs, his mouth curving into a sly smile. "Looks like we're about to find out."

"The fuck does that mean?"

I whip around at the sound of a door slamming. The shop is

twenty minutes out of town. The only people who come around are employees, customers, and us. I like it—the quietness, the peace.

I follow Hudson out of the garage to find Stella coming our way while holding up a bag.

"Lunchtime!" she yells, stomping across the gravel parking lot.

Willow circles the car, slowly dragging her feet in our direction, making it clear she'd rather be anywhere but here.

Hudson slaps me on the back. "Would you look at that, brother? Perfect timing." He jogs forward to meet Stella halfway and plants a kiss on her lips.

I follow his lead but trail a few feet behind in hopes of sparing myself from their lovesick hellos.

I'm a miserable bastard, but that doesn't mean I'm not happy for my baby brother. He went through a messy-ass breakup. His ex fucked him over by screwing his best friend and used their scheduled wedding date to marry the so-called friend. Hudson ditched town, took over my job as Stella's bodyguard, and somehow convinced her to fall in love with him.

"I'm starving, babe," he tells her with another kiss. "Did you bring enough for my pain-in-the-ass brother?"

Stella throws me a look with a smile. "Sure did. I also brought a friend." Her chin tips toward Willow when she makes it to us. "Do you two know each other?" She slaps her knees. "My bad, you knocked her up."

"Funny," Willow grumbles, throwing her a dirty look. "You remember that two-weeks' threat?"

"You have anything going on tomorrow, Willow?" Hudson asks.

She peeks over at Stella. "No. Stella said I have the day off." Her green eyes flash between the couple in confusion.

"You do," Hudson replies. "You're probably going to be pretty bored, so I have good news for you. Dallas has to go out of town for work and needs some company. You feel like tagging along?"

She bites her lip and shoves dirt around with her shoe, dirtying them up. "I have a busy day. I need to unpack."

"Weird. You told me you were finished unpacking yesterday," Stella says, exchanging a glance with Hudson, confirming this isn't some last-minute idea.

Willow shoots her a death stare. "I have baby books to finish reading."

"Read them on the way," I suggest.

She sucks in a breath at the sound of my voice and finally acknowledges me.

"As a matter of fact, how about you read them to me?" I go on.

My jump into the conversation has shocked everyone, including myself. Making an eight-hour round trip alone sounds like a fucking nightmare.

Willow's mouth presses together in a grimace. "You can't be serious."

"Sure am. I'll bring the doughnuts. You bring the baby lit." I grin. "I'll be there at eight."

CHAPTER NINETEEN

Willow

I SPENT last night drafting texts to Dallas that I never sent.

The keeping-my-distance plan I made at the first positive pregnancy test is backfiring in my face. I can't stop myself from reaching out and clasping on to every hand he holds out even though I know he'll do nothing but drop me at the end. My heart is begging for a repeat of that soul-to-soul connection we shared.

Dallas gets me in a way no one else seems to. He understands what it feels like to have your heart ripped out and torn to shreds. He understands the way love can throw you into a pit of denial. He wouldn't come to terms that Lucy was sick until it was too late, and I couldn't grasp that my boyfriend since high school had been cheating on me for years.

Our hurt is the polar opposite. I know losing someone is nothing compared to a breakup. My pain doesn't even register on the scale of his. His hurt snuck up on him, wearing him down on short notice, and I'm terrified he'll drag me into the dark place with him.

We run from the truth because it's easier to live a lie than face the monster. I was content with living with my struggles … until that positive test. I won't allow my babies to be raised by two broken people. One of us has to be strong, and I can't do that with Dallas Barnes playing with my heart.

The doorbell rings at eight sharp. Like me, Dallas is punctual. You learn to be that way when you're working with tight schedules and dealing with celebrities who have no regard for time. I've had to drag people out of bed, brush their teeth for them, and even buckle them up in their private jets.

"I'm surprised you didn't run off this morning," he says when I open the door.

Me, too, buddy. Me, too.

Three red travel cups are stacked in one hand, and a white paper bag is clutched in the other. A pair of heels is tucked underneath his armpits. I reach out to help him with the cups when he slides past me to get into my apartment. I inhale his woodsy scent while following him into the kitchen.

He drops the bag on the counter and then holds up the familiar black peep-toe heels. "These belong to you."

The shoes I left at his house.

The ones I thought I would never see and didn't care to see again. He'd be on my mind every time I slipped them on. *Where did he keep them? Did Maven see them?*

I grab them from him and toss them onto the floor. "Thank you." I take in all of the cups. "Someone joining us today?" I sound more disappointed than I should about having a third-wheeler on this trip.

He shakes his head. "All I know about your morning drink of choice is coffee is a no-go, so I had to get creative and bring options."

"By creative, you mean …"

"Asking the woman behind the counter at the doughnut shop."

I lean against the wall. "And what did she suggest?"

"Hot chocolate, decaf green tea, and passion fruit something." He counts off the list with his fingers. "I have no damn clue what the last option was, but she said health nuts have been going crazy over it. Thought I might as well give it a go."

His answer is so Dallas.

"Green tea for one then, please."

He frowns. "Well … fuck."

"What?"

"I didn't take you as a green-tea lover, so I chugged it down on the way here."

"*A green-tea lover?* I don't see you as one either, considering you once told me not liking coffee was an abomination."

"It truly is." I keep staring at him until his lips crack into a smile. "I'm only fucking with you. Green tea is in the middle cup." He snags the doughnuts. "We'll eat on the way. Let's hit the road."

"I LIKE THE SHIRT TODAY," Dallas says.

We've been on the road for about an hour and have covered the weather, the latest news, our ideas for where Stella and Hudson should get married, and what the best movie that came out this year was.

Everything but baby talk.

Which I'm totally okay with.

I pull at the bottom of my *You Had Me at Tacos* tee. Graphic tees are my thing. "I thought I'd give you a hint of what we're having for lunch."

"Can we delay that until dinner? There aren't that many stops on the way, and I doubt any of them serve quality tacos."

I nod. "I can settle for dinner."

It's not like I have anywhere to be. It's either hang with him or sit, bored, in my apartment. You can only watch so much Netflix before you're ready to pull your hair out.

"I'll find you the best damn tacos you've ever had for tagging along today." He grins while peeking over at me. "I woke up this morning, expecting a text from you, bailing."

I cast a curious glance from my seat. "Disappointed I didn't?"

"Hell no. I told you I'd enjoy the company."

I study his driving position. He's leaned back in the seat, right arm stretched out and steering. It comes across so casual, so laid-back, and I never thought I'd be so turned on by the way a man drove.

"What made you change your mind?"

His question smacks me out of my eye-fucking-him moment. "A change of scenery sounded nice."

He chuckles, faking offense. "Not the company?"

I bite the side of my lip. "I haven't decided on that yet."

"I admire your honesty and pledge to give you the time of your life, so you can make that decision at the end of this trip. The drive is beautiful. We won't hit any of that bullshit LA traffic you're used to."

"How long are we talking?"

Now that I think about it, I should've asked more questions before jumping into his truck. It seems I have a habit of jumping into things with this man without considering what could happen first.

"Eight-hour round trip. We'll be at the auction for an hour or two. My eyes are only on one piece of equipment, which will be at the front of the line. I bid and fill out the paperwork, and then we'll be back on the road."

"Sounds like a whole process. How often do you do this, and why do you do it?"

"Once or twice a month, depending on what they have for sale. Hudson and I buy machinery that needs to be updated. We fix it up, modernize it—that kind of stuff. Then, we sell it to farmers and construction companies around the area."

Interesting. I knew he and Hudson did some type of machinery work but never knew what exactly it was.

Stella's explanation consisted of, "They fix stuff and sell machines," which wasn't as thorough as his answer.

"How did you get into it?" I want to draw out every detail of his life that I can.

"My grandfather started the business decades ago. My dad ran it after he passed and while I was in LA and Hudson was in the military. He's ready to retire, so he asked us to take over. Since we're home for good now, we figured it was the perfect time. We've already expanded the business and doubled our clientele."

"So, you bid on the machines you want and then take them to the shop if you win?"

"Most of the time, I bring a trailer and tow the machine with my truck, but today, I'll have a contractor pick it up and deliver it to the shop."

I squint my eyes at him. "Why not tow it today?"

"It's not only uncomfortable, but also a longer trip when towing a piece of heavy machinery. I want you to be comfortable."

Dallas might have had parts of his heart shattered, but fragments are still shoved in there, beating. He's kind even though he's heartbroken. He's miserable, but he manages to consider other people.

"I've been on eighteen-hour flights and gone straight to work without sleeping for another twenty-four," I tell him. "It's nothing compared to traveling with Stella."

"You get paid for that. You're not getting paid for this, and quite frankly, even if you were, I'd still want to make it comfortable for you." He shakes his head and whistles. "I sure don't miss traveling with Stella."

I nod in agreement. "At first, it was a blast, but it's not always glitz and glam, working for Hollywood's finest."

His fingers close around the steering wheel, and he stares at the road. "Seemed like a good idea then, but I have my regrets."

"Regrets about working for her or not moving back when Lucy did?"

"Both, to be honest." The ease of his laid-back mood evaporates. We've moved from the weather to an intimate conversation. "Moving to LA was Lucy's idea. I was fine with staying in Iowa, but she wanted a change."

I've been curious about Dallas's story since he started working for Stella. She filled me in on small details, and I picked up information here and there, but we never ventured into personal conversations, never let our real life seep through the cracks of our professional one.

"You moved for her?" I ask.

"I loved her." So much was said in those three words.

"Why did you stay when she moved back?"

Dallas had been working for Stella for three years when Lucy moved back home. Stella was a stressed mess, worried about finding a new bodyguard as good as him, but he decided to stay, relieving us both.

Sadness. Regret. Tension. All of those emotions pass over his face. "I offered, sometimes even begged when the loneliness of missing my family barreled through, but Lucy insisted I stay. The money was too good to pass up. Our plan was to save enough money, so I could move home after a few years. We'd be able to live more comfortably." More waves of sadness smack into him, and he pauses. "Fuck it."

I stay quiet, not sure if he's going to shut down or break down.

He expels a long breath before going on, "I've never told anyone this, not even Hudson. We ..." He hesitates again. "We were trying for another baby. Maven was unplanned, so we wanted to do things the right way. Expand our family. Funny how life works. We could conceive when we weren't ready but couldn't when we were. Her doctor suggested IVF, which costs a fucking fortune, so we decided to save money and try it in a few years."

Wow.

My heart breaks at his confession. He was desperately trying to have another baby with his wife and failed. Then, I got pregnant after a one-night stand with him. His wish for more kids has been granted but with the wrong woman.

"You regret not coming back," I say, my voice thick, my throat hurting.

"Every fucking day of my life."

I wanted his reality, his secrets, but I now wish for a dead end. This road is too heartbreaking, and I'm roaming along the sidewalks of guilt. He has to go through all of the motions with me now even though he wanted to do them with someone else.

"You don't expect to lose your wife that young," he continues. "You don't expect your daughter to be motherless at six. We were fucking robbed, and I didn't take advantage of spending all my time with her, protecting her, until life broke in and took her from me."

His vulnerability shocks me. It's comforting to see a flash of something other than anger spark out of him. His hurt opens up emotions in me, and I'm holding myself back from bursting into tears at the sight of this broken man. I'm fighting back the urge to reach out and console him. To let him know everything will be okay.

But I can't, for fear of falling harder for a man who's unavailable. When I fall in love, I fall hard, and that's my weakness. People that love as deep as I do get their hearts shattered harder when it all falls apart.

He blows out a stressed breath and focuses on me in pain. He tilts his lips up into a forced smile. "And here I said I'd give you a good time."

"You're fine. I like this Dallas," I answer, honestly.

He rubs the back of his neck. "You like me being a miserable bastard?"

"I like you being real," I correct. I've never evoked emotions like this out of anybody.

"This is as real as it gets. This is me, and I wish I could be someone better for you."

"What you're giving me is enough." *He wants to be a better father, not a better lover, not a better man for me.* I repeat that to myself over and over in my head, hoping it'll drill the reality through. "I mean ... what you're giving the babies."

"I hope that never changes."

CHAPTER TWENTY

Dallas

"WOOHOO! WE WON!"

I can't stop my lips from breaking into a smile, watching Willow jump up and down in excitement after the auctioneer yells, "Sold," and points to me.

The men around me are either staring at her in annoyance or desire, and I want to slap all their thoughts from their heads.

I've managed to snag the excavator and got a better deal than I planned. An overweight man wearing a business suit had me worried for a minute when he started driving the price up, but lucky for me, he gave up early.

I know his kind. The men who are only in business for profit and for retail-fucking people with no concern about how they bust their asses every day to keep food in their families' mouths. Barnes Machinery and Equipment isn't like that. We give a shit about people, about their checkbooks, never high gross.

Willow insisted on tagging along with me at the bidding yard. I offered to let her wait in the truck or hang out in the coffee shop across the street since there's a lot of standing and waiting around for your item to come up. She wouldn't have it and refused to decline a ticket into my world.

She hasn't complained once, which doesn't surprise me.

She's a hard worker, who scored a job with one of the most prestigious celebrity PR and assistant firms in LA at twenty-one. She worked with Hollywood's elite and impressed Stella so much, she hired her full-time. Even though Stella isn't as hard on her, Willow works her ass off to make things easier for her boss.

Hell, most of the time she goes above and beyond what is asked of her. She works long hours, does the shit no one else wants to do, and fixes any problems that come along.

"How about some jams?" Willow asks when we get back into the truck.

I paid for the machine, filled out all the necessary paperwork, and scheduled the delivery. We'd gotten lunch before the auction started, and now, my goal is to find her some kick-ass tacos for being such a good sport.

"You be the DJ," I answer.

Music comes blaring through the speakers when she turns the radio on. I haven't used it since dropping Maven off at camp and cringe at the same time she bursts out into a fit of laughter. Since her laugh is contagious, I can't stop myself from doing the same.

"Whoa," she says when she catches her breath. "Didn't peg you as a Bieber fan, Barnes."

I turn down the volume a few notches. "I'm not. *Maven* is a Bieber fan."

"Blaming it on the kid, huh? How convenient." She smacks her palm against her forehead. "Oh. My. God."

I lift my chin. "What?"

"My baby daddy is a Belieber."

"A what?"

"A Belieber. A member of Justin's fan club."

For fuck's sake.

Not only do I have to listen to this shit, but now, Willow also thinks I'm his biggest fucking fan with posters of his mug splattered all over my bedroom wall.

"I'm not, let me repeat, I'm not a member of his fan club."

"I believe you." A smile still dances on her moist lips.

"Appreciate it."

"You're the President of it."

I can't stop myself from smiling as a light chuckle echoes from my chest. "Oh, come on, you honestly can't believe I listen to this shit."

"The evidence is clear, counselor. His music is on your radio."

Thunder roars through the sky so loud, I can't hear Bieber, and rain smacks into my windshield. *Fuck.*

"And look at that. God knows you're lying, too."

"Or the weather predicted a seventy percent chance of thunderstorms, but I hoped it'd be in our favor."

At least it waited until after the auction to pour hell down.

The windshield wipers squeak when I shift them to high, and Willow turns down the music, reading my mind so that I can focus better on the road. My headlights shine brightly as the sky turns a deep shade of black even though it's only after six.

I lower my speed and get better control of my view on the road when a loud pop rings out, and my steering wheel starts to shake. The ride gets bumpy, and Willow hangs on to her seat belt for stability.

I pull the truck over and park it before slamming my hand against the steering wheel, causing the horn to blare out.

"Motherfucker," I mutter.

"What?" Willow asks.

"We have a flat."

She stares at me as if it's not a problem. "You know how to change a tire, right?"

I nod. "It helps if you have a spare though."

Her jaw drops. "You're kidding me."

"I wish I were." I feel like a defeated asshole.

This puts a damper on our almost perfect day. We're

stranded in the rain, and instead of tacos, I'll be giving her Maven's fruit snacks as the final course.

"No big deal. We'll call a tow truck. I've been in bigger messes than this in my sleep."

"One problem with that." I pull out my phone to show her the screen. "No service. Tell me you have something."

She snatches her purse from the floorboard and rifles through it before finding her phone.

Horror takes over her face when the screen comes to life.

"For real?" she shrieks, throwing her hands up in the air. "We're in the ass crack of no-man's-land stranded with no spare tire. This is straight out of a horror movie." She turns around and lays her gaze out the back window. "Swear to God, if a meat-truck-driving serial killer pulls up, I'm making a run for it."

I grind my teeth, my heart crashing with anguish and guilt from putting her in this situation. I gave my dad my spare last week and forgot to replace it.

Her face softens when she peeks over at me. "Shit, sorry," she whispers over the pelting rain hitting the windshield. "That was too dramatic for this situation. I tend to do that at times."

"You're fine. I'll take dramatics over you wanting to kill me." I turn around in my seat and snatch a jacket from the backseat. "I'm going to see if I can manage to get service in the field over there."

She points out the window. "It's pouring. There are no streetlights. We should wait until the storm calms before going out."

I put the jacket on. "What if it storms all night?"

She starts to unbuckle her seat belt. "Then, I'm coming with you."

I stop her and snap it back in place. "The fuck you are. Stay here, and I'll be back in a flash."

I jump out of the truck despite her protests and hold my phone in the air while sprinting toward the field. The rain comes at me sideways while I wait for the service bars to light up on my phone.

Come on! Come on!

I jump, nearly losing my phone, when a crack of lightning bites through the dark sky. I can barely make out the truck in the downpour and am still messing with my phone when I notice the bright shine of headlights getting closer.

My attention snaps away from the car to the truck at the sound of a door slamming. I scream her name and race toward her when she starts running to the side of the road, waving her hands in the air. The car flies by, splashing her with water, and her shoulders slump in failure.

Fear and anger splinter through me like the storm.

"Have you lost your mind?" I scream, snatching her by the waist from behind and swinging her into my arms. I hover my body over hers to protect her from getting more soaked and tighten my hold on her shivering body while walking us from the street back to my truck. "They could've run you over!"

My breathing halts, dying in my throat, and a chill colder than the rain zips down my spine when she rotates herself in my arms. My hands stay on her wrists as she glares at me before jerking out of my hold with a huff.

"I was flagging them down for help!"

"You running out in the street, waving down some stranger, does not fucking help me. You keeping your ass in the heated seat in the safety of my truck is what helps me."

"It was worth a try!"

The way her voice cracks makes me feel like shit. We lock eyes. She's staring at me like she's searching my soul, assessing the situation in my eyes, unsure of what my next step will be.

I suck in each breath she expels, inhaling her sweet scent, nearly panting at the sight of her dripping wet in front of me, neglecting the shitty situation we're in. Her shirt is soaked to her skin, her hard nipples peeking through the thin tee, and I lick my lips, mentally tasting her.

My next step should be getting her inside the truck, out of this chilly ambush of rain, but goddamn it, I can't break away. I run a hand through her hair and smooth it down before lowering my fingers to her cheek. She shuts her eyes and relaxes into my touch.

I inch forward, my chest brushing against hers, and she lets out a soft moan. The sweet sound runs straight to my dick.

"Dallas," she whispers, eyes still closed, "what are we doing?"

I can't stop myself from chuckling. "We're standing in the rain."

"No," she croaks out. "What are *we* doing?"

CHAPTER TWENTY-ONE

Dallas

WILLOW'S QUESTION shakes me back into reality, and I drop my hand from her face.

She wants to have this conversation now.

In the pouring rain.

I chuckle.

This situation sums up our relationship.

Bad timing. Unexpected. Not sure what the next move is.

I run my hands down her arms when her teeth start to chatter. "We need to get you in the truck," I say, squeezing her shoulders.

I move around her to open the door. She nods timidly, her front teeth biting into her soft lip, and turns her back to me to climb in. I stand behind her, helping her up, and make sure she's secure.

"I managed to get one bar in the middle of the field. I'm going to try to get in contact with a tow company, so I need you to refrain from leaving the car. I don't give a shit if a parade starts coming down the street." I nod my head toward the dashboard. "Turn the heat on high. I have clothes in my gym bag in the backseat for you to change into."

"Got it. No getting out of the car." I go to close the door, but she stops me. "What if a serial killer is running toward you with a knife?"

This woman and her fucking questions. *Where does she come up with this shit?* "You lock the doors and let me deal with it."

"I'm trained in martial arts, you know. I was a junior green belt. I would be a great help."

"Look at you, badass. Keep your eyes out for killers and promise me you'll stay in here." I can't believe I'm standing in a fucking storm and taking the chance of getting struck by lightning to entertain this conversation. Willow gets me swept up into her world, her words, and I can't seem to walk away. "Promise me you'll stay in here."

"My promises don't mean shit, remember?"

"Make them mean something."

I slam the door shut and let out a sigh before jogging back to the field. I ignore the rain as I hurry back to the same spot and dial the number as fast as I can, hoping that not only the service stays connected, but also that Willow keeps her ass planted in the truck.

I make it through and give the tow company our location. Then, I shove my phone into my pocket. I stop to search the dark sky and twist my wedding ring while rain drips from the tips of my fingers to the mud underneath my boots.

I don't move. I only think.

My mind hasn't been fighting back the painful thoughts of missing Lucy today. I haven't felt like a failure of a husband since I knocked on Willow's door this morning. I haven't cursed the world for my loss. The constant guilt and anger didn't seep through me when I saw the happy family in the booth across from us at the small diner we ate lunch in.

The presence of Willow blocks out that dark tunnel in my brain and gives me a way toward the light and out of my hole.

I open the back door when I get back to the truck, toss my mud-covered boots in the backseat, grab my tennis shoes from the floorboard, and slide into the driver's side.

My attention shoots straight to Willow. She's still in her wet clothes and slipping her fingers through the strands of her dripping hair. She sighs, grabs her purse, and digs through it until she scores a hair tie.

I gulp as she lifts her hair up, exposing her long, sleek neck.

Fuck, she's breathtaking.

"You good?" I finally ask.

She bashfully runs a hand along her pale cheek. "Sorry about that. Minor freak-outs tend to be my thing during stressful situations."

Her answer is a shot of relief. Relief of not scaring her away. Relief she's not broaching the conversation she started outside.

"Don't worry about it. Tow truck will be here in ten to fifteen minutes."

"They'll take us back to Blue Beech or fix the flat?"

"Depends. If he can change it in the rain, he will. If not, he'll take us to the closest repair shop. Flats typically are a quick fix."

Minutes of silence pass through the cab until Willow says something. "We missed you when you left, you know." She snorts, and I'm unsure of where she's going with this conversation. "The temps they sent when you left were terrible, and Hudson was a total asshole for the first month."

I perk up in my seat. She's talking about when I quit working for Stella. I didn't give much notice. I left a day after Lucy told me the diagnosis.

"He was mending a broken heart," I say, sticking up for my brother.

"Hmm, so is that what happens when men are *mending a broken heart?* It justifies them acting like assholes?" Her face is playful, but her tone isn't. It's built up in hurt, betrayal, and also confusion.

Fuck. Where is this tow truck? I should've offered more money to get it here sooner.

"You trying to insinuate something?" I brace myself for the impact she's about to give me.

"Damn straight I am."

I swallow down my guilt. "Care to elaborate?"

"People get their hearts broken. People lose people. No offense, but it happens every day. Every minute. That's no excuse to act like a dick. You were a dick to me. Hell, *all* men are dicks if you're not letting them give you theirs. That's when they're nice and comforting."

"I'll apologize again for my dickdom. Hurt people don't always intend to hurt other people. That's not my intention. Trust me, I'd never want anyone to go through the hell I'm going through."

Her attention moves to the back window as headlights pull up behind us. Perfect timing to end this conversation. Intimate conversations with Willow are high risk for me. I'm a man of few words, and it seems I always choose the worst ones with her.

I grip the door handle. "Don't get out of this truck, headlight-chaser."

I meet the man in the middle of our trucks. He's sporting a parka and black boots.

"Nice day out here, huh?" he asks, thrusting his hand my way.

"For a duck," I mutter back, shaking his hand.

"It's about to get worse for ya."

Of course. The day goes more to shit.

Instead of asking why, I wait for him to elaborate.

"I can't work in this weather," he says. "It's dangerous, and they're talking about possible tornados." He whistles. "Half of the town's power is out due to the storm. Our mechanic went home to his family 'cause of it, but I'll ask him to come in first thing in the morning to fix this."

"Fuck. You've got to be kidding me."

He takes a step closer while chewing on a toothpick. "Wish I were. If it helps, I can give you a ride to the motel a few blocks down from the shop."

I slap him on the shoulder. "Appreciate it." I nod toward his truck. "You happen to have an umbrella in there?"

"Sure do."

"Thanks, man."

I jump back into my truck with the umbrella in my hand, ready to hear Willow rip my head off when I tell her we'll be having a sleepover tonight. I open my mouth when reality cuts through me. *How am I going to handle a sleepover?* I grind my teeth. This is a small town. They'll no doubt have more than one room available. I jumped the gun with the thought that we'd be sharing.

She's relaxed in the leather seat with her bare feet resting on the dashboard. I can't stop myself from giving her a once-over. Her soaking T-shirt has been replaced with a rose-colored lace tank top that showcases her cleavage. Her breasts are small, but that doesn't mean they don't excite my dick. They fit perfectly in my hands that night.

"Everything okay?" she asks.

I jerk my chin up, my throat tight. "He's giving us a ride into town."

"Perfect. How long will it take them to fix it?"

"Till tomorrow."

Her legs drop from the dashboard faster than Maven comes running when I mention ice cream. "What?" she shrieks. "Where are we supposed to sleep?"

"There's a motel a few blocks down from the repair shop."

"Can't we take an Uber back home and then pick it up in the morning?"

I smirk. "Ubers don't go to Blue Beech, babe."

"SORRY, but we only have one room available."

Go fucking figure.

Stranded. Check.

Having to share a room. Check.

What else can happen that's not going to make Willow wish she'd never stepped foot into my truck?

"We're always booked up on auction days. It's even worse today," the woman with steel-gray hair says in a hoarse, cracked voice while shaking her head at us like we're in the principal's office. "People don't want to travel in this mess. Here's a piece of advice for next time: book in advance."

"Thanks for the tip." I don't give two shits about her advice. She's our last resort. "We'll take it."

I grunt when Willow edges into my side to push herself in front of me. She faces the woman with a *Harriet* name tag.

"That's a room with two beds, right?" she asks.

"Sorry, honey. All we have is one queen." Harriet releases a bland smile. "Again, book in advance next time."

Sharing a bed. Fucking check.

Willow shoots me an innocent smile. "This will be interesting."

CHAPTER TWENTY-TWO

Willow

IF DALLAS BELIEVES I'm calm, I'll be asking Stella for a job tomorrow because I deserve an Emmy.

I'm doing everything in my power not to freak out right now.

We've shared a bed before.

Granted, we fucked each other, but no alcohol will be present tonight. We'll keep our hands to ourselves and build a pillow wall to separate us, and everything will be okay.

No touching. No sex. Fingers crossed he won't freak out tomorrow morning and leave me stranded.

On the bright side, we can't do anything stupid enough to make a baby again.

Shit. Babies. My mind still hasn't wrapped around that.

Dallas plays with the room key in his hand, circling it around his thick fingers, while we stand in front of room 206.

"What are you thinking?" he asks.

This seems to be our go-to question.

"That we have no other choice," I answer, signaling to the door in a hurry-it-up gesture. "This is our only option unless we decide to be a pain in the ass and have someone pick us up, and then they'll have to drive you back tomorrow to get your truck."

I scowl at the door like it's my worst enemy. "Open sesame. Let's do this."

He obliges in what seems like slow motion while I look around. It's not exactly the Ritz, but I don't see any vermin running about, so that's a plus.

As Harriet pointed out with her stupid, smug smile, which I wanted to slap off, there's only one bed. What she failed to mention was that she's a liar because the bed is not a queen. It's a full, which means I have even less room to build my cockblocking fort. I briefly wonder if Dallas would be opposed to sleeping in the bathtub.

It's a standard room with a fake-wood-paneled bed topped with a generic comforter, a desk complete with a Bible and phone, and an older flat screen TV. I shuffle into the room, as if I were on my way to lethal injection, and Dallas stands in the doorway, his hypnotic eyes trained on me.

I sit on the edge of the bed and chew on my nails. "Oh, shit," I say. "Where's, uh … Maven?"

This is only now hitting me. *Jesus, am I going to be one of those mothers who forgets her kids at the supermarket?*

He chuckles while stepping into the room, and I tense at the sound of the door clicking shut. It's official. We're slumber-partying it up.

"I didn't forget about my daughter, if that's what you're thinking. She's spending the week at summer camp," he answers.

"Camp? Like on *The Parent Trap*? That's a real thing?"

"It looked real when I dropped her off." He tosses the key on the desk.

What hotel still uses actual keys these days?

"Which side of the bed do you want?" he asks.

"It doesn't matter."

He points his chin at where I'm sitting. "I'll take that side. It's closer to the door, and you'll be closer to the bathroom."

He opens up the desk drawer, shuffles a few papers around,

and shuts it. His next destination is the nightstand. He does the same thing and drags out a piece of paper ripped on both sides.

He blows out a breath. "Room service menu is tempting."

My stomach growls at the mention of food. I'm eating for three, and my appetite hasn't done anything to make me doubt it.

"I'm apologizing in advance for not feeding you quality tacos, but you have some superior choices here."

I bet. "And what would those be?"

He starts to read them off while fighting to keep a straight face. "Ramen noodles—"

"There's no way it says that," I interrupt.

"I'm not shitting you." He holds out the wrinkled piece of paper for me to read. Sure enough, ramen noodles is on there. "The other world-class options include grilled cheese, corn dogs, tomato soup, and sloppy joes." He frowns. "I'm not a picky person, but none of these sound exactly appetizing."

I agree. "So many options, such a small stomach." That's not *exactly* true.

The bed descends when he sits next to me. "Again, I'm sorry about this."

"Don't be. This will be a good story to tell our kids one day."

He smacks the paper. "So, what'll it be?"

"A corn dog might be my safest option."

"I owe you plenty of taco nights after this," he mutters, shaking his head. "Fucking corn dogs."

"Hey now, I have nothing against corn dogs."

He doesn't need to feel guilty about this. Shit happens that's out of your control sometimes. It's not like he planned to get a flat in the middle of nowhere.

He hands me the paper. "Anything else you want?"

I skim my finger down the page. "Might as well add some French fries while you're at it."

"Got it." He gets up from the bed and picks up the phone connected to the wall with a cord. "Room service, please." He orders my food and throws in ramen noodles for himself.

My stomach grumbles again, and I throw a pillow to get his attention, smacking him in the head. "I'll take some of those, too!"

He nods, rubbing his head. "Make that two ramen noodles." He hangs up. "Dinner is ordered. Get comfortable. I'll grab some drinks from the vending machine I spotted on our way in."

He snatches the keys from the desk, and I pull my phone out of my purse to see three missed calls and texts from Stella, asking how things are going and when I'll be back in town.

Me: Not until tomorrow. This is me officially calling in late. We're stranded because of a flat.

My phone beeps seconds later.

Stella: Stranded where?

Me: Neverland, for all I know. I'd say thirty minutes from the auction. Doubt it's on a map.

Stella: You need us to pick you up?

Me: No. Dallas got us to a motel. We're okay for the night.

My phone abruptly rings.

"Hello?"

"You're staying the night together?" she shrieks. "This is the best day ever."

"You damn liar!" I hear Hudson yell in the background. "You told me the same thing last night when I made you orgasm four times in a row."

"Ignore him," she mutters. "*Sooo* ... what are you guys doing?"

"Dallas is raiding the vending machine, and I'm sitting on the bed. No excitement over here." My response is along the lines of pathetic.

"You can always make it exciting."

I sigh. "I'm hanging up now."

"Call us if you change your mind and need a ride."

"I will. See you tomorrow."

"Damn straight you will. I'll be sitting on your doorstep, waiting to drag every detail out of you."

As I'm ending the call, Dallas walks in with drinks in his hand and a duffel bag draped over his shoulder. He sets the cans on the desk to hold up the bag on display.

"You didn't take me up on my clothes offer earlier, but I keep my gym bag in my truck. You need something to sleep in?"

"Are they dirty or clean gym clothes?" Not that it matters. I'll gladly sleep in anything that smells like him—dirty, bloody, stained, you name it.

"Filthy. Dirty. Sweaty." He chuckles, and I fake a horrified look. "I'm kidding."

I blush at the thoughts running through my head. "I know."

He drops the bag next to me on the bed and starts to rummage through it. "What's your preference? Pants? Shorts?"

"Shorts, please."

He holds up a pair of blue shorts with a red stripes down the sides. "These okay?" He pulls out a T-shirt next.

"They'll work." I play with the fabric in my hand when he hands them to me. "I'll go, uh … change in the bathroom."

I'm getting my pervert on when I shut the door behind me and smell his shorts. Fresh linen. I never knew what that smell was until my mom bought me the scented candle for Christmas. It was my favorite scent until I got a whiff of Dallas's *fresh linen*.

Even with my growing stomach, I have to tie the drawstring tight around my waist to keep the shorts from falling to my ankles. I grab the shirt and contemplate taking off my bra. It's usually the first thing I dispose of when I walk through the front door, but I'm not alone.

I unsnap it, snap it back, hesitate, and decide to leave it on. I pull the shirt over my head and pause to take in my reflection in the mirror before going back out. I grimace and smooth my hands over my hair. Rain turns it into a frizzy mess.

"Dinner is served," Dallas announces when I walk out. "It didn't take them long to microwave it."

I laugh. "Gourmet ramen at its finest."

He scoots out the desk chair, so I can sit down, and he places the corn dog, French fries, and the Styrofoam bowl of noodles in front of me.

"I lived off this stuff when I moved to LA and was looking for a job. Hell, even after I found a job, I ate it more than I should have because I was lazy." I grin and kick his foot when he sits down on the bed. "Meanwhile, your lucky ass got to live in Stella's guest suite that was complete with a gourmet chef."

He hooks his thumb toward his bowl. "This might be giving him some competition, and don't act like Stella didn't invite you to move in every month."

"That's true, but I wanted my own place, you know? My own space. Believe it or not, I'm an introvert at heart."

Stella also despised Brett, and they couldn't be in the same room for five seconds without wanting to rip each other apart.

"Makes two of us. Lucy was the extrovert to my introvert. She could make conversation with anyone in the room. Me? I was cool with standing to the side and people-watching."

I stiffen in my seat. *Lucy.* Her name always sends a bolt of mixed emotions through me.

Guilt from sleeping with Dallas. Jealousy that she was the one he adored, the woman he loved and shared a bed with without freaking out in the morning.

I nod and slurp a noodle into my mouth, attempting to appear relaxed. Dallas sets his bowl on the nightstand and slides to the edge of the bed until he's only inches from me. I slurp my noodles louder and faster, sounding obnoxious, and act like I don't notice how close he is.

He stays quiet until I swallow down my bite. "I was in a dark place then."

I drop my spoon into the bowl. "What?" *Why is he bringing this up? Abort mission. Please.*

"That morning. Hell, for months."

I fish the spoon out of the bowl, and my heart sinks at the pained expression on his face.

"Sometimes, I still am." He scrubs his hand over his face. "Sorry for sneaking this shit on you after the nightmare of a day we've had, but I can tell it bothers you when I mention her."

It's only fair I'm honest back. "Hearing her name makes me feel guilty."

He pats the space next to him, and I take the invitation, sliding between the small space between us and sit down next to him.

"If anyone should feel guilty, it's me," he says.

"I obviously played a part in it."

He didn't fuck himself.

"And today was not a nightmare. I enjoyed myself," I add.

"You don't have to lie to make me feel better."

I smack his arm. "You know I wouldn't lie about that. I'll take every chance I can to bust your balls."

"Point made. I enjoyed myself, too. To be honest, lately, the only time I seem to be in a happy place is when I'm with you." He lets out a heavy breath. "You took me out of my stressed out, broken world and gave me a good day. Same with the night we spent together. I like myself when I'm with you. I forget about the loss and the hurt. You make me feel alive again."

I nod. He misses Lucy and will always miss her but is opening up a portion of himself for me to discover.

Keep going.

No, stop. Red light. Don't drag me down this tunnel if it ends in hurt.

Keep going.

Why can't I think straight? I need to think with my head, not my heart.

"If I could take it back, I would," he goes on.

"Take us back, sleeping together?"

"No, take back my behavior. I might've not been all there,

but I didn't bring you to my home for a simple fuck. I promise you that."

I bump his shoulder with mine. "It's my turn to say you don't have to lie to make me feel better."

"Babe, no bullshit. The opportunity for a quick fuck has been open to me several times, but I've never succumbed to any advances. Not one. Drunk. Sober. Horny as hell. It wasn't only my dick that felt a connection with you. I didn't want to admit that to myself that morning." He shakes his head. "I'm still having trouble with admitting that you pulled something out of me."

I wring my hands together. "Yes, there's an attraction between us, but that's as far as our relationship can go." I refuse to be second best to another woman.

He rests his hand on my knee and sucks in a breath. "I know. We'll stick to staying friends and co-parents. I didn't say that in hopes of having sex again. I said it, so you'd know I never meant to disrespect you, and what happened that night seems to be what makes us uncomfortable most of the time. I don't want that."

"Me either," I whisper.

"Good. Then, it's settled." He wraps his arm around my shoulders. "We're new besties."

IT'S ALMOST MIDNIGHT.

Even though we had the no-more-awkwardness conversation, it has yet to leave the building. Everything was fine while we finished eating, when we had to share a toothbrush because there was only one in the vending machine, and even when we watched endless episodes of *Cops*, which I learned is his favorite show.

Our problem now is going to bed.

We have to make ourselves comfortable and slip underneath

the sheets. The lights will go off. There's intimacy involved in this whether we like it or not.

"You ready to admit, you're tired?" Dallas asks when I'm on my eleventh yawn. He chuckles. "Come on, go to sleep. You're not going to miss anything exciting here."

"Fine," I groan out. "If you insist." My shirt rises when I slide down until my head hits the rock-hard pillow. The air in the room grows thinner when I peek up and notice his eyes pinned to my exposed stomach.

He lifts his hand. "Can I?"

I nod in response since I'm struggling for words. My stomach flutters at the same time he presses his steady hand against it. It dawns on me that he's never touched my stomach like this before. Not even during the ultrasound.

His touch comforts me, the opposite of what I thought would happen, and I settle myself on my elbows to watch him. He's gentle, treating me like I'm expensive china, and he cradles my skin with his hand in awe.

"I can't believe we have two babies growing in here," he whispers.

I smile when he shifts, so he's eye-level with my stomach.

"It's beautiful." He lifts up to focus on me with compassionate eyes. "You're fucking beautiful." He lowers his head and places his lips against my stomach. "Fucking perfection."

I miss his touch as soon as he pulls away and makes himself comfortable on his side. The smile that's been plastered to his lips since I gave him the okay is still there while he stares down at me.

He's waiting for me to tell him not to call me beautiful, to make a sarcastic comment, because that's what I do when conversations get heavy.

"What are you thinking?" he finally asks.

That your touch calms me more than a lavender bath and an expensive massage. That I wish we hadn't agreed to keep things platonic because the things I want to do with you right now are far from that.

"I'm thinking …" It takes me a second to come up with something. "I'm thinking today is officially the weirdest day of my life."

He cocks his head to the side. "That's what's heavy on your mind?"

I gulp. "Yep."

"You seemed to be in deep thought about that," he argues, running a finger over his chin.

"It's a deep subject." *Oh, hell. Let's put our attention back on people getting arrested, please.*

"Fuck, I wish I could read your mind right now, but I'll run with your answer."

I scrunch up my brows in question.

"I'll act like I'm convinced with the weirdest-day-of-your-life lie." A grin plays at his thick lips. "Today was weirder than the time one of Stella's stalkers broke into her house, dressed as a housekeeper, and begged her to wear black lipstick while going down on him?" He chuckles. "And, if I remember correctly, you tasered him before I even made it into the room."

"Asshole deserved it," I mutter.

He bursts out in laughter. *Real laughter.* I feel like I've hit the jackpot every time I get that from him.

"I'll have to call it a tie between the two."

"I'll take that and agree that getting stranded with you has been eventful. The plus is, I'll always remember this. We've formed a stronger relationship and learned more about each other in a day than we did throughout years of working together. So, thank you for the good memories and not bailing on me. Eating ramen noodles and watching a *Cops* marathon all alone wouldn't have been nearly as much fun."

I lower my head to hide the cheesy smile biting at me. He needs to stop talking like this if he wants to stay on the just-friends level. I lift my gaze when he scoots in closer, wiping out the small distance between us, and his eyes soften as he drinks me in.

I play with the chain of my necklace. "What are you thinking?"

It's my turn to ask the questions. Hopefully, he won't lie like I did.

His jaw flexes. "You want to know the truth?"

"Of course."

"What I'm thinking is, how bad I want to kiss you right now," he answers with no hesitation.

Anticipation drives through my body and straight between my legs, but I keep a calm face. "Then, what's stopping you?"

Adios, platonic, co-parenting plans. Hello, making shit complicated.

At least it'll come with an orgasm. Hopefully.

He grins. "Good point."

My tongue darts out to wet my lips at the same time he presses his mouth to mine. He sucks on the tip of my tongue before dipping his into my mouth. I've never found the taste of generic toothpaste so delectable. Our lips slide against each other, as if we'd been doing this for years.

My heart pounds when he lifts up to move over me, keeping our lips connected, and I open my legs to allow him enough room to slide between them. I take in a deep breath when his mouth leaves mine to trail kisses down the curve of my neck.

He's slanted over me, careful of my stomach, and all I'm staring at is his erection straining through the thin gym shorts. My pulse races when I remember how big he is and how electrifying he felt inside me last time. No time is wasted before he rubs his fullness against my core to hit my most sensitive spot. I'm close to having an orgasm before we've even started.

It won't take much. I haven't been touched in forever, and if he's telling the truth, neither has he. We need to take this slow if we want it to last.

Unfortunately, what I need isn't what my body wants.

I need to get off.

I need this to last longer.

Why does this man constantly seem to drag out mixed emotions?

"More," I beg and squirm underneath him. *So much for wanting this to last longer.* "I need more."

More touching. More kissing. More of him everywhere.

My back arches when his mouth returns to mine. This kiss is different than the soft one before. It's greedy. Untamed. Eager.

"Where do you want more?" he asks against my lips.

"Everywhere," I moan out.

He groans deep from his throat when I run my foot up and down his leg and start moving into him more aggressive than what's appropriate. I shift until his cock hits me in the perfect spot, and then I grind against him.

He uses a single finger to untie my shorts, and I wiggle out of them in seconds, desire blazing through me. He doesn't bother removing my panties. Doesn't see them as a challenge.

Instead, he pushes the lace to the side and gives my clit the attention I've been dying for, rubbing it with the pad of his thumb.

I gasp when he slowly slips a finger inside me while still giving me the feel of his cock. His thick finger gracefully moves in and out of me. Not how I want it. I move against him harder to tip him off on how I need it.

"Slow down, baby," he says with a laugh. "You keep doing that, and my dick is going to explode. You probably want this to last longer than a few minutes."

"I don't care how long it lasts if I get what I want," I mutter.

He chuckles and shoves another finger into me without warning. He gives me rough. "That better?"

"God, yes," I moan out in response.

"I have something you'll enjoy even more."

He dips his fingers out of me in order to grab the strings of his shorts.

Finally. This is what I need.

The sound of a phone ringing startles me.

His hand drops from his shorts, and he curses under his breath. My heart beats wildly when he places them in his mouth and sucks on them on the way to his gym bag. I can't stop staring at the outline of his swollen cock when he opens the bag and grabs his phone.

We were right there.

Right freaking there.

My vagina does not deserve this.

He checks the caller before answering.

"Hello?" He drops down in the chair and expels a stressed breath. "Hey, honey. How's camp?" he croaks out. "What's wrong? You're feeling homesick? That happened to me my first time there, too." He pauses. "I promise."

I catch my breath when he falls quiet again.

"You know what helped me? I wrote my parents a letter, telling them all the cool stuff I was doing there. I'll ask your counselor to mail it out for you, and I should get it before I pick you up."

I pull my shorts up at the next pause. We won't be finishing this.

"Good. I'll be waiting for the postman every day."

I sit up on the bed.

"Call me if you need anything, okay? Good night. I love you."

He ends the call and tosses the phone on the desk. His eyes are pinned to the floor while he sits there, looking tortured. His chest heaves in and out, and the only sound is coming from the police sirens on the TV.

"Dallas," I finally whisper.

He lifts his head, and my chest aches at the unease on his face.

"Shit, Willow. I'm fucking sorry."

He pushes out of the chair, his erection not as visible as before when he was about to screw me but still there, and then he storms out of the room.

Tears slip down my face.
Another rejection.
I'm done lying to myself.
I'm done thinking he'll change.
Fuck Dallas Barnes.

CHAPTER TWENTY-THREE

Dallas

I DESERVE the rain pouring down on me in front of our hotel room. I deserve to get sucker-punched in my fucking face, mugged right here on this sidewalk, and stabbed in the back for how I treated Willow *again*.

My cock is hard. The taste of Willow's sweet pussy is on my tongue. My head is not only blasting with thoughts of how turned on I am, but also of how terrible of a man I am.

I did it again—treated her like shit and walked away while in the moment.

Willow deserves someone better than me, someone who isn't a mess. But why does it kill me to picture her having that someone? Why can't I get her out of my head and stay in this miserable place, as I promised myself I would months ago?

I shake my head in agony. What would it look like to Lucy if I fell for someone else? That would hurt her memory, show I was a shitty husband, make it seem like she was replaceable in my eyes.

I bang my palms against the motel's brick wall. *But, Jesus, fuck, what about me?*

I clench my hands and stalk back and forth, depicting a serial killer.

Would it hurt Lucy if I moved on?

She's gone.

Hell, knowing Lucy, she's probably smiling down at me. She begged me to find someone else to love and made me promise I'd eventually move on, for my daughter's sake and mine. I agreed, lying to her on her deathbed.

But who wouldn't when time was running out and you didn't want to waste your last words arguing about giving your heart to another woman?

I never thought it was possible. The thought of touching another woman made my skin crawl.

Until Willow.

Can I stay confined in my miserable bubble? Keep my heart in reserve because I'm terrified of losing someone I care about again?

I tilt my head up to stare at the dark sky.

"Lucy, baby, tell me what to do. Am I making a wrong move or being a fucking idiot?" I whisper while a million thoughts rush through my mind.

The bed is empty when I walk back into the motel room. I look at the window first, like a dumbass, considering the window is right next to the door, and I would've seen her leave. The bathroom light shines through the bottom of the door, and I hear the shower turn on.

Lucky for me, the door isn't locked. My hand is shaking when I open it while taking a deep breath. I make out her breathtaking silhouette through the thin shower curtain at the same time I hear her crying.

Damn it! I'm a fucking asshole.

I take a step into the room and say her name.

She doesn't reply.

I repeat it, louder this time.

Silence.

I strip out of my wet clothes, and when I climb in across from her, she pushes me back.

"What the hell, Dallas?" she shrieks. "You scared the shit out of me."

"I'm sorry," is all I can muster. Sorry for scaring her, for turning her down, for acting like an asshole. *Why am I always fucking up with her?*

Her tears get lost in the water. "I'm sick of your *sorrys.* I'm done, Dallas." She throws her hands up. "Done with your bullshit games. I refuse to be some toy for you to play with when it's convenient for you."

She winces when I stretch my arm out to move her fiery-red hair from her face, so I can see her beautiful green eyes better.

Today was a good day. We had fun. I told her shit no one else knows. I felt our babies in her stomach for the first time. We kissed. I had my hand in her panties and fingers in her pussy.

Then, I fucked it all up.

"No more bullshit," I whisper. "I promise."

"Your promises don't mean shit," she says with a snort, throwing my words back at me. "It only makes you look like more of a jackass each time."

I am a jackass.

"Tell me what you want me to do. How can I make this right?"

"Let yourself live!" she shouts. "Get it through that thick skull of yours that it's okay to move on, for your sake!" She stabs her finger into my chest. "For your daughter's sake!" Her finger moves to my stomach. "For my fucking sake!"

I cup her cheeks with both hands. "I've tried," I ground out. "I've tried telling myself I shouldn't do this with you, but maybe that's where I'm going wrong. I'm not supposed to be fighting it." I caress her soft skin. "Neither one of us is supposed to be fighting it because the only thing that feels natural is this. Us together."

"No," she breathes out. "You only fight shit that you don't want to happen."

"Trust me, fighting it means, it's *all* I want to happen." She shakes her head, and I wipe away her tears. "Say the word. Tell me you don't want me. Tell me you want me to leave this shower."

She breathes in deep breaths and stays quiet.

"Do you want me to leave?" I stress.

She pinches her lips together and won't answer.

"Or would you rather I did this?"

She gasps when I fall to my knees and inch her feet apart. I run my hand up her leg and straight to the opening of her pussy.

"Answer my question," I demand.

Instead of pushing me again, she slips her hand into my hair and moans. "That. I'd rather you did that." Her nails dig deep into my scalp before I make another move. "Keep going."

And that's what I do.

I situate one of her legs on the edge of the bathtub, and her body trembles at the first swipe of my tongue.

The taste of her is sweet.

Fucking heavenly.

I could eat her out for the rest of my life and never go hungry.

I apologize with my tongue.

Own her with it.

Beg her not to turn her back on me and plead to her to give me another chance.

If my words aren't convincing enough, I hope my tongue can do the trick.

"Shit, that feels so good," she mutters when I drive two fingers into her pussy and flick my tongue at her opening at the same time.

My dick stirs when I peek up at the image I'm getting. I'm on the verge of combusting from the view of Willow grinding her pussy into my face. I don't stop until I know she's on her way to falling apart.

"I'm close," she chants over and over again. Her foot arches off the edge, and she holds the back of my head in place as she lets go, her juices running onto my tongue while she moans out her final release.

So fucking gorgeous.

So fucking delicious.

My cock is hard as a rock. I'll be taking a cold shower and jacking off to thoughts of what happened in here when Willow goes to bed.

"Does that at least make up for some of my dickness?" I ask, looking up at her.

She spreads her fingers a few inches apart and massages my scalp. "A little. You still have some making up to do. I can take payment with your tongue a few more times."

I stand up, rub my hands down her sides, and then squeeze her hips. "Lucky for you, I don't mind paying interest."

She laughs. "Good to know."

I jerk my head toward the outside of the shower. "You ready to hit the sheets? It's late, and I know you're beat."

She nods. "You did just lick all the energy out of me."

I grunt when she wipes her mouth, and my hands are shoved off her hips. This time, she's the one dropping to her knees.

I stop her when she opens her mouth and bobs her head toward my dick. "No, this was about you."

I've turned down blow jobs on more than one occasion, but my body has never physically ached when I did, like it is doing now. I eye her full lips, the way she's licking them and staring at my cock like she can't wait to taste it.

"Trust me," she says. I tense and moan when she licks the pre-cum from the tip. "Me sucking your cock is just as much for me."

Her lips wrap around me before I can even come up with a response. My cock twitches, growing even harder, and I let her set the pace even though I want to plow my cock in and out of her mouth, fuck it until she can't breathe.

She takes me in, sucking me hard, and adds her hand to stroke me.

I throw my head back. "Shit, Willow. This is amazing."

She devours my cock, not stopping to catch her breath once, as water pours down over us. I thought the sight of pleasuring her with my tongue was my favorite, but her on her knees, sucking my cock, is running in close second.

I can't wait to fuck her again.

I know that'll be number fucking one.

"So fucking good."

My plan of not controlling her speed annihilates when I feel it coming. I jerk my hips up, and she moans against my cock, exciting it more.

"So good." I swipe the hair away from her face, so I can see every inch of her and give her a warning when I come, but she doesn't pull away.

The water turns cold at the same time she swallows my cum with a smile.

CHAPTER TWENTY-FOUR

Willow

"AND THEN WHAT HAPPENED?" Stella asks, nearly jumping off the couch in eagerness.

I'm back at work, and we're hanging out in her over-the-top trailer while she's making me do *another* rundown of what happened last night. She knows everything but the part where we dry-humped each other and had an oral face-off.

She'll get that story another time. It's still fresh in my mind, and I don't want questions to ruin the image yet.

Nervousness is an understatement of what I felt when I woke up this morning. The bed was empty. A bad sign. I grabbed my phone, and my heart settled when I heard the shower running. Joining him crossed my mind, but I'm not as gutsy as him.

When he got out, he said the truck was ready to pick up, and a shop employee would give us a ride there.

An hour later, we were back on the road.

No more kissing, hugging, or talks of what went down, *literally*, last night. It gave me relief yet also fried my brain at the same time. I'm concerned. Scared. Terrified.

We made light conversation. He told me about Maven's call last night. She was homesick and wanted to hear his voice. We listened to the radio, and I let him choose the music. It was *not* Justin Bieber.

"You know what happened," I answer.

Stella gives me a puppy-dog look. "No, I don't," she whines. "More happened than what you're telling me. I know you better than you believe."

I throw my arms out and fall back on the couch. "You've pulled every detail out of me. What more do you want? I can start making stuff up if it helps your weird imagination. We got married. Adopted kids to go with the baby on the way. Bought a house with a four-car garage. Surprise!"

She rolls her eyes. "No one copped a feel while you were sleeping *together?* Surely, the two of you are horny as hell, considering you've both been celibate for a minute. There you were, stranded in the rain, cold and lonely. How romantic."

"Now, you're making shit up. We weren't cold and lonely."

She clips a dark strand of hair behind her ear. "Work with me here." She narrows one eye at me, studying, like the answer she wants is marked across my skin. "You have every side effect of an orgasm."

"Side effect? Since when did you get into the pharmaceutical business?"

"I haven't seen a smile that bright on your face in a long time. Your skin is glowing. You look like you've been wandering around Wonderland all day."

"Pregnancy gives me mood swings. I could get crazy angry in three seconds."

She jumps up from the couch to lock the door, and I squirm in my seat when she joins me again.

"Uh, what are you doing? Keeping me hostage until I give you what you want?"

Her lips curl up. "How'd you know?"

I rub my hands together. "You have to promise you won't tell Hudson."

"Jesus, Willow," she moans out, her smile collapsing. "Do you not trust me anymore?"

My cheeks burn. "The whole scenario at your party scares the crap out of me."

She sucks her cheeks in before answering, "The only reason Hudson found out was because he was eavesdropping, not because I told him. I would've kept your secret."

She rises from the couch again. I'm afraid I've pissed her off when she unlocks the door and sticks her head out the door.

"Hudson?" she yells, looking around before slamming it shut, the lock clicking back. "No fiancé in sight. Half of the cast and crew have left for the day. You have my word that my lips are sealed."

I inhale a long breath before giving her the real rundown of what happened. She squeals, claps her hands, and is on cloud nine with every word.

I SNAG my phone from the nightstand when the doorbell rings. No missed calls or texts, and I didn't make plans with anyone.

Dallas texted earlier, asking me to go out for tacos, and I declined. Getting stared down while eating isn't on tonight's agenda. It's getting more difficult, hiding my baby bump. I'm going to have to get more creative.

I throw my post-shower wet hair into a sloppy ponytail and peek through the peephole when I reach the door. Dallas didn't give me a heads-up that he was coming, which is irritating because my baggy gray sweatpants and three-sizes-too-big T-shirt isn't the most attractive outfit to greet the guy who gave you a fantastic orgasm the night before.

He moves into my apartment with grocery bags covering half of his face. His muscular arms are securely wrapped around the bags, and he nearly runs into me when I stand in the middle of the doorway because I can't take my eyes off them.

"What are you doing?" I ask when he sets the groceries on the kitchen counter.

"You didn't want to go out for tacos, so I brought the tacos to you." He winks. "I promised tacos, so they're coming your way, and you can bet your ass that they're better than anything you'd get at a restaurant."

Shit. Fingers crossed he's not expecting me to help him.

We'll be eating grilled cheese by the end of the night. Burned grilled cheese.

I watch him while he digs out the groceries and starts moving around my kitchen as if he were my roommate. He sifts through the cabinets before pulling out pans and bowls.

"You know how to cook?" I stupidly ask.

He cuts open the hamburger, drops it in the pan, and turns a burner on low. "I'm a single dad."

"Good point," I mutter.

This soon-to-be mom had better take some notes. Takeout has always been my main food group, but that doesn't mean I eat like shit. I get healthy takeout—at least, I did before, but there's not a big market for that here.

"I cook dinner every night. Come over and eat anytime you want."

That's a big hell no. Any appetite I build up will be lost when I step into his house, and the memories of his freak-out flood me.

I take in my T-shirt and pull at the bottom. "I wish you had told me you were coming over."

He snags a cutting board and starts cutting the bell peppers. I slide into his spot, pushing him away and causing him to grin, and take his place. I start slicing the peppers, the simplest task for me to take over, without saying a word.

"You would've bailed," he replies.

"No, I wouldn't have." That's the truth. I bailed on going out to dinner but would've been up for his company. "I would've made myself not look like a train wreck."

"You look gorgeous." He nods toward my belly. "You've been hiding it well. Anyone know about the twins yet?"

I shake my head. "You spill the beans to anyone?"

"I'm waiting for you to give me the green light. You do know, we have to tell everyone sooner or later, right?"

"I do, but why does it feel like it's shock after shock? Guess what?" The knife waves through the air when I dramatically throw my arms up. "I'm pregnant. Guess what? It's with twins!"

"Put the knife down, Mike Myers." He laughs while peeling an avocado and then mashing it in a bowl. "You realize, life is full of surprises as you get older. You grow wisdom with age."

I click my tongue against the roof of my mouth. "Appreciate the insight, *old man.*"

"Whoa, who are you calling old?" He smirks and bumps his hip against mine. "You want to be on dish duty tonight?"

I slide the peppers off the board and into a glass bowl. The lettuce is my next victim. "I'm calling *you* an old man."

"Sweetheart, we're six years apart."

"Six years is a long time. You were in kindergarten, learning how to write your ABCs, when I was born."

"You seemed to find this *old man* attractive enough to sleep with."

"Eh, let's blame it on the alcohol."

"I'll keep waiting for you to admit it."

I drop the knife. "Admit what?"

"Admit this so-called *old man* made you feel better than any *boy* you've been with your age." He rests the spatula on the stove, and his eyes fix on me. "You lose a taco for every lie you tell, so I'd suggest you stick with the truth if you have an appetite."

Fucking tacos.

Are they worth honesty?

My stomach growls.

Hell yes.

"I don't have much to compare since I've slept with only two men. Brett cared about pleasing me in the beginning." I sigh.

"That changed in the end. He'd get off, slap my ass, thank me, and then go back to his video games."

"Shit, you dated a fucking loser," he grumbles. "LA is saturated with men, and you stuck around with him? I never understood that."

"That's what everyone says."

"Why'd you stay with him then?"

"I don't know. Convenience?"

"That's a piss-poor excuse to stay in a relationship."

"You're telling me, you've never stayed with someone because starting over sounded too rough?" My voice is filled with defensiveness. I'm not alone on this.

"Fuck no. I'd never be with someone I didn't love. I stayed with Lucy for so long because my life would've been a nightmare without her. I loved her more than my own air. I would've given my life for her, taken her cancer, given her my health."

"It might not be with Lucy, but you're doing it now." I shift around him and go to the fridge for a bottle of water.

My response *really* catches his attention.

"What was that?"

I take a drink and slowly swallow it while he stares at me in confusion.

"Nothing," I mutter. I place my water on the counter and go back to my chopping duty.

He plucks the knife from my hand. "Not so fast. Tell me what you mean."

Here goes nothing. "You're doing the same thing!"

He raises a questioning brow and reaches back to turn the stove off.

"You've accepted being alone because the thought of starting over without Lucy seems too rough. *Convenience.*"

My eyes pierce his, and I wait for him to turn around and leave me with a half-cooked dinner. I should feel guilty about what I said, but I don't.

His shoulders draw back while he takes a pained breath. "She was my wife. You're not supposed to get over the love of your life."

My mention of Lucy has put a damper on taco night, but it needed to be said. His answer will tell me if last night was just sex or if he's ready to open his heart and try something with me.

"I'm not saying you have to get *over* her but more of coming to terms that she's gone. I stayed with Brett because the thought of something new scared the living shit out of me, and you're doing the same. Don't throw stones at glass houses."

He wipes his hands down his jeans. "How'd you do it then?"

The fact that he's still standing here shocks me. "Do what?"

"Let your heart move on."

"It wasn't easy. It was one of the hardest decisions I'd ever made."

His jaw twitches, and his eyes are downcast on me. I suck in a breath. "I'm trying, trust me. I'm fucking trying for you." We're so close, I can feel his heart beating against my chest. "You've opened up what I feared for months. It doesn't seem as fucking scary, exploring with you."

I POINT my fork at my plate. "This is delicious." Screw those fancy taco joints. Dallas Barnes kills anything they serve. "Seriously, the best guacamole I've ever had."

He showed me how to make it step by step. I'm in charge of taco night next time.

"Told you I knew my way around a kitchen," he says proudly and then takes a drink of water.

I offered to run upstairs and grab a beer from Lauren's fridge for him. Tacos always taste better with beer. He wouldn't let me because it wasn't right for him to drink when I couldn't.

"How was work today? Stella drill you about our trip?" he asks.

Yep, drilled me as hard as his tongue did in the shower. I give him my best *duh* impression, and he laughs.

"Hudson pulled the same shit with me."

"They're more invested in our relationship than their own." I scrunch up my face. "I can't blame them though. I did the same thing with them."

"I'll admit, it's fun when you're on the other side." He tilts his water glass my way. "Did I thank you for the company the night we got them back together?"

A while back, Stella and Hudson broke up after the tabloids went after their relationship. I called Dallas, and we set up a plan to get them back together. It worked, and Hudson and Dallas flew to New York to surprise her.

I didn't want to be a cockblock during their making up, so I hung out in the lobby. That was where Dallas found me. We spent the night tasting food at every food cart, and I showed him my favorite spots in Times Square.

"You gave me my first good night in a while," he says. "No matter how shitty I'm feeling, you seem to always bring me back to the light." He runs his hand over his jaw. "Since we're talking about fixing relationships, about last night ..."

"I know, I know. It was a mistake," I rush out, sensing his regret. *Did he make tacos to soften up the blow?* "We were tired, not thinking clearly, horny *again* because we hadn't been laid in months."

"Whoa, hold up. I wasn't tired, and my mind was crystal clear." He stretches his shoulders back and grins. "Although you hit the nail on the head with the horny part."

What's he saying?

"I didn't eat your pussy last night just to get off. I don't do pity sex or pity *oral* sex." His tone turns serious. "In fact, I thought my sex life was over, but then you sat your perky ass across from me at the bar with your sexy-as-hell red hair pulled back to show off your contagious smile." He chuckles and leans in to rest his elbows on the table. "So, let's quit using the horny-and-not-thinking excuse."

Why do my words always come back to bite me in the ass? I'm judging him for pushing me away yet doing the same.

"In case you forgot, I was there in the morning," he continues.

"'Cause you were stranded."

Why can't I stop pulling away? Rejection still scares me.

"That was part of the reason, yes, but the other was you."

"Good. So, we can confirm we're both sexually attracted to each other. Maybe we should explore that and leave our feelings to the side for now."

"You want this to only be about sex?"

I nod.

"You sure about that?"

"Positive."

We'll screw for now and get each other out of our systems. In my head, I want to believe the only reason I'm pursuing him is that he gives me the best orgasms I've ever had. I want sex, and then we can worry about a relationship later. The opposite of what I was taught as a kid, but whatever.

He wipes his mouth, throws the napkin on his plate, and gets up from the chair. "Let's see if I can change your mind." He holds his hand out to me.

I stare at him in shock. I wasn't expecting this to go down now. "What?"

His eyes grow wilder every second he stares at me. "A warning, sweetheart. Don't challenge me and then be surprised when I rise to it."

I take his hand and let him pull me up. He doesn't give me a chance to take another breath before he hungrily captures my mouth with this. I moan when his tongue slips into my mouth. The kiss makes it clear that he's going to make me regret saying that all I wanted was his cock. It explains he'll make me beg for it until I admit that I want more.

I gasp for those lost breaths when he grabs a handful of my ass and draws me in closer. I waste no time in pushing his shirt up and over his head. I didn't have the chance to thoroughly appreciate his body last night in the shower. His tongue between my legs consumed my every thought.

My mouth waters at the sight of his firm chest, muscles galore, the six-pack finely sculpted. He's right about one thing. He might be older, but his body and his cock outweigh Brett in every way. He tenses when I run my lips down his chest and flick my tongue against his nipple. His cock swells under his jeans, him *rising for the challenge*, if you will, and I drop to my knees to frantically pull it out.

I'm taking control before he gets the chance to.

Blow jobs have never been my thing. I saw them as a chore with Brett, but everything is different with Dallas. The thought of his hard dick inside my mouth excites me. Pleasing him pleases me.

I wet my lips, drinking in the sight of his large erection twitching in front of me, pre-cum dripping from the tip. His head falls back when I take the full length of him in my mouth. He's so big, it stabs me in the back of my throat. I bring my mouth back, drawing his dick out to catch my breath, and then eagerly suck him back in.

"Fuck, that mouth, Willow," he croaks out when I sink my nails into his ass to blow him better.

His hand dips down to wrap around his cock, and he jacks off in sync with my mouth. The hottest fucking thing I've ever experienced. I take him in, more excitedly.

He's close, I can tell, and I can't wait to taste his cum again.

Can't wait to swallow him down but still have the taste of him lingering there.

I wait for it, my mouth moving faster, but he pulls away right before we reach the finish line.

The hell?

His face burns with desire as he stares down at me on my

knees. "I'll never get the sight of this out of my mind. It's better than anything I've imagined while jacking off."

Chills climb up my spine. "You think about me when you're jacking off?"

His hand is still wrapped around his cock, and he goes back to slowly stroking it. "Every fucking time," he grits out.

"Let me finish the job then," I say with a pout.

He shakes his head. "I'm going to finish the job in your tight pussy. I know you enjoy sucking my cock, but that'll be nothing compared to sliding inside you." He catches my chin between his thumb and forefinger. "Now, stand up, so I can put you on this table and eat you as my dessert."

I shyly bite my lip. "How can a girl deny that?"

"You'll never want to deny me when I give you this dick again. You'll be coming back for more."

He picks me up underneath my elbows and settles me on the table. I open my legs the second my ass hits the edge. I'm ready for this. I *need* this.

"Put your hand over my mouth before you start," I breathe out.

He cocks his head to the side. "Didn't know you were into that."

I shake my head and laugh. "We have to be quiet. Your sister lives right above me, and the walls are thin."

"I don't give a shit. I want to hear you scream my name."

My sweatpants and panties are off in seconds, and he disposes of my bra and T-shirt. He licks his lips when he takes in my breasts. He cups them and leans down to draw a nipple into his mouth. He sucks hard and releases me, and not another word leaves his mouth before he drags my legs over his shoulders. My breathing hitches when he falls to his knees.

The first lick sends jolts through my body, and I would fall off the table if he wasn't holding me in place. His tongue is an expert, dipping in and out of me, before he slips it out to suck on my clit. When he uses it to separate my folds for a better angle, my toes arch toward the ceiling.

Ache blossoms through my chest, and the need for an orgasm pushes at me even harder. His hands move up and down my legs as he pleasures me, and I make sure I'm balanced well enough before reaching down and pushing a finger inside myself. I work in sync with his tongue the same way he did when I was sucking him off earlier.

Our connection is what ends me. My back comes off the table, my legs buckling against his shoulders, and I never want to come down from this orgasm as it shoots through me.

"Say my name," he groans, still working his tongue in me.

I do as I was told—not screaming it at the top of my lungs, but repeatedly gasping it out.

He slowly releases my legs with a shit-eating grin on his face. "Damn, I love the sound of that when my face is shoved in your pussy."

He gets up and goes to help me down from the table, but I stop him.

"I want to fuck you."

He's shocked at my outburst. "Don't worry, sweetheart. I fully plan on doing that—*multiple times*—but let's save the table sex for another time. I want you in your bed."

I grunt when he picks me up in his arms, newlywed-style, and he races to the bedroom. As badly as I want this, I still have nervousness riding through me like a hurricane. We're taking a big step here.

This isn't a quick blow job in the shower.

This is *sex*—something so intimate for the both of us. Neither one of us sleep around, so this is a big deal, especially for him.

I don't want him to freak out this time and feel like he's betraying Lucy by sleeping with me.

"Are you sure about this?" I ask when he carefully lowers me onto the bed.

He doesn't respond until I give him full eye contact. "I've never been surer." He situates himself between my legs, and his cock impales me with no warning.

I constrict around him while he gives me time to adjust to his size. I know the situation I'm getting into with his first thrust. His first moan tells me I'm not making the wrong decision.

He starts out slow, which frustrates me. This is something I've wanted for months. I tilt my hips up to give him a better angle, excite him, and hint that I want more.

Harder. Faster. More.

It works.

He pounds into me rougher, sweat building up along his forehead, and groans with every stroke.

"Say my name," I whisper. "Tell me who you're in bed with." It's my turn to show ownership.

"Willow," he says, his eyes drinking in my face … my body.

We slow down when he stretches forward to take my lips with his, and he devours my mouth.

"I'm in Willow's bed, fucking Willow, and Willow is about to make my dick explode."

I kiss him until he pulls away to fuck me harder. That's when I place my hands over my stomach to hide it. I've never been an insecure person, but I've gained weight. *A lot of weight.* My stomach is no longer flat. I see myself as less attractive.

"Don't," he demands in a raspy voice. "Let me see what we did together."

I slowly drag them away, and he grasps my hands in his, placing them over my head and tightly holding them.

I shudder underneath him, coming undone, and scream out his name again.

There's no doubt everyone in the building heard that one.

He jerks and gives me two more thrusts before releasing himself inside me.

"Fuck," he grunts, breathing as hard as I am. "That was fucking amazing."

I'm still catching my breath when he collapses next to me. We're a sticky and sweaty mess. Pretty sure I've burned off every calorie of those tacos.

I turn my focus on him. "You work an appetite back up?"

He smirks. "I had a very filling dessert."

His answer makes me tingle. *Tingle.* This is the first time I've ever felt myself do that.

"I'm starving, and I don't like eating alone if I don't have to. Lucky for you, I have a pantry full of ramen noodles."

He chuckles. "Fucking ramen noodles."

I'm falling for this man who is broken, a little ruined, a bit of a disaster … and who gave up on love.

CHAPTER TWENTY-FIVE

Willow

I TENSE when the bed shifts behind me.

He yawns.

Then, he heads to the bathroom.

What happens now?

God, why am I so paranoid every morning after?

We went back to the kitchen last night and didn't have ramen noodles. Instead, we had ice cream, and then he did fuck me on the table after licking our dessert off my chest. We were exhausted, and I'd reached my exercise goal for the month, so he suggested a movie. I introduced him to my favorite black-and-white film, *Casablanca,* and we passed out before reaching the end. He carried me to bed, kissed me good night, and wrapped his arms around me. It felt good to be held, relaxed me, and I was back to sleep in seconds.

His next move this morning will tell me everything I need to know about our relationship—or possible lack thereof. Him not bailing at the hotel doesn't count, doesn't ease my mind, because he had an obligation to stay with me. He didn't have a working car, and Stella would've kicked his ass if he'd left me stranded.

I brace myself for whatever is about to happen when he comes around the bed and drops to one knee, so we're eye-level.

His lips curl up as he edges closer. "I didn't want you to assume I was sneaking out. I have to pick up Maven from camp."

I smile. "Do you mind if I come along?"

What the hell am I thinking?

"You up for another road trip with me?"

"Why not?" I want to spend all my time with him.

My smile grows when he kisses my forehead.

"All right, get dressed, and we'll be on our way. I'll grab my clothes from the truck."

I hop out of bed like I'm ten and it's Christmas, and I scurry to the bathroom.

Our relationship shifted into something last night—something that exceeds friends but isn't quite into the whole relationship thing yet.

Friends with benefits?

Co-parenting with benefits?

Sex, not love?

"OH MY GOSH, this is so cute," I say when we pull into the camp parking lot. "It's not like the movies but still cool."

Dallas cocks his head toward my stomach. "Can't wait for our little ones to join Maven here in a few years."

"A few years? You mean, six?"

"I started coming here in Pampers."

I slap his shoulder. "You are such a liar."

Maven comes running our way as soon as we get out of the truck.

"Daddy!" she screams. "You brought Willow! This is the bestest day ever!"

I lose a breath when she rushes into me and wraps her tiny arms around my waist.

"Hey now," Dallas says, coming up behind her and peeling

her away from me. "What am I, chopped liver? You haven't seen your dad in a week, and you roll right past me."

She giggles and jumps into his arms. "You know I missed you, Daddy!" When he releases her, she pulls a stack of papers from her bag. "I made all of these for you and wrote letters like you said!" She snatches the top piece from Dallas's hand and holds it out like she can't wait for me to see it. "This one is for you."

"Wow, thank you," I say with a smile. It's a hand-drawn picture of her and a tall redhead holding hands and walking around what resembles lights. "It's so pretty."

Her eyes sparkle with pride, and she bounces on her tiptoes. "It's us at the fair. I had *sooo* much fun and can't wait to do it again next year!"

I squat down and give her another hug. "Me either. Maybe, next time, I can gain some courage and join you on the rides."

"I would love that so much!" She turns around. "Daddy! Willow said she'd get on the big-kid rides with me next year!"

Dallas smiles and winks at me. "Oh, really? We'd better hold her to that."

"Dallas, I thought that was you," a feminine voice calls out.

Maven loses my attention when I see a woman walking our way. A pretty blonde dressed similar to what Lucy used to wear, and she gives me a once-over, sizing me up to see if I'm competition.

Sure am, sweetie.

She thrusts her hand in my face when she reaches us, and I can't stop myself from rolling my eyes. Her face scrunches up into a sneer to assure me it wasn't missed.

"You must be Willow. It's nice to finally meet you. You're all everyone in town has been talking about."

Her eyes drop down to my stomach, and I pull my arms around it to block her view.

Really? I cross my arms. *Let's see her squirm.*

"Like what?"

I've only gone to the fair and the diner for lunch once. The only other times I've left my apartment is to go to work, and Stella's show is filmed thirty minutes out of Blue Beech. I've kept to myself, but I'm sure she's heard about me from the videos taken at the fair.

My question surprises her. I don't mean to be rude, but the way her eyes scrutinize me is rude in itself.

She signals between Dallas and me. "That you two have been spendin' an awful lot of time together." Her smile is bright and phony. "You're from the big city, like Hudson's little fiancé, right?"

"Sure am. I'm her best friend and assistant."

"I see," she clips. "How long do you plan on staying here? You probably miss LA. It's pretty boring around here."

"Cindy," Dallas warns.

She whips around to smile at him. "What? I'm only introducing myself to the town's newest ..." Her attention moves back to me. "Visitor? Resident?"

"Resident," he growls to her back. "Willow is a new *resident* of Blue Beech, so you march on and relay that to your gossip club and quit interrogating her."

She throws me a flat smile, turns around to give him her attention, and slides her hand across his chest. He jerks away.

"You want me to make y'all dinner tonight? I can bring that fried chicken of mine you love so much." She glances down at Maven with a faker smile than she gave me. "Didn't you say it was your favorite, honey?"

Maven shakes her head. "My grammy's fried chicken is my favorite."

Dallas glares at Cindy. "As much as I'd love to chat and deny your company, we have places to be. Enjoy our day."

"Call me," she sings out to him.

This time, she wraps her arm around his, and he pulls out of her grip, narrowing his eyes on her.

"Stop." He gives her his back and grabs Maven around the waist. "You ready to go, sweetheart?"

I throw *Cindy* the dirtiest look I can manage before getting into the truck.

She brings him dinner? He said he cooks every night.

Dallas gets into the truck and leans into my space. "Don't let your head go there. Give me the benefit of the doubt, and we'll talk about it."

I nod. My heart aches with jealousy, terror, and betrayal.

Dallas starts the truck with fire in his eyes.

"WALKERS! WALKERS! WALKERS!" Maven chants twenty minutes into the drive home. "Daddy, you promised!"

Dallas pats my thigh. "You hungry?"

"The waiters are rude to you at Walkers!" Maven says. "It's *so, so, so, so* funny! They told Daddy he had a nose bigger than a rhino's horn one time."

I laugh and twist in my seat to smile at her. "No way." I fake lower my voice and place my hand on the side of my mouth. "I totally see what they're talking about though."

Maven bursts into a fit of laughter.

"Hey now," Dallas cuts in. "That's supposed to be the part where you stick up for your dad and argue that I don't have a nose like a rhino." His hand moves to rest on my leg this time when I turn back around. "You cool with stopping?"

"I'm not passing on this, rhino man."

MAVEN AND DALLAS sit across from me in the booth.

Walkers is an old-fashioned diner where the waiters wear ridiculous uniforms with unusual, most likely made-up names.

The waitress tells me I'm cheap when I order a water. Maven cracks up.

She says Dallas isn't man enough for real beer when he orders a root beer. Maven cracks up.

She gladly takes Maven's order for a milkshake without saying a word. Maven still cracks up.

At least they're nice to kids.

Not only does Maven take over all the conversation, telling us everything she did at camp, but she also takes my mind off what happened with *Cindy*.

Fucking Cindy. I can't be pissed at Dallas for hanging out with another woman when we're not officially anything. I can't call dibs on him just because I'm carrying his babies.

Wait … yes, I can.

I can because, last night, he was in my bed.

I'm calling dibs.

I'M STUFFED AFTER LUNCH, but Maven insists we share a dessert.

"My birthday party is next weekend," she tells me, scooping up a bite of the brownie sundae. "Will you come? Pretty, pretty please with cherries on top?"

I swallow my bite down. "Sure." My attention goes to Dallas. "I mean, if that's okay with your dad."

"I'd love for you to come," he answers.

"It's at my grammy and grampy's," she continues. "They have a giant yard, and Daddy promised to get me a princess bounce house, so all my friends can play in it. Didn't you, Daddy?"

Dallas ruffles his hand through her static-filled ponytail. "Sure did."

"A princess bounce house?" I say with high enthusiasm. "I can't say no to that."

Maven bounces in her seat. "Yay! I'm so excited!"

We finish our dessert, and Dallas leaves the table to pay the bill.

"Do you have any kids?" Maven asks as soon as he's out of earshot.

I nearly spit my water in her face and cough a few times before managing to swallow it down. It takes me a second to get over the shock and tilt my lips into a smile.

"I don't," I croak out.

CHAPTER TWENTY-SIX

Dallas

FUCK, it's been a day.

After I dropped Willow off, I helped Maven unpack her bags. We went through all of her painted pictures, letters, and worksheets she'd created. There were several she had drawn with her family doing activities she enjoyed. I flipped through them with a smile, and my heart crashed into my chest when I got near the bottom of the stack.

She and I are standing together, holding hands, and a blonde angel is flying above us. *Lucy* is flying over us.

The next one was a picture of us with Willow.

My daughter is confused.

Willow is confused.

Shit, I'm confused as a motherfucker.

Cindy's comments when I picked up Maven didn't help. Dinner went well until I went to pay the check. After that, Willow froze me out.

I can't wait to collapse on the couch and go over all the shit I need to fix. I need to clear up the Cindy situation with Willow before shit falls apart.

My day gets even more complicated when I finish Maven's favorite bedtime story and tuck her in.

"Willow is nice," she says. "I'm glad she's coming to my birthday party."

I kiss her forehead. "Me, too, honey."

"And she's really pretty."

I nod, hoping I can make it out of the room before she starts her favorite game of a million questions.

"Is she your girlfriend, Daddy?"

She never fails to catch on to something.

I shake my head and fake a laugh. "Now, that's a silly question."

She frowns. "It's not a silly question."

"Your daddy can't have a girlfriend."

I need to tread lightly here. I can't get her involved in something that could break her heart. I'm already growing attached to Willow, constantly thinking about her. *But can I throw my daughter into the mix?* I'm more worried about her heart getting broken than my own.

"Why not? Mommy told me, when she was gone, you'd someday get a new girlfriend who'd be a good mommy to me. Willow would be a good mommy, don't you think so?" She sighs. "Maybe I'll ask her."

Oh, fuck. Holy fuck. This is heading into territory I'm not ready for. Territory Willow isn't ready for.

I squeeze her sides over the blanket. "Honey, Willow is just Daddy's friend."

"*And* my friend," she corrects.

"And your friend."

"She rubs her belly a lot. Marci's mommy did that all the time when she had a baby in there. Does Willow have a baby in there?"

And shit just got even more complicated.

CHAPTER TWENTY-SEVEN

Willow

"YOU'RE OVERTHINKING THIS," Stella says on the phone. "You can't seriously believe Dallas is messing around with some other chick named fucking Cindy. I've never heard of a Cindy, which means she doesn't get thought of around here."

I thought the night at the hotel was a crazy one.

That's nothing compared to today.

I spent a morning with Dallas. We hung out with his daughter. A woman told me he'd been hanging out with her. Maven asked me if I had kids, and I somewhat lied to her. I don't have kids ... *yet.*

"She said he's been eating her food. Fried chicken, to be exact," I argue.

"And?"

"And?" I shout. *Why does she not agree that this is a problem?*

"Does eating her food mean eating her vagina or something? Is fried chicken a code phrase I don't know about?"

I slump down on the couch and groan. "I don't know. I just ..." *Just don't want him falling for another woman.* I'd better start whipping up some food Betty Crocker–style to compete with this chick's fried chicken. Time to call KFC for their secret recipe.

"Trust me, you're the only woman I've seen Dallas hanging out with. Shit, even talking to."

"You not seeing it doesn't mean it's not happening. You don't see me witnessing you screwing Hudson, but I know you guys are."

"Holy shit," she bursts out.

"Holy shit what?"

"You're falling for him, aren't you? This isn't about your hook-up the other night or about you wanting to get along for the baby. You're into him."

"What?" I yell. "No! Absolutely not!" I'm getting good at this whole lying/denying-my-feelings thing.

"Oh, come on. It's obvious. You've been hanging out, having dinner, giving each other oral before having sex, and picking up his daughter from camp. All that is falling-for-each-other stuff."

"It's not *obvious*." I take a deep breath to change the tone of my voice to sound more self-contained. "Don't take me making sure my baby daddy isn't a psychopath for me falling for him."

She sighs dramatically. "You owe me a hundred bucks when you two become official. I can take it out of your paycheck. I'll ask Hudson if anything is going on with Dallas and fried-chicken chick."

I snort. "Like he'd tell you. Dallas is his brother. Bro code."

"I can be very persuasive with my man. Trust me."

I stretch my legs out and measure my stomach—something I've been doing every night to track my progress. "I'm beginning to second-guess my decision of forcing the two of you to get back together. All this lovey-dovey crap makes me sick."

She laughs. "It's the morning sickness making you sick. I can't wait until you and Dallas admit you're in love, and I can throw all of this back in your face. I'll be the one rolling my eyes at your lovey-dovey shit."

"Whatever. Dallas is in love with his wife, who passed away." I'm acting like a brat, feeling sorry for myself, but this is where I start to push him away again. My heart is ready to go back into solitude. You can't have your heart broken if you don't give it out. "He'll always be in love with her, and I doubt that's going to change anytime soon."

She expels a long breath. "People move on. He can still love her *and* you."

"People can move on, yes, but a man in love as deep as Dallas was? No." A call beeps through, and I pull my phone away to check the caller ID before she keeps up with her argument. "Let me call you back. I have a call coming through."

"Is that call from Dallas?"

"Good night, best friend."

She's laughing when I end the call to answer his.

"Hello?" I throw my hand over my mouth, regretting taking the call. I haven't prepared myself for this conversation yet. I have to get myself together.

"Hypothetical situation," he breathes out, sounding stressed. "What would you say if I told you Maven knew you were pregnant?"

I don't even have time to *think* about what I would say before I screech out my reply, "I'd say you were out of your mind, and there was no way she'd know unless someone—say, her *father*—told her."

"Another hypothetical situation. What would you say if I told you Maven knew we were having twins?"

"What?" I shriek. *Him and his big mouth.* "You've lost your mind!"

He groans. "I couldn't help it! My six-year-old is apparently the damn baby whisperer. She asked me if you were pregnant because you rubbed your belly like fucking Marci's mom."

"Marci's mom? Who's that?"

"Another pregnant woman, I'm assuming."

"Let me get this straight. She asked if I was pregnant because I rubbed my stomach like another pregnant chick?"

"Correct."

"And you felt it was important to confirm it?"

"Correct again."

"Are you nuts?" I scream.

"I didn't know what to do. I can't lie to my daughter."

The hell he can't. I'll be lying to my children all the time about stuff they have no business knowing yet.

"Oh, really? So, you've told her Santa Claus isn't real and the Easter Bunny is you?"

He chuckles but tries to keep his voice serious. "You know what I mean."

"Well, you could've maybe, I don't know, changed the conversation to fucking Barbie dolls or something? Asked her to have a tea party? Talked about anything but my uterus."

"We can't have tea parties before bedtime," he explains.

"That fake caffeine is bad for children and their stuffed dogs after the streetlights come on, huh?"

"Smart-ass," he mutters. "I don't see why you're pissed. You should be thanking me. This saves you from having to be there when I planned on telling her."

"At least one good thing to come out of this." My heart stammers, and confusion flickers through me. Why am I upset that I wasn't there? Why am I sad I didn't get to see her reaction?

"You still pissed?" he asks a few seconds later.

"Not pissed. Shocked."

"If it makes you feel better, I made her promise she wouldn't tell anyone until I told her it was okay."

"I'm not sure how much I trust a promise coming from a six-year-old."

"It helps when you add an extra birthday gift as a hush bribe. Some parenting advice to a mommy-to-be—nothing works better than bribery with extra doll clothes."

"Bribery is okay, but lying is off the table? Makes sense. I'll have to keep that in mind." *While mine is going fucking crazy right now.*

"Now that I know you're not pissed, *just shocked,* I need to ask for a favor."

Seriously? This co-parenting relationship with benefits is getting demanding.

"Haven't you thrown enough at me tonight?"

"This one will be a fun one."

"Shoot." I cross my fingers that it doesn't involve any more pregnancy announcements.

"Will you go shopping with me for Maven's birthday present? Lauren planned on going with me, but she's been pulling double shifts to save up for a house. I don't want to put more stress on her."

"Maybe you should ask *Cindy.* You can go shopping, and then she'll feed you some fried chicken casserole." I'm acting petty, but this is how I bring up my problems. I use my sarcasm to tell people how I feel.

"What?"

"The smiley chick who came over when we picked Maven up." *Is clarification needed?* "The one who thought her fried chicken was the best thing since sliced bread."

"Wow," he says with a laugh.

"What?".

"Surely, you don't believe I'm hanging out with her?"

"No," I stutter out. "I mean, I don't know."

He sounds like he's enjoying this now. "Would you be upset if I were?"

"Nope. Not at all. Eat her fried chicken. Get heart disease. It's all good."

"Willow," he draws out in warning, "would you be upset if I were?"

"Would I upset? Nope. Pissed? Yes. Will I have sex with you again if you are? Definitely not."

"I'm not hanging out with her, I swear. She came around and dropped off food when Lucy passed but hasn't been around in months. Even then, it was nothing. I accepted the food, so my daughter wouldn't starve until I got my shit together. When I managed to perfect grilled cheese, I put a stop to it."

I roll my eyes. "Whatever."

"You're the only woman I'm hanging out with. Hell, other than my sister and mother, you're the only woman I even talk to. So, now that that's done, when do you want me to pick you up for shopping?"

"We're not going anywhere in town, are we?"

"No. I figured we could take a trip into the city. She asked for an American Girl doll?" He says it like he's unsure if that's the right name.

"Oh, I had one of those, growing up. Which one does she want?"

"Uh ... one that looks like her? They have a store in the mall near the airport."

"Another road trip, huh?"

"Seems to be our thing. My mom is taking Maven to her bake sale, and then they're going shopping for her party decor on Saturday. That okay?"

"My Saturday looks open." Like almost every day.

Stella is on break from filming and hasn't been asking much of me, so getting out of my apartment sounds refreshing.

"Then, it's a date."

I grin. "It's a date."

CHAPTER TWENTY-EIGHT

Dallas

"DO you remember the doll I want, Daddy?" Maven asks for the umpteenth time.

I tap my finger on the side of my head. "Sure do." I have it written in my phone notes. I pulled up the doll website last night, and there's a shit-ton of options. I pause and cock my head to the side. "And you don't even know if you're getting a doll."

Yes, she does.

She bounces from foot to foot. "I *really, really, really* hope so." She skips up the steps to my parents' porch to meet my mom standing outside. "Grammy, don't I need an American Girl doll?"

My mom draws her into her side. "Of course you do, sweetie."

Maven wags her finger my way with a smile on her lips. "You have to listen to your parents, just like you tell me."

"Oh, honey, your daddy was not a good listener when he was your age," my mom replies with a laugh. She squeezes Maven's shoulders. "Now, go wash up for lunch, and we'll go to the bake sale and then shopping for your party decorations."

"Yay! Princess Jasmine all the way!" she shrieks. She pulls the door open and disappears into the house.

"Thank you for watching her, Ma," I say.

She nods. "Anytime. You going to the city to get the doll?"

I scrape my boot against the steps. "It's what she wants."

She can't contain her loving smile "And her daddy always gets her what she wants."

"It's the least I can do. She lost her mother. She deserves the world."

Her smile drops. "You're getting her a doll in the hopes that she won't be sad every day?"

I grew up with parents who refused to sweep shit under the rug. If there was a problem, we talked about it. If they wanted to know something, they asked and expected honest answers. I grew up, facing my challenges, but this isn't a problem easily fixed. No amount of parenting or life lessons could've prepped me for losing Lucy.

"That's not the ultimate reason, but it has something to do with it," I answer. "I want her to heal and enjoy her childhood. If that means spoiling her right now, then that's what I'll do. Whatever my daughter needs to put a smile on her face, I'm willing to do it."

A tear slips down her cheek. I hate seeing my mother upset. I take the few steps up to wrap her in my arms. She sniffles for a second before she continues her impending lecture.

"It'd help her much more if her father started working on the healing process as well," she says when she slips out of my arms.

I clear my throat to bring out my kindest warning voice. "Ma …"

She wipes her eyes and then places her hand on my shoulder. "Dallas, honey, I loved Lucy. We all did. We all miss her, but she's gone."

"She was my *wife*." I'm using all my power not to get pissed with her. "You'd be lost without Dad."

"I would. The difference between you and me is, I'm in my sixties. I have thirty years on you, son. A whole life is waiting for you. Happiness is out there, but you're never going to find it if you're blocking it out. Find someone for Maven. Find someone for *you*."

My mother is the best person I know. She's beautiful. Selfless. Caring. There will never be another woman with a heart as kind and nurturing as hers. She raised us to be strong, fearless, and independent.

Her age doesn't show, and Lauren is the spitting image of her. They're both short and have long brown hair. Lauren keeps hers down most of the time while my mom's stays in a bun. They also have a personality with enough spark to light up a city. Mom doesn't make it easy to get upset with her.

"Can we talk about this another time?" I ask.

"Of course." A smile plays on her lips. "Are you going shopping by yourself?"

I shake my head. "Willow is coming with me."

"Stella's assistant?"

I nod, and her lips form a sly smile.

"Word on the street is, you've been spending an awful lot of time together. Beautiful girl, I must say. The few times I met her, she was such a sweetheart."

"I see the Blue Beech gossip is still alive and kicking," I mutter.

"You go have fun, honey. If it gets too late, stay there, and have a nice dinner. I've already told Maven she could spend the night, so we have plans."

"You spoil her too much."

"That makes two of us." She pulls me in for another hug. "Now, I'm ready for some more grandchildren. I don't know why my children are taking so long to give them to me."

Oh, shit.

She's about to be surprised.

THE AMERICAN GIRL store is packed with moms and daughters, and I have no idea where to make my first move.

Willow cracks up before grabbing my hand. "Come on. I'll try to lead the way the best I can. It's been about two decades since I had one of these dolls, but surely, not that much has changed."

We don't lose our connection and dodge people while migrating through the loud crowd.

"We're looking for one that resembles her!" I yell over the noise, as if it were normal to be hunting for the incarnation of your child.

I scan the aisles and stop her each time I think I've found it, but Willow shakes her head and continues her search.

Good thing she came with me, or I would've grabbed the first doll I saw and bolted out of here. Lauren most likely wouldn't have had the patience to deal with this crowd either. She didn't play well with dolls. She drove my mom crazy because she popped all the heads off them, so she could play outside with Hudson and me.

Unlike us, Willow is thorough. She'll assess every doll until she finds the perfect fit.

We've been in the store for thirty minutes when she spots the one and clutches the doll to her chest for me to see. "What do you think?"

It eerily resembles Maven. The dark brown hair, a bow clipped to the side of it, bright purple sunglasses, and a checkered dress.

I tilt my head toward the doll. "Sold."

"Now, we need to find clothes for her."

I point to the doll. "She has clothes."

"She needs more than one outfit. *Geesh.*" She pulls on my shirt. "Do you live with only one outfit?"

"No, but unlike this doll, I'm a living, breathing human."

"She needs outfits." She pivots around, and I follow her into another section.

Willow picks out three outfits for the doll, and a sense of happiness jerks through me when she demands to pay for the clothes. I've been terrified of letting someone else around my daughter. I didn't want her to feel neglected or jealous. I didn't think another woman could make Maven feel as loved as Lucy did. But Willow thinks of my daughter, smiles with my daughter, enjoys her company. And my daughter enjoys hers.

"One more stop, and then we'll head home." I snag her hand after paying for the doll and hope I'm taking her in the right direction. I haven't been here since Lucy was pregnant.

"I'm in no rush." She's more at ease in this crowd than she's ever been in Blue Beech.

She stills when we reach our destination, and I'm not sure if it's a good or bad thing. It's a baby store, the largest one in the state, and it has everything you need from clothes to furniture to supplies.

"I thought we could look around. See if there's anything we like," I tell her. She nods in hesitation, and I throw my arm out. "After you."

"Are you sure we're ready for this?"

"One hundred percent."

"IS it bad that I have no idea what some of this stuff is?" Willow asks. "I've read every baby book I could get my hands on. Researched for hours and made lists of every necessity needed, but this all seems too overwhelming."

I still have Maven's nursery furniture in the attic. We kept it in hopes of having another baby and saw it as a good-luck token. As much as I want to pull it out, along with the memories, it wouldn't be right for me to do that to Willow.

"It is at first. I Googled everything of Maven's to figure out how to use it." I point to the cribs on the other side of the store. "One thing we know our little tykes will need for sure is somewhere to sleep. Let's start there, and we'll work our way through the store."

She grins. "Sounds good."

CHAPTER TWENTY-NINE

Willow

DALLAS LEANS against the doorway to the guest room I'm converting into a nursery. "There's still time to change your mind and set the cribs up at my place."

"Yes, you've mentioned that several hundred times," I reply.

Our shopping adventure ended with bags of baby items. We spent three hours shopping and had to get two of everything. Dallas shoved my card away when I tried to pay and nearly threw my wallet out the window when I tried to give him half of it in cash when we got in the truck.

He wraps his arms around my waist from behind and drags me into his firm body. "I'll give you the master and crash in the basement. I'll be the nanny. I'll get up in the middle of the night and change diapers. Feed them. Bathe them. Whatever you want."

"Give you the master."

The room where he freaked out on me.

No freaking thank you.

It'd help me physically with the babies but not emotionally. It'd obliterate my heart. Two babies is hard work, but I'd rather risk being sleep-deprived than take him up on that offer.

I'll fuck him but not walk through his front door.

I'm a hot mess.

He scrapes his hands together. "You want to start setting everything up?"

"Can we leave that for another day? I'm exhausted, my feet hurt, and I'm sore everywhere."

"You want me to give you a massage?"

"Can you do it with your tongue?"

He smirks. "I'd love to."

STELLA SITS DOWN NEXT to me with a plate of cake in her hand. "Hudson said Dallas spilled the baby beans to Maven."

We're at Maven's birthday party, and she's started opening gifts. I showed up early, sat down so that the table would hide my stomach, and haven't moved since.

Maven's face lights up with excitement as she opens each gift, and she thanks the gifter before moving on to the next. Dallas is saving ours for last. I peek over at him and smile at the happiness on his face as he watches her.

He's a good dad.

He might be broken, but he managed to repair part of his heart and opened it up for her. I'm hoping he'll do the same with our babies.

Half of Blue Beech's population is here, eating the food Rory, Dallas' mom, made—which is enough to feed the entire NFL—chasing their screaming children around, and staring at me like I have a nip slip. Maven has attempted to drag me to the bounce house dozens of times, and it looks like Disney vomited everywhere.

"She figured it out herself," I answer.

"No shit?"

"Apparently, I rub my stomach like some other pregnant chick around here does. She put two and two together." I laugh.

"Dallas broke the news because he couldn't handle fibbing to a six-year-old."

"Damn, kids are getting smart these days. I was still under the impression storks dropped babies off on doorsteps when I was her age."

Maven squeals and jumps up and down when she opens Dallas's gift. She screams again when opening mine, and then she runs over to give me a tight hug. "Thank you!" she yells, still jumping up and down. She sits down next to Stella and starts ripping open the doll box and all of the accessories.

Stella bumps my shoulder with hers. "You sure you don't want to take a run in the bounce house? It'll be a first time for me."

"You've never been in a bounce house?" I ask, looking horrified. *Who hasn't been the kid who fell down and tried to get up while the others bounced harder to stop them?*

"Nope. My mom considered having a childhood was an abomination, and all I needed to do was work." She puts her hands together. "So, *please.*"

I point to my stomach. "No sudden movements, remember?"

"Oh, crap, I keep forgetting about"—she pauses and nervously looks around—"*that.*"

"She can't go into the bounce house, Aunt Stella!" Maven shouts with a gasp. "She has to be very, very careful because there is a baby in her tummy." She stops to correct herself and holds up two fingers. "I mean, two babies in her tummy because she and Daddy are having twins!" She slaps her hand over her mouth. "Uh-oh." Her gaze sweeps over to Dallas with wide eyes. "Sorry, Daddy. I broke our secret. I'm so, so sorry!"

The noise in the backyard comes to a halt, and Rory's cup falling to the ground is the only sound I hear before I freak the hell out.

CHAPTER THIRTY

Dallas

HOLY FUCK.

This isn't how I imagined this going down.

Willow looks like she's about to vomit. My mom looks hurt. My dad looks like he's ready to lay into my ass. Hudson is grinning like a motherfucker.

I clear my throat, ignoring every set of eyes on Willow, and bolt her way. I kiss my daughter on the top of her head. "It's fine, May Bear. Why don't you go show your new doll the bounce house, okay?"

"I'm sorry, Daddy," she says again. "I've just been so excited." She throws her hands out. "It just blurted right out of my mouth."

I kiss her forehead. "It's okay."

Willow jumps out of her chair when her eyes start to water. She doesn't want anyone to see her cry. "If everyone will please excuse me for a second." Her voice breaks. "Or a few minutes. Possibly a few hours ... or days."

She turns and dashes into the house. Stella jumps up to follow, but I stop her.

"Let me have this one, okay?"

She stares at me with a hard look and hesitation before

nodding.

As soon as I leave the crowd, I can hear the voices erupt into chaos. Question after question is being fired off, one after the other, to my family. I feel sorry for leaving them to the Blue Beech gossip wolves, but I have to make sure Willow is okay.

I find her sitting on the bed in my childhood room with tears in her eyes. I shut the door and bend down in front of her. I take her chin in my shaky hand and lock eyes with her.

"I'm so fucking sorry, do you hear me?" I whisper. "I made a mistake."

She tries to pull away from my touch, but I don't let her.

"Please," I hiss. "Please don't fucking run from me because of this."

Willow is a pro at helping other people with their problems but terrible at facing her own. It's easy for her to turn her back on situations she doesn't want to deal with.

She sniffles. "This is humiliating. Did you see their faces? All the jaws dropping?"

"They were surprised, which we expected. I mean, we haven't exactly been forthcoming about your pregnancy or *this*." I signal between the two of us. To be honest, I'm relieved it's out there. I wish it had happened in a better situation, like us sitting my parents down and spilling the news, but at least the secret is off my chest now.

"*This?*" she questions, scrunching up her face and reenacting my movement. "What do you mean, *this?*"

I get up and sit down next to her on the bed. "We're doing something here. I'm as confused as you are about it, but we are. You're the only woman I've looked at since I lost Lucy. I can't …" I pause. "I can't stop thinking about you. Whenever I leave your apartment or drop you off, the excitement from when I get to see you next keeps me high. Hell, I can't wait until the next time I even get to talk to you. You're something I look forward to every day. The thought of seeing you, talking to you, and spending time with you gives me so much fucking happiness." My revelation only makes her cry harder. "What can I do to make this better? Anything. I'll do anything."

Except let you walk away.

Please don't fucking walk away.

"Turn back time to months ago," is all she whispers.

Fuck. I want to beg her not to go there.

"Tell me you don't mean that. You might've thought that at first, which I don't fucking blame you, but tell me, after all this time we've spent together, after seeing the beautiful babies we made on that monitor, that you don't mean that."

She sighs. "I ... I don't." She covers her face with her hands. "I thought I would. Sometimes, I wish I still felt that way. I thought it was the end of my happiness when I found out I was pregnant after our night together, but now ... now, I can't think of a time when I've been happier. A time when I thought I was doing something so right." She rubs her stomach. "These past few months have changed my life, too."

"These past few months have dragged me out of the darkest hole I thought I'd never escape." Not all the way. I'm still there, and I'll never be the same man, but Willow has brought out parts of me I thought would never come out again. And I can feel myself healing as the sun rises each day.

I drop down to my knees to take in the sight of her and show her the honesty in my eyes. "You brought me to the light. We might not have expected this, but it's somehow made us stronger, brighter, happier."

I cringe at the knock on the door that interrupts us. Stella pokes her head in, apology on her face, and takes in the scene in front of her.

Me on my knees in the begging position, and Willow crying.

Willow wipes away a tear and nods her head, silently permitting Stella to come in and shut the door behind her.

The door opens again seconds later, this time without a knock, and Hudson appears with brows knitted in concern. "I know this is bad timing, brother, but Maven is in the bounce house, crying, and insists on only talking to you or Willow."

"Fuck," I snap, averting my attention to Willow. "Will you be okay for a minute?"

She nods. "Go ahead. I'll be fine." I get up, but she grabs my arm to stop me. "Actually, I'd like to come with you, if that's okay?"

"I'm not sure you'll be ready for eyes on you," Stella says.

"How about I try to get her to come in here?" Hudson asks, leaving the room before waiting for our answer.

Willow sniffles again. "That's a good idea."

Stella starts to go toward the door but stops and darts over to Willow. "I love you," she says with a hug. "Know that I'm here, no matter what, and I love you."

This brings a small smile out of Willow. "I love you, too."

Stella pokes her shoulder. "And you know you have some explaining to do. *Twins?* You couldn't even let a girl know she's having two godchildren now?"

"I was waiting for the right time," Willow replies.

The door opens again, and a sobbing Maven comes running into the room and crashes into my arms. "Daddy, I'm sorry!"

I keep my arms around her and rub her back. "It's okay, May Bear."

She turns around, still in my arms, and shyly peeks over at Willow. "Are you mad at me?"

Willow's eyes go soft, and her tone turns soothing. "Of course not, honey. Just shocked, is all."

She composes herself, gets up, and runs a hand down her dress. I can't stop myself from grinning at the sight of her stomach showing through. Fingers crossed, she'll let it be on display more now. "I need another slice of cake."

I grab her elbow to make sure she's stable and dip my mouth to her ear. "You sure you're okay with going back out?" I ask. "We can leave, if you want?"

"We'll have to face them sooner or later," she says.

"We'll be out in a few minutes," I tell Hudson. "Tell people no questions until we're ready."

Maven wraps her hand around my leg. "I know you promised extra doll clothes if I kept our secret." She pushes her lower lip out. "Do I still get to keep them?"

Willow snorts before bursting out into a fit of laughter. "God, I needed that."

CHAPTER THIRTY-ONE

Willow

"I KNOW my son demanded no baby talk, and I respect that, but can I give you a hug?" Rory asks.

I nod, and she pulls me into her tight, patting my back. "Congratulations, dear. I am incredibly grateful for you. So is John, who's around here somewhere, waiting to corner his son and lecture him on keeping secrets from his mama." John is Dallas's father.

The majority of the crowd has ventured home, but a few people are still hanging around. Since we came back, Dallas stayed by my side until minutes ago when I finally convinced him to go to the bounce house with Maven and her doll. Some people have been pretending not to stare at me, others have refused to acknowledge me, and the rest have shamelessly watched every move I make.

"Don't worry about them," Rory says when she pulls away. "If anyone asks too many questions, you let them know they'll have to deal with me." She grabs a slice of cake and hands it to me. "You deserve this. I told Dallas to give you my number. Don't hesitate to call if you need anything."

I nod. "Thank you."

She throws me another smile, pats my shoulder, and then

walks over to a table of women hunched over while talking in hushed voices. Most likely about me.

"Holy shit," Stella gasps, wrapping her arm around my shoulders. "That was seriously something out of a movie. I need to use that in a script."

"No benefiting from my problems for your career," I mutter, leaning into her.

"How are you feeling?" she asks when we sit down at a secluded table.

"A million things at once. Mortified that this is how everyone found out. Relieved that we no longer have to hide it."

She smirks. "He's a good dad, Willow. He'll be good to you and your baby." She winces and pouts. "I mean, *babies*. Why do I feel like I'm not your first call anymore?"

"Sorry. It's just been so overwhelming. I'm still digesting it myself. There hasn't even been a call to anyone else." I shake my head. "Hell, all of these people found out before my mom did."

"You'd better call her. Blue Beech news makes national news."

I laugh. "I saw the town's newspaper. The front page was about some ribfest cook-off. I'm sure my mom subscribes because who can go about their day without finding out Sandy May's special recipe?"

"Sandy May makes killer ribs. I'd never even had ribs until Hudson dragged me to that festival."

"I'm sure there's a plan in Dallas's head to drag me to the next one."

"It'll be fun." She pokes my side. "Now, if you get any more baby news, you'd better let me know. If I find out you're having quintuplets from another six-year-old, I won't be happy."

"Maven didn't tell you? It's actually sextuplets. We're waiting for another party to shock everyone."

"Very funny." She glances around. "By the way, I'm pretty sure Rory is over there, planning your baby shower."

"God, her reaction was dramatic. Her fruit punch fell to the ground in slow motion. I thought she wanted to kill me for not telling her."

"Oh, that was just the shock. You didn't see the bright-ass smile on her face after you left. She's not pissed. She's fucking elated." She laughs. "The only people who weren't over the moon were the women who wanted to be the one Dallas had knocked up. You got knocked up by Blue Beech's finest bachelor. You go, girl."

"SO, THE NEWS IS OUT," Dallas says.

"The news is out," I repeat slowly.

Maven is passed out in the backseat, snoring like a man in a nursing home, and it's almost eight o'clock. She apologized to me countless times for her outburst, but I couldn't be upset at a girl sporting a *Birthday Girl* tiara and sash.

"You want to come over?" he asks. "Hang out for a bit? I have leftover cake."

Jesus, does everyone think all I eat is cake?

The thought of spending more time with him excites me, but the problem is, going to his house doesn't. It terrifies me. The memories from our night together might slash a hole in the connection we've been making. We've already been through enough today. Reliving those memories isn't something I want either one of us to do.

"Not tonight," I answer. "I'm exhausted."

"You sure?"

I nod at the same time he pulls up to my apartment building, and I stop him from unbuckling his seat belt. "Don't wake her up. I can walk myself in."

"Okay. I'll wait out here until I see your light come on, and you call me to let me know you made it in okay."

And that's what he does.

IT'S seven in the morning, and someone is banging on my door.

"What is up with your family knocking people's doors down at the butt crack of dawn?" I ask when Lauren walks in.

"Good morning, my future sister-in-law," she sings out while walking into my apartment. "I brought doughnuts and green tea."

Seriously?

"What do you want?" I mutter in my best cranky voice.

"You didn't believe it'd be that easy to dodge me, did you, neighbor?" She plops down on a barstool at the island. "I was upset enough that I got called into work and missed my niece's birthday party, and then I find out you're having *twins*, and you didn't tell me." She crosses her arms. "As the girl who lives above you, I am extremely offended."

I take a gulp of the green tea. *Yummy.* "We were waiting. No one knew."

"Except the six-year-old."

"Except the six-year-old," I mutter. "Your brother apparently can't lie to his daughter."

"Yeah, he sucks at saying no to her. She's got him wrapped around her finger. Now, if it's a girl, I'd like her name to be Lauren."

I side-eye her. "It's too early to argue about baby names."

"It's never too early to hash it out over baby names. *Trust me.* I've heard stories from the maternity ward nurses about the kind of drama and chaos families have over baby names."

"I'm naming them after my pet goldfish—Goldie and Nemo."

She rolls her eyes. "Now that we've got Lauren Junior covered, what's going on with you and my big bro?"

My brows lift. "Other than the fact that we're having twins together, nothing."

"His truck was here the other night when I got home at *four in the morning.* It seems to be here pretty frequently, if you ask me. Since we know you weren't discussing *baby names* at four in the morning, what were y'all doing?"

"Discussing nursery decor."

"You suck," she grumbles.

I perk up. "You love me."

"I do. But can I say something serious?"

"I don't think I can stop you."

"Don't hurt him."

This really catches my attention. "Huh?"

"You know exactly what I'm talking about. Don't hurt my brother. He's been through too much to lose someone else he loves."

Deflection time. "I've made it clear, I won't ever keep the babies from him."

"I'm talking about *you*, girlfriend." She annoyingly shakes her shoulders while drinking her smoothie through the straw.

"Your brother most certainly does not love me."

She grins. "Not yet. From what my mother tells me, it's getting pretty damn close, and my mama knows everything."

CHAPTER THIRTY-TWO

Dallas

THE EXCAVATOR I bought from the auction is kicking my ass. Even though I do my due diligence the best I can, you never know what you're going to get when you buy an item as is.

It's an easy fix but fucking time-consuming, and Hudson ran off for a staycation with Stella for the day—whatever the fuck that is—at the local bed-and-breakfast. I tried to fight him on it, telling them they could eat Cheerios at their kitchen table, and then he could come into work, but he agreed to give me as much time as I needed off when Willow had the babies.

Almost a week has passed since Maven's birthday party, and I've talked to Willow on the phone a couple times a day but not in person.

The machine loses my attention when the music is cut off.

I look down and grin. "This is a nice surprise."

Willow holds up the cooler in her hand. "Thought I'd bring you some lunch."

Good. I'm fucking starving, and I was planning on skipping lunch, so I wouldn't have to spend time driving into town and then back today.

I carefully move down the ladder and wipe my forehead with the back of my arm while coming her way. I laugh when

JUST ONE NIGHT   201

she licks her lips while brazenly eye-fucking me at the same time I'm eye-fucking her.

She's not wearing her usual baggy clothes today. I'm not sure where she got the maternity clothes, but she's breathtaking in her jean shorts and T-shirt that says *Tacos for Two, Please.*

Her and her tacos.

I run my hand down my sweaty chest. I have the air on high, but I get hot, no matter what, when I'm working on machine engines. "You like what you see?"

She lifts her gaze back up my body and grins playfully. "Oh, I *love* what I see."

"You know, I'm more than just a hot, lean body."

I curl my arm around her shoulders to pull her into me and plant a kiss on her lips. She doesn't even flinch. Us touching has become so natural. Not only does it feel good, having her here, but she also showed up without my asking. She took the time to make lunch and came to surprise me. She can deny it all she wants, but she's falling for me.

"I'm starving. What did you whip up for us?"

She glances around the room. "It's a surprise."

I gesture toward the other side of the garage. "We have a table and shit in the office, if you want to eat in there, or we can go outside?"

"Outside. I've been quite the hermit lately. I could use some sun."

"You know the remedy to that problem?"

She wrinkles her cute nose in annoyance. "Funny. I'll start venturing out of my apartment when the time is right."

"I hope it's before our kids turn sixteen."

She shoves my side and pulls away when we reach the picnic table underneath two weeping willows. My grandfather built the table decades ago for when my grandmother would bring him lunch.

I rub my hands together when we sit down. "So, what have we got?"

Her eyes widen in reluctance. "They say it's the gesture, not the gift, right?"

Did she bring cheese and crackers? A Snickers bar and Sunny Delight?

"I'll enjoy whatever you brought."

She draws in a breath when I open the cooler and start dragging out its contents. There are plastic bags with sandwiches in them.

"I love me some peanut butter and jelly," I say upon further inspection. The next item is a bag of tortilla chips large enough to feed Maven's entire preschool and then a covered bowl. I open it and can't stop the cheesy smile from hitting my lips. "And guacamole."

"I'm giving you a run for your money on the best guac in Blue Beech."

"Let's taste-test it, shall we?" I open the bag of chips and dip one into the guacamole.

It's good, definitely not as good as mine, but I can tell she worked hard on it. She analyzes me chewing it likes she's a contestant on *Top Chef.*

"You killed it. I'll bring over my trophy for you later this evening."

She raises a brow. "You're just saying that because we're having sex."

"There are better things I could say to you to get laid than" —I stop to fake a smoldering gaze I saw on *The Bachelor* once— "*Hey, girl, you make excellent guacamole. Let's fuck in a bed of guacamole, have it served at our wedding, and name our children Guac and Mole.*"

She throws a chip at me while trying to contain her laughter and then slides the sandwich in front of me. "Now, eat your PB and J and shut up. I slaved all day, making this."

I scarf down the two sandwiches she made me and make sure I moan with every bite of her guacamole.

She looks from side to side. "So … is there anyone else here?"

"No. Just me today. I'm sure you know, Hudson is feeding Stella strawberries in bed."

She laughs. "I booked the room for them. Stella's been coddling me since our secret came out. I couldn't handle it any longer."

"What secret?"

She leans forward. "You know."

"Which one? I believe we have a few."

She narrows her eyes my way. "You know exactly which one I'm referring to."

"The one where we're having twins?" I give her a shit-eating grin. "Or the one where I've been eating your pussy?"

She blushes. "You've been doing that? I think I'm in need of a reminder."

I smirk. "Oh, I see what's going on here. You thought you could come here and butter me up with PB and Js to get laid?"

She shrugs. "Just a little."

I point to my chest. "You do know I'm sweaty as fuck?"

"Let me make you even sweatier," she whispers with a wink.

I surge to my feet. "You don't have to ask me twice."

Willow slips off her seat and speed-walks to the garage. Her mouth crushes to mine as soon as I lock the shop door behind us. Adrenaline speeds through my blood as she demands more of me, pressing her tongue into my mouth. I'll never be disappointed to come to work again. This memory will hit me every time I walk in.

I grunt when I'm pushed back against the wall, and she kisses me harder, owning me, as our tongues slide together. She consumes me. The need of wanting her takes over every thought in my mind. I seethe at the loss of our connection when she runs her lips over the line of my jaw.

She's running the show.

She needs this.

And I'm a willing participant—anytime, any-fucking-where, any way.

My hands trail down her body to cup her perfect ass and lift her off the floor. I spin us around, so I have her against the wall now. She wastes no time in grinding against my cock. I do the same against her pussy.

"God," she whispers. "Please fuck me. I need it."

"Where do you want it?" I grit out.

She jerks her chin toward the parked car on the other side of the garage. "There."

We don't usually work on cars here, but I'm doing it as a favor for a buddy.

He's the one doing the fucking favor now.

"You want me to fuck you on that car, baby?"

Her breathing is labored, and she has to speak between breaths. "Yes"—inhale—"right"—exhale—"there."

"You want it hard or soft?"

"Hard. Really hard," she says against my mouth.

Heat radiates through my chest when her teeth graze my tongue, and she bites it.

Oh, yeah. She wants it hard. Rough. Dirty.

We fumble around until we're both naked, and I race across the garage and lower her bare ass on the '67 Chevelle.

I brush her hair back from her face and don't make another move until her eyes meet mine. "Willow, you're beautiful."

A bright grin spreads across her mouth when she hears her name, and I tense when her soft hand wraps around my aching cock. My heart hammers against my chest when she guides me into her. My head throws back as a roar rips through me.

The first move is made by her tilting her waist up, slowly taking in the length of me, and I'm close to losing it when my gaze drifts down to our connection.

Her pussy juices cover my cock. Her legs are open wide as she takes me in again and rolls her hips in the process. Nothing describes the feeling of watching the girl of your dreams lying on the hood of a car and taking your cock like she owns it.

"Fuck, you feel good," I grind out.

No more taking it slow. I grab her ankles, pull her down the car until she's on the edge, and slam inside her. She clings to my shoulders and rests her weight on me.

"I'm there," she says, her body going weak. "Oh God, I'm there."

I keep my focus on her to watch her face. Her mouth opens, a loud moan escaping her, and she clenches around my dick.

The view of her getting off sets me off.

My body shakes when I bury my face between her breasts and release inside her.

We stare at each other, breathing heavily, and she cracks up laughing.

"Not the best reaction after someone gets you off," I say, unable to hold back my smile.

"I so buttered you up with my guacamole."

I join her laughter.

Willow Andrews isn't just working her way inside me. I'm also falling in love with her.

CHAPTER THIRTY-THREE

Willow

TWO PAINT SAMPLES are in my hand as I hold them against a wall in the nursery.

Red or yellow?

I want to go with a neutral theme since we don't know the sex of our babies yet. I drop them onto the floor when my phone rings.

"Hello?" I answer.

"Hey," Dallas says on the other line. "You busy?"

"Nope, just unpacking the rest of the stuff we bought for the babies and trying to decide what look I'm going for in the nursery." I balance the phone between my shoulder and ear. "What's up?"

"Maven's preschool called. She's sick. I'm swamped at the shop, and my parents aren't available until this evening. Any way you can pick her up and hang out until I get a break from here?"

"Sure, that's no problem."

He lets out a relieved sigh. "Thank you. I shouldn't be any later than five. There's a spare key under the planter on the porch. Make yourself comfortable. There's plenty of food in the house. Let me know if you need anything, okay?"

"Okay."

I throw my hair up in a ponytail, change into shorts and a T-shirt, and hop into my SUV. I don't realize what I'm about to do until I pull into the parking lot of Maven's preschool.

I'm going to his house.

Holy shit. I should've told him I'd bring her back to my place.

Stepping foot in his house again is something I've been putting off even though he's invited me countless times.

I take in a breath. *I have to get over this fear, right?*

There's no way I would've gotten away with it for too much longer. At least it won't be in front of Dallas in case I have a panic attack.

"HELLO. YOU MUST BE WILLOW," the older woman behind the desk greets me when I walk through the front door and into the lobby. "Dallas said you'd be picking up Maven." She picks up the phone and tells the teacher I'm here.

I look up at the sound of heels coming down the hallway. I recognize the woman from Maven's birthday party but don't recall seeing her again after the pregnancy outburst.

She stops in front of us and rests her hands on Maven's shoulders. "Hi, Willow." She gives me a red-lipped smile and holds out her hand. "I'm Mrs. Lawrence, Maven's teacher."

"She's my aunt Beth," Maven corrects.

I freeze up and blink a few times, noticing the similarities between her and Maven ... and Lucy. Mrs. Lawrence—*Beth*—squeezes Maven's shoulders.

She nods. "That I am." Her voice turns soothing. "I'm Lucy's sister."

I shake her hand. "It's nice to meet you."

Damn, Dallas has thrown me so many curveballs today, I'm dizzy. I'm meeting the sister of his dead wife *and* going to the house he shared with said wife.

"She's had a fever for the past hour. Thank you for picking her up. It seems everyone is busy or out of town today, and I couldn't find a sub to come in for me."

"It's fine. I was, uh ..." *Getting a nursery together for my babies with Dallas.* "Off work today."

"I feel no good, and I'm sleepy," Maven whines, rubbing her eyes.

Beth kisses her cheek before releasing her. "Get some rest, sweetie." Her attention moves to me. "Please ask Dallas to keep me updated, and don't hesitate to call if she needs anything."

I nod, pressing the back of my hand against Maven's forehead. She's warm.

"Of course."

I help Maven into the backseat of my car, and she falls asleep the first few minutes into the short drive to Dallas's house. Even though I haven't been back inside of the house since that night, I know where it is. We've driven by it dozens of times, and Maven has pointed it out to me.

I admire the large white farmhouse he restored years ago. There are large gray shutters on each side of the windows and planters under the ones next to the front door. It's perfectly landscaped with bright pink roses and daisies. It's a beautiful home.

The key is under the planter, like he said, and I follow Maven through the front door.

"Mommy and Daddy always let me sleep in their big bed when I no feel good," she says, stomping down the hallway. "It's right down here."

Oh, honey, I know where it is.

I gulp when she opens the door. This is the moment of truth where I find out if I can go forward with Dallas or if I can't get over him loving another woman. This is where I find out if I'm a quick screw because he's horny. You don't have to love someone. Hell, you don't even have to like them to fuck them.

The familiar whitewashed wood bed sits in the middle of the

large master bedroom. The plaid comforter is the same as it was that night. The scent in the room smells like him. Nothing has changed. My hands are on the verge of shaking as I help Maven into the bed.

That's when I see it.

The picture of him and Lucy on the nightstand. There's another of Lucy by herself on the other nightstand. Her ... or another woman's perfume is sitting on the dresser next to a white jewelry box with her name branded on the front. There's a chair in the corner with a woman's sweater draped over it.

Was that Lucy's?

Or is it Chicken Chick's?

"Will you put on cartoons for me?" Maven asks with a yawn.

"Sure." I snag the remote from the nightstand and flip through the stations until I find her favorite cartoon.

She slides underneath the blankets and relaxes against the pillows.

I tap the bed as my heart thumps against my chest. My throat grows tight, and the room feels warmer than Maven's forehead. "You let me know if you need anything, okay?"

"Will you stay?" she asks. "And watch with me?"

I nod even though all I want to do is abort mission and hang out in my car until Dallas gets here. I take off my shoes and sit down next to her, over the covers. That night haunts me as the opening of the cartoon lets out some annoying song. Maven snuggles into my side.

"Willow," she whispers, hesitation layering her voice.

"Yeah?" I ask.

"Will you be my new mommy?"

I blankly stare at her, fighting off the desire to flee the room, and try to give her the most comforting smile I can manage.

"You're going to be my brother or sister's mommy, so maybe you can be mine, too, since my mommy is in heaven."

A knife digs into my heart, and I take in a deep breath to stop the tears. Maven looks just as upset as I feel.

I kiss the top of her head and then smooth my hands over her hair. I don't know what to say. I don't know what to do. I don't even know my name at this point because my brain is spiraling out of control. "We'll talk about it when you feel better, okay, honey?"

"Okay," she whimpers.

She only lasts five minutes into the show before she dozes off. I slowly and quietly pull away from her and get out of the bed to grab my phone.

I catch my breath when I make it into the kitchen and drop onto a chair. I glance around the kitchen. More pictures of Lucy on the refrigerator. Another one by the coffeemaker. A grocery list that's not in Dallas's handwriting is stuck under a magnet on the fridge.

Will I always think everything is Lucy's here? That Dallas wants to keep and display every part and memory of her, so he won't forget ... so he won't move on?

It's petty of me to think these things. He wants to keep those memories of her alive because he was a good husband.

But I can't stop myself.

That's why I need to take a break from him. Why I need to consider the consequences before throwing myself into a situation this serious. His daughter asked me to be her new mommy. That's big. *Huge.* A little girl's heart is on the line, and I can't break it if everything doesn't go well with Dallas.

I grab my phone and text Stella.

Me: You busy?

She got home from the bed and breakfast yesterday, and nothing was on her schedule for the day.

Stella: Nope. Just going over some scripts. What's up?

Me: I picked up Maven from school for Dallas because she was sick, and now, I'm not feeling so hot myself. Would you be able to watch her until Dallas got home, so I could get some rest at my apartment?

Stella: I'll be there in 15. You need anything?
Me: I'm good. Thank you.

Her answer slows down my heart rate. Now, I need to make sure she doesn't notice anything is off with me. I need to put my actress face on and hope the actress herself doesn't find out I'm a fraud.

I'm still in the kitchen when Stella walks in. She rushes into the room and falls down in the chair across from me.

"You feeling any better?" she asks with concern.

"Not really," I mutter. "I just need to lie down. I've been working on the nursery all morning, and I think I overdid it. That, or the twins are pissed that I fed them a healthy breakfast this morning."

She laughs and gets up to wrap her arms around my shoulders. "You take care of yourself, girlfriend. Call me here soon."

CHAPTER THIRTY-FOUR

Dallas

IT'S BEEN a hell of a day.

The shop's phone has been blowing up all day with people wanting maintenance on their machines that weren't scheduled in. I took them, of course, but I'm feeling overwhelmed.

I can't wait to get home to my girls. Willow texted me a few hours ago when she picked up Maven, but I haven't heard anything from her since even though I've tried calling. I'm guessing they fell asleep when Maven made her put on cartoons.

I wasn't sure how Willow would react when I asked her to take Maven to the house, but she didn't seem to have a problem, which is a fucking relief. I don't want her to feel like she can't step foot through my front door. I don't want her to feel uncomfortable in my home. I want her to feel so fucking good there that she decides to move in.

I start my engine and then kill it a few seconds later.

Fuck. She's going to see them.

She's going to see all of Lucy's stuff. I haven't built up the courage to move anything related to Lucy. Her toothbrush is in the holder, her clothes are in the closet, her touch is everywhere. I haven't moved anything because it's comforting, knowing there's a part of her there. I can't forget about her if her bracelet is still on the kitchen counter. I can't forget her if I see her favorite pink top when I open the closet.

I don't want that to change. I don't want to forget the woman I loved. I don't know if I can move her things yet, but I have a feeling that Willow won't be comfortable until I do.

I call her again. No answer. I text her next.

Me: You doing okay over there?

I start my truck again and head home. She still hasn't answered when I pull into the driveway, and instead of parking next to her car, I see Stella's red BMW. I walk in, check in on Maven sleeping in my bedroom, and then meet Stella in the kitchen. She's at the table going over scripts.

"Hey," I greet, tossing my keys onto the counter.

She presses a finger to her lips. "We don't want to wake her up. She's been knocked out for a few hours."

I nod, lowering my voice. "Where's Willow? I've tried calling her a few times but no answer." Anytime Willow goes MIA, I go into nervous-wreck mode.

"She texted me and asked me to come hang out because she wasn't feeling well. She wanted to go home and lie down."

I lean back against the counter, resting on my elbows. "Huh. I wonder why she didn't mention anything to me."

She chuckles. "You know Willow. She doesn't want to inconvenience anyone."

"You heard from her since she left?"

She shakes her head. "She seemed like she couldn't wait to get out of here. I wish I had more for you, but she's been distant with me lately. It most likely has something to do with her fear of sharing anything with me since it will get back to you because my fiancé has a big-ass mouth."

"Fuck, sorry 'bout that. I don't want to come between the two of you. If it helps, I don't expect anything from you. Your loyalty is to her."

They've been close for years, and I hate that she has no one to turn to right now.

She gets up. "No worries. She's used to dealing with shit on her own. Brett made her that way. She kept all of their problems inside because she was sick of us telling her to break up with him every day. It's hard to vent to people when they agree the guy you're venting about is an asshole."

"I get it."

"I have to head out. I have a reading for the new season of my show in an hour." She kisses my cheek. "Let me know if you hear from Willow, okay? And I'll do the same for you. I'll call her on my way to set and ask if she wants to come with me. Maybe I can get something out of her."

I hug her. "Thank you for watching Maven. Be careful, and keep me updated."

"You're welcome, and of course."

Maven is sound asleep and snoring when I go to check on her again. She insists on sleeping in my bed if she coughs the wrong way. Some might find it annoying, but I enjoy that she considers my space a healing place.

I turn off the TV and do a once-over of the room.

Then, a twice-over.

Willow didn't run because she was sick.

I was right.

She ran because Lucy was everywhere.

CHAPTER THIRTY-FIVE

Willow

EVEN THOUGH I don't know where I'm going, I packed an overnight bag. All I'm sure of is, I need to get out of Blue Beech for a minute and clear my head.

Is it sad that Lucy's stuff upset me?

I've been second best to Stella for years. Her assistant. The second choice to hang out with and only when someone wants to get closer to her. People have looked past me to see the celebrity. I can handle not being the star in the spotlight, but being second place in someone's heart isn't an option.

My SUV's sunroof is open. The music is up while I drive down a deserted road. I didn't turn on my GPS. I'm just driving. I'm blurting out the words to my favorite song when a sharp pain shoots through me, causing me to buckle forward. I swerve to the side of the road when another one hits me just seconds later. Tears well in my eyes, and the pain overtakes me. This isn't a baby kicking or morning sickness.

It's something else.

Something I haven't been expecting.

Something I haven't read about.

Something not normal.

I dump the contents of my purse out in the passenger seat to find my phone and then power it on.

Please have service. Please have service.

One bar. All I have is one bar.

I dial the three digits as tears start crawling down my cheeks.

"Nine-one-one, what's your emergency?"

"My name ..." My voice trembles, and I struggle to come up with the right words. "My name is Willow Andrews. I was driving." I stop and double over, holding my stomach and groan. "I'm pregnant and having severe abdominal pain."

"Okay, ma'am," the woman says on the other side. "Do you know your location?"

I urgently search for a street sign, mile marker, anything that can help them. *Nothing.*

"I ... I'm not sure. There's hardly any traffic." I open the Maps app on my phone to get the exact location and recite it to her.

"Thank you. We have an ambulance on the way. Stay with me, okay? Take deep breaths, Willow. Are you experiencing any bleeding?"

I'm sobbing louder. "I'm not sure." I'm not proud of this, but I dip my hand into my panties and gasp when I drag it back out. There's not much of it, but it's there. And it's bright red.

Tears fall down my face faster.

"You doing okay, Willow?" she asks.

"Yes," I croak out, the words barely audible. "Yes, I'm bleeding."

I should hang up and call Dallas. Call Stella. Call my mom. *Somebody.*

But I can't move. I'm frozen to the spot, imagining every nightmare that could happen.

Please let everything be okay with my babies.

Please let everything be okay with me.

Please. Please. Please.

CHAPTER THIRTY-SIX

Dallas

I'VE BEEN PACING the floor in my kitchen for what seems like hours. I fed Maven dinner, and she passed back out an hour ago. Her fever has gone down, which is a relief.

I've tried calling Willow countless times. At first, it was going straight to voice mail. It's ringing now, but she's not answering, so I get her voice mail again.

When my phone rings fifteen minutes later, I quickly hit the Accept button without even looking at the caller ID. "Hello?" I rush out.

"Dallas!" Lauren screeches. "You need to get to the hospital right now."

"What?" I stutter out. "What's going on?"

"Willow is here. They brought her in about ten minutes ago."

My stomach drops. "How do you know? Did she call you?"

"Oh, gee, I don't know, maybe because I work here. Get here fast, and I'll explain everything. I've got to get back to my patients."

"I'll be there as soon as I can."

I hang up, and my hands are shaking when I dial Hudson. "You busy?"

"Nope, just parked on the couch, watching sports and waiting for Stella to get home. You want me to come hang out with you and my sick niece?" He must've not heard the urgency in my voice.

"Can you come watch Maven for me?"

He catches on now. "What's going on?"

"Lauren said Willow got admitted to the ER."

"Fuck," he hisses. "What for?"

"I don't know. Lauren wouldn't tell me over the phone." *That means, it's not fucking good.*

"I'll be there in five, sooner if I can."

"Thank you."

I call Willow's phone again. It rings. Then, voice mail. A million reasons why she's there flash through me. If it were contractions or something small, Lauren would've told me to ease my mind.

Why didn't Willow call me? Why didn't she let me know what's wrong with our babies? It's just as much my information as it is hers.

Because she's fucking selfish, and I'm fucking pissed.

THIRTY MINUTES LATER, I'm pulling into the hospital parking lot. A bad taste fills my mouth as I run through the sliding glass doors. The last time I was here was when I said good-bye to Lucy.

I nearly collide with the front desk and ignore everyone standing in line, cutting straight to the front. "Willow Andrews," I blurt out. "I'm looking for Willow Andrews. Redhead. She's pregnant."

The middle-aged woman stares up at me in annoyance. "You family?"

"The father of the twins she's pregnant with. My sister is a nurse here and will vouch for me. Lauren Barnes." Never thought I'd use that to my advantage of getting in somewhere.

The way her face falls confirms it's not good news. She picks up the phone. "Will you please tell Nurse Barnes her brother is here?"

The doors open, and Lauren comes sprinting into the waiting room. "Dallas!" she calls out, nearly out of breath, and waves her hand. "Come with me."

We speed-walk through the crowded hallway, and she knocks on a door before opening it. Willow is lying in the bed, tears and mascara running down her face, while the nurse checks her vitals. Her eyes are puffy from crying. She's exhausted. Broken. Worn out. Like she's been through hell. I'm positive I'm about to go there, too.

I rush over to her side, take her shaking hand, and slowly massage it with my thumb when she starts to cry harder.

"I don't know what happened. I was driving down the road, and all of a sudden—" Her free hand flies to her mouth, stopping any words from exiting.

"All of a sudden what?" I ask, swallowing hard, my voice breaking, my heart breaking.

The nurse hits a few buttons on the monitor and scurries out of the room. Lauren shuts the door and leans back against it.

Willow moves her hand, so I can understand her. "All of a sudden, I got these sharp pains in my stomach." She plays with her admittance bracelet over my hand and glances at Lauren in torture. "Can you ... will you ..."

Lauren takes a step forward with a pain-stricken face. "They did an ultrasound. It's the first thing we did when the EMTs brought her in."

My eyes pierce hers. "The EMTs. An ambulance brought you in?" I've already heard more than I want to, but I know it's only going to get worse.

"There was only one heartbeat," Willow whispers.

A knot forms into my stomach, tightening every muscle, and

I gag, positive I'm about to vomit. I squeeze her hand before pulling away to sit down.

"One heartbeat? What do you mean, one heartbeat?" I ask, practically begging for the answer I want even though I'm not going to get it. "We have two babies. *Twins.* I saw them with my own two eyes at our ultrasound!" My lip trembles, and I lock eyes with Lauren. "Tell them to do it again." My tone is demanding.

"I already had them do it again. They showed me ten times!" Willow cries out. "I begged them to keep doing them, so I could prove them wrong. There were two heartbeats during our last ultrasound. I swear there was!"

"There was," I gulp out.

"They did multiple ultrasounds," Lauren says, wiping her eyes. "Trust me when I tell you, they wouldn't put an expecting mother through this unless they were positive about it." She moves across the room to rest her hand on my shoulder. "I'm sorry, but the second baby is gone."

"The fuck you mean, the second baby is gone?"

There's a knock on the door that gains our attention, and Lauren tells whomever it is to come in. I've been to too many doctor visits and had too many hospital stays with Lucy to know when a doctor is about to deliver bad news, and the doc that walks in is about to deliver some bad news. I prepare myself for the blow.

He shoves his glasses up his slender nose. "Hello, I'm Dr. Jones." I stand up, and he holds his hand out for me to shake. "I'm deeply sorry for your loss. I've talked to Willow, but I wanted to come back when you arrived in case you had any further questions for me."

"Sure do," I reply. "Where's my other baby?"

He doesn't seem surprised at my aggression. No doubt, he was expecting it. "We performed an ultrasound on Willow. She immediately told us she was pregnant with twins when she was brought in, but we could only find one heartbeat. I double-checked. Another doctor did, too." He looks over at Lauren. "Your sister did also."

Lauren's face falls.

"Willow experienced symptoms of a miscarriage. She lost one of the fetuses from what appears to be vanishing twin syndrome."

She lost a baby.

One of our babies is gone.

Gone. I'm so sick of that word.

If I could set that word on fire and kill it, I would. Risk doing time. Risk going to hell. Risk anything not to hear that fucking word again.

Everything good in my life gets taken from me.

"What about the other baby? There's a heartbeat?" I rush out.

"Yes, there is a heartbeat for the surviving fetus."

"And everything is okay with that one?"

"So far, yes. The prognosis of the surviving twin is hopeful, but it can be more difficult since she's in her second trimester."

"So, what do we do now?"

"The ultrasound didn't show any remains of the lost fetus, so we won't have to perform any additional procedures. Again, I'm sorry for your family's loss." He hands me a card. "If you have any additional questions, please feel free to call anytime. Day or night."

I grip the side of the bed from my chair and stare down at Willow when the doctor leaves. "How did this happen? Where were you?"

She hesitates before answering me, looking deflated and hugging herself. "Taking a drive."

Lauren moves to Willow's side to kiss her on the forehead. "I'm going to give you some privacy. Let me know if you need anything."

"Taking a drive?" I ask. "I thought you didn't feel well. Why were you taking a drive when you were sick?"

This stops Lauren from leaving, and she whips around to stare at me. "Dallas, none of this is Willow's fault, so don't you dare go there. There was nothing she could've done to stop the miscarriage."

"I'm not blaming her," I hiss.

I'm blaming myself. I'm fucking blaming everyone and everything.

"Well, you're not convincing me of that," Willow fires back. "Sure sounds like it."

"All I asked was, why you were out driving in who the fuck knows where when you knew you were pregnant, and you told Stella you were sick!" I reply.

Her face lights up with anger, and she jabs a finger in my direction. "Don't talk to me like that. Don't you think I'm hurt about this? I lost a baby, too!"

"Okay, *now*, I'll give you two some privacy," Lauren says. She points to me before leaving. "Don't be a dick."

When Lauren shuts the door, I stare at it for a few seconds to calm down. Arguing with Willow isn't going to help either one of us. It'll only make shit worse.

"What happened?" I ask softly. "Why did you leave my house? I could've been there for you."

She blows out a breath. "I needed to clear my head. Get some air."

My voice starts to break. "Why?"

"I just did. It was all too much. Too much was happening, and I couldn't keep up. Stella said she could watch Maven, and I needed to get out of there."

I can tell she didn't mean to say that last sentence.

"You needed to get out of there?" I repeat.

She nods.

"Are you going to tell me why?"

"It doesn't matter."

I rub my eyes to fight back the tears. "It was because of Lucy's stuff, wasn't it?"

"That was one of the reasons, yes." She's not shocked I knew what it was. She knew I'd know.

This is my fault. If I had picked up Maven myself or taken down Lucy's stuff or told Willow to take Maven to her place, this might've never happened.

"Fuck. I'm sorry. It didn't even cross my mind before I asked you."

She shrugs. "It's fine. She's a part of your life. She was your wife. I get that now."

"What do you mean, you get that now?"

"I understand the loss of someone you love. I now understand, sometimes, you can't get over it." She rubs her stomach as the tears fall. "I know I'll never get over this, just like you'll never get over Lucy. I don't blame you for it. I'm not mad."

"What are you saying?" I ask, simmering with fear.

Her eyes are vacant. Dull. She's here physically, but she's not *here*.

"I'm saying, we should spend some time apart."

I feel my pulse in my throat. "Are you ... are you saying you're done with me?"

She shakes her head and rubs her forehead, like I'm stressing her out. Like it's the last conversation she wants to have.

Me, too.

"I can't be done with you. We're having a baby together, but we should take a step back from everything else."

I can't be hearing her right. I lost Lucy. I lost one of my babies. Now, I'm losing her.

"Take a step back from the relationship we've been building? Take a step back from feeling happiness? Take a few steps back from making love?"

She cringes. "Don't call it that."

"Don't call it what?"

Her jaw clenches in anger. "Making love. We don't *make love,*

Dallas, because we don't love each other. We fuck. That's it. You and I both know it."

"You know that's not true!" I grind out, fighting the urge to raise my voice. "If I were only interested in *fucking* someone, do you think I'd do it with the most complicated woman in the world?" I shake my head and lean in. "I do it because I'm falling in love with you. Not for a quick fuck!"

"Oh, shit!"

I stumble back at the sound of Stella's voice and look at the doorway to find her standing there with my parents.

"Bad timing?" Stella asks regrettably, tears lining her eyes. "Sorry, I suck at knocking."

Tears are falling down my mom's cheeks. My dad has his fist against his mouth to fight his own hurt.

They know before even asking questions.

I stride across the room to hug my mother, rubbing her back as she lets out her hurt, and then move to my dad next. He's not much of a hugger, but he keeps a tight hold on me, understanding my pain.

I lean back on my heels. "Will you give us a moment?"

They nod, and I'm back at Willow's side when they're gone. I scrub my other hand over my face and try to control my breathing. "You honestly can't believe I'm not in love with you. I've been trying to show you how damn good we are together."

Her chin trembles as she prepares herself to break my fucking heart. "I might be younger than you, but I'm not stupid, Dallas. We have fun together. We like each other. We're attracted to each other. But your heart isn't ready for anyone else. And my heart isn't whole enough to give someone a piece I'm not sure I'll get back. We were caught in the moment, moving too fast, even though we told each other in the beginning that a relationship was off the table."

"That was before I brought you into my life, before you showed me how wonderful you were with my daughter, before you showed me what it was like to be happy again."

She stares down at her stomach without saying another word. She said what she needed, and now, she's done.

"So, this is it, huh? Where you want us to go? I've lost two people in my life that fucking meant something. No, make that three if you walk away from me."

She keeps her head bowed and grimaces.

"Please, look at me. Goddamn it, look me in the eyes and tell me you don't want me."

She appears almost frail while slumping down on the bed. "I understand you're upset about our baby, but please don't try to act like you're hurt because I'm asking for space. We would've never worked because you're not ready to open your heart to me."

"Glad I know where I stand with us." I push off the railing on the bed. "I need some air."

I speed out of the hospital without stopping to talk to anyone else, get in my truck, and slam my fist against the steering wheel, taking all of my anger out on it. The pain hits me like a brick. I let the tears fall freely, and I'm certain my heart is dying in my chest.

My tears were finally starting to dry from losing Lucy.

I'm back at square one.

My life keeps falling apart.

CHAPTER THIRTY-SEVEN

Dallas

ELEVEN MONTHS AGO

YOU DON'T KNOW what you have until it's gone.

It's a bullshit cliché.

But fuck me if the reality of those nine words isn't smacking me in the face.

I knew what I had.

I cherished what I had.

But I sure as hell didn't plan on it getting ripped away from me at thirty-one years old.

The beeping of the machines next to Lucy is the only noise in the room. I have a love-hate relationship with them. They're her helping hand, her strength, but they won't be here much longer.

And neither will she.

A relentless surge of panic rips through my veins like a drug when I grip my hand around hers. Watching someone you love die is like your flesh torturously being stripped from your bones, inch by agonizing inch, baring the most vulnerable parts of yourself.

I wipe away my tears with the back of my arm, pissed at them for blurring my limited view of her. I haven't cried like this since I was in Pampers.

I'm a Barnes boy. We're known for our resilience, for our strength in the most desperate times. Emotions don't bleed through our skin. We hide them underneath and let them eat us alive.

At least, that's what I thought until I had to shoot myself with the truth. She is going to die, and there is nothing I can do. No one I can fight. No amount of money I can pay to stop it.

That shit does something to a man.

I tilt my head up to painfully stare at the tiled ceiling and wish it'd cave in on me. Her lips are a bruised blue when I bore my eyes back to her.

Metastatic breast cancer.

It spread fast, too fast, and was caught too late. There was nothing we could do. Chemo didn't work. Praying didn't work. Her liver is failing. Her body is shutting down.

I've followed her wishes. This is where she wanted to do it— not at our home where our daughter lays her head. Here, with just the two of us, so that's what I'm giving her.

"Take me," I plead to the good man above. "Take me, goddamn it!" My chest aches, my lungs restricting airflow, and I pound my fist to my chest. "Let her fucking stay! Take my last breath and give it to her!"

My throat is scratchy and sore, like I've been screaming my pleas, but they've merely been coming out as a whisper.

I tighten my grip on her, wishing I could be her lifeline, as she starts to let go. I gulp down the urge to beg her to hold on, beg her not to leave me, but the thought of her enduring more pain kills me just as much as losing her. I have to let her go in peace even if I selfishly don't want to.

I don't know how to live without her.

I sob as the radiant eyes I fell in love with dim.

No!

Take my light! Take it all from me!
Let her keep shining!

I slump down in my chair like a fucking coward when the machine starts to fire off.

And, with her last breath, she takes me with her.

CHAPTER THIRTY-EIGHT

Dallas

GONE.

I was on the verge of a panic attack when they brought me to the hospital. I cried. Man, did I cry. I'm shocked I have any tears left. I didn't know what was happening—if I was miscarrying, if it was something serious, if I was overreacting. The pain told me something was off, and I was hoping that it wasn't the something that happened.

I shrank into my bed, a cry escaping my lips, when they couldn't find the second baby's heartbeat. They checked it once. Checked it twice. Nothing. Blame wrapped around me like a blanket when Dallas walked in. I shouldn't have been on the road in the middle of nowhere. I shouldn't have been stressing myself out over a man when I had babies to worry about.

At first, I blamed myself.

Then, that blame shifted to Dallas.

He shouldn't have asked me to go to his house.

It's not my fault we lost the baby.

It's not his fault we lost the baby.

But, sometimes, you want to blame someone because you can't handle knowing they're just gone. Even though I haven't been pregnant that long, I've already started to fall in love with my babies, and now, one of them has been taken away from me. My heart is hurting, like someone stuck a knife inside and is twisting it until every part of me has ruptured.

I still have a baby relying on me. I'm not going to put myself into any other stressful situations. I won't be worried about Dallas's heart because I'm only going to focus on keeping mine sane for the baby, and trying a relationship with him isn't going to do that.

I need space. I need to step away. I stare at the door, wondering if he's going to come back or not, and tense up when a knock comes.

Stella peeks her head in. "Cool if I come in?"

"Yes," I answer. I need someone right now.

She smiles and sits down in the empty seat next to me. "Have you called your mom yet?"

I shake my head. "I honestly don't want to tell anyone. She'll want to fly here and take care of me, which is what I don't want. I need time to breathe on my own, to accept this, to take it in." I rub my stomach. "Can you give me a ride home when they release me?"

She squeezes her hand over mine. "Of course." She opens her mouth and then shuts it. She wants to talk about Dallas, most likely wants us to patch things up, but that's impossible right now.

Like I told Dallas, I understand now. I know how it feels to lose someone you love so much, someone you thought you'd spend years with.

And I understand never wanting to let them go.

THREE DAYS HAVE PASSED since Stella brought me home from the hospital.

I'm sore. Exhausted. Hopeless.

Calls and texts have gone ignored, and the only reason I've seen Lauren is because she has a spare key to my apartment and lets herself in, uninvited. I'm selfish because they're worried about me, but I want to be left alone. I asked Dallas to give me some space, and except for a few texts, he has. But no words, no lecture, nothing will stop me from feeling some blame in this. I was too stressed. I wasn't eating right. I should've been resting more. The guilt that my body is the one that lost my child kills me.

I called my mom the day I got home. We cried. She prayed. She begged to fly out here to be with me, and I begged her not to.

I'm reading another article on vanishing twin syndrome when I hear my front door open. I turn around on the couch and shut my laptop at the same time Lauren walks in, wearing her scrubs, going straight to the kitchen like she owns the place.

"Hey, girl," she calls out when I meet her. "I hope you have an appetite." She starts the oven and begins pulling out containers of prepared food. "Tacos are on the menu for tonight."

I do a scan of all the items laid out on the counter. Meat. Lettuce. Cheese. Salsa. Guacamole. "You made all of this?" I ask. "Didn't you have to work?"

She laughs, removing the lid from the meat and pouring it into a pan. "Sweetie, you know my cooking is shit. Although my reheating game is pretty good." She turns the burner on. "Dallas did all of this last night before going to work and asked me to bring it over."

I snort. "Why? Is he scared I'm not feeding myself well enough, and we'll lose the other baby?" The words come out before I can stop myself.

She narrows her eyes at me. "No. And we both know he doesn't think that, so quit acting like a brat."

"Excuse me?" I snap.

"You heard me," she says, her attention going back to the stove. "Quit acting like a brat."

I huff. I puff. I want to kick her out of my apartment, but she keeps going, "I get you're going through pain, but don't forget you're not the only one experiencing this loss. So is my brother."

I press my finger to my chest. "He's the one who tried to blame me for losing the baby."

"Did he say those words?"

"Well … not exactly."

"The only thing that's exact about your argument is that he never said you're to blame. Not once. You're pissed at him because you have no one else to be mad at—because no one is to blame. *No one.* You heard the doctor. The miscarriage would've happened, no matter what."

"I don't blame him for the miscarriage."

"But you blame him for what occurred before the miscarriage. You need something to blame for losing the baby, so you're blaming it on Lucy's stuff at his house."

"Don't do this, Lauren," I mutter. "I'm not talking to you about this."

"Then, don't talk to me. Talk to him. *Please.*"

"I have. We've texted a few times."

"Maven has a sleepover tonight. Let him come over."

"I can't," I whisper, and my voice starts to crack. "It'd be too hard."

"Going through a hard phase in life is a lot more difficult with no one at your side. It starts getting softer, gentler, when you have someone else with you. Trust me."

DALLAS KNOWS food is the way to my heart. The tacos and the slice of blueberry pie he sent over are making me reconsider seeing him. Lauren's right. We've barely said a few words to each other since our argument at the hospital. I've run our exchange through my mind hundreds of times, staying up late because I can't sleep, and I've tried to dissect every word that fell from his lips.

I shut my eyes and remember what he said.

"Take a step back from the relationship we've been building? Take a few steps back from making love?"

He said *making love*. I corrected that and said we were only fucking.

I'm the only one being honest with myself, with our relationship. We were both in a sensitive place the night of our one-night stand, and I'm afraid we're only pulled to each other because of that and my pregnancy.

But bad days, bad months, don't last forever, and eventually, we'll get over our bad times and realize we were only using each other as a Band-Aid until we healed. He'll go back to being a widower mourning his wife but still be getting laid. And I'll go back to being a woman who doesn't want anything to do with love but still getting laid.

We're having sex for the need of it, the connection of it, for desire. Not for love, like he said. I gulp. Not for love on his part because the more time I spent with him, the more I knew I was falling into the pit of somewhere I didn't want to go. A hole of falling for a man not interested in falling for me other than in the sheets. I'm afraid to admit, I'm in love with this broken, beautiful, loving man.

There's a knock at the door when I'm taking a tray of cookies out of the oven. Dallas cooked for me, so I wanted to return the favor. Making the cookies has also helped keep my mind off everything I'm going through. Granted, I used a premade box mix, but a girl has to start somewhere.

Dallas said he'd be over after dropping Maven off for her sleepover. I take a deep breath and don't bother looking through the peephole before answering the door.

"What the hell are you doing here?" I yell.

Brett is standing in the doorway with flowers. *Yes, fucking flowers again.*

His blond hair is swept back in a baseball cap, and a T-shirt and jeans cover his tall and scrawny body.

My asshole ex has a history of bad timing—having a girl in our bed when he thought I was out of town, sending dick pics without putting a password on his phone, being on a date with another woman when I ran into him at the frozen yogurt shop.

I stumble back when he takes a step forward and shuts the door behind himself.

"I heard about what happened to our baby."

"I'm sorry. What did you just say? Our *what?*" I'm dreaming. I have to be dreaming. This isn't happening.

Brett is out on bail. He shouldn't even be leaving the county, let alone the state.

He tilts his shoulder in a half-shrug and walks into the living room, placing the flowers in the middle of the coffee table and sitting down. "I've gotta say, I'm unhappy you kept this from me, but I'll forgive you … for the sake of our family."

"Have you lost your mind?" *Does jail make you imagine things?* I take a step closer to look him in the eyes. He has to be high to consider this to be a good idea. "Are you on drugs?"

"No, Willow, I'm not on drugs," he mocks in annoyance.

"You need to leave."

"I'm not leaving until we talk about our dead baby."

"There is no *our* baby, dumbass."

My breathing labors, and my fist itches to connect with his face. He just referred to my baby as *dead.* He gets up and struggles to grab my hand, but I fight him off.

"Leave before I call the cops. You know this baby isn't yours. I haven't touched you in almost a year."

"I don't care. I'll take on the responsibility if it's another man's because I love you." He arrogantly looks around the room. "I don't see anyone here to help you. What'd you do? Get knocked up by some random dude while traveling with Stella?" He clicks his tongue against the roof of his mouth and shakes his head. "You know, that's why I said I didn't trust you working with her. You'd get mad at me for cheating when I knew you were doing the same."

That's a lie. He was always jealous of my job.

"Fuck you. Do you honestly believe I'd ever have a baby with you? You almost killed a child."

He points to my stomach. "I want a paternity test on the one that's still alive."

God, could his words be any more horrible?

"Excuse me? You admitted the baby wasn't yours seconds ago."

"No, I didn't."

I don't have the time or the patience to deal with this asshole today. Or ever. "Screw you. I just had a miscarriage, for fuck's sake, and you thought it would be a good idea to fly thousands of miles and harass me?"

We look at the door at the sound of a knock. Brett goes to answer it before I can stop him. I make it at the same time Dallas walks in, bumping into Brett on his way, and his attention bounces between Asshole and me.

"Did I miss something?" he asks.

"Stella's old bodyguard?" Brett spits with a bitter laugh. "The fuck is he doing here?"

"The better question is, why are you here?" Dallas fires back, moving into his space.

"Stop!" I hiss. "I have neighbors!" I gesture for Dallas to close the door behind him. I can't lose my apartment because of this.

Brett points to my stomach again. "This is my baby, and I've come to take care of my family."

Dallas looks straight at me. "What is he talking about?"

"How do you even know about the baby?" I finally ask Brett.

"My father told me after your mom asked the church to

pray for you. Your mom wouldn't tell me where you were, so I took matters into my own hands. I figured you were still working for Stella, stalked her social media, and found you." He shrugs like that's not creepy at all and then throws his arm out toward a fuming Dallas. "You never answered my question. What are you doing here, bro?"

"Don't fucking call me bro," Dallas snarls.

He smirks. "Jesus, fuck, this is the dude you're banging? This is the dude trying to take you and my baby away from me?"

Dallas takes a step closer. "You better get the fuck out of here before I throw you out."

"So, you were cheating on your dying wife with her? You guys have been fucking around this entire time." He laughs. "This is fucking perfect. You're not such a good man, are you? You walked around like you were this perfect husband who then left his job to take care of his dying wife, but you were cheating on her and fucking my girl." He glares at me. "You're nothing but a lying cunt."

I jump when Dallas punches Brett in the mouth. Brett pushes him back. Dallas wraps his hand around Brett's neck and traps him against the wall.

"What the fuck, dude?" Brett struggles to breathe out, wiggling to get free. "I'm pressing charges!"

"You're not even supposed to be here!" I yell. "Call the cops, please. Let them take you back to where you belong—behind bars."

We don't have to call the cops because they knock on my door seconds later.

"Blue Beech Police Department!" one yells.

Dallas moves his hand from Brett's throat to open the door, and Brett dramatically collapses on the floor, holding his throat and fake choking.

Two officers step in. A young guy and an older gentleman.

"Hi, I'm Officer Barge," the older man says.

The younger cop tips his head forward. "Officer Layne." He

surveys the room. "We received a noise complaint about two men fighting." His eyes cast a look straight to Dallas. "What's going on, man?"

"He punched me!" Brett screams, stumbling to his feet and sticking out his chest. He's a badass now that there's protection. "I want him put in jail."

"I punched him," Dallas says. "Because he was harassing her. She's pregnant with my baby, and he was giving her trouble. He's out on bail, and he shouldn't even be out of California."

"That true?" Officer Barge asks.

"No," Brett lies.

Officer Layne holds out his hand. "Let me see some ID."

Brett flinches. "Are you going to ask him for ID? He's the one who assaulted me!"

"Already know who Dallas is," he answers and then tilts his head my way. "I know who she is. Now, how 'bout you let me get acquainted with you?"

"I'll tell you who I am. I'm the son of a mayor in a very affluent California town."

"Cool story, man," Officer Layne replies. "But this ain't California, hipster boy. I don't care if your father is the president. Let me see some ID, or I'm going to have to bring you in for failure to cooperate."

Brett pulls out his wallet and reluctantly hands his driver's license over.

"I'll go run this," Officer Layne says while Officer Barge keeps his eyes narrowed on Brett.

The officer and Dallas make small talk until Officer Layne comes back.

"It appears you broke the stipulations of your bail. We're shipping you back to that *affluent* town of yours where you can enjoy your time in a cell." His upper lip snarls in disgust. "I can't believe they even gave you bail for what you did."

Brett throws every name at me while they cuff him and force him out of my apartment. "He doesn't love you!" he screams before the door shuts. "He'll always love that dead bitch!"

Dallas stalks out of my apartment, ready for round two, but the police officer stops him from getting to Brett.

"Let it go, man," Officer Layne says. "He isn't worth it." He looks at me. "Congratulations on the baby, you two."

Dallas slaps him on the back. "Thanks, man."

He hands me a card. "Willow, you let me know if he gives you any more trouble."

Dallas's defeated gaze focuses on me after he shuts the door, and his jaw twitches. "That fucker telling the truth?"

"Huh?" My brain is so exhausted, I don't catch the severity of his question.

"Is he telling the truth about him being the father?"

My heart races. "Are you kidding me? You believe him?"

"I don't know what to believe. He seemed pretty damn adamant about it."

"If you want to believe him, be my guest. Leave. I planned on doing this by myself from day one, and I have no problem going through with that plan. I don't need you or Brett. I'm a woman who has her shit together. I have a good job and don't need to fucking baby-trap a guy." I shake my head. "Fucking trust me, it would've been much easier to do this on my own."

"Don't say that," he growls.

I cock my head toward the door. "Leave. I'll take care of this supposed illegitimate baby on my own."

"Don't." He grabs my hand in his. "Don't say that. You can't be pissed at me for asking. I asked, you told me the truth, I believe you."

I release his hold and shove him away from me. "The fact that you even doubted me is bullshit."

This is too much to handle right now. My hands are shaking in anger. I should've punched Brett in the face.

Dallas throws his arms in the air. "I'm sorry. It's been a

rough fucking week. I came over to make things right with you, and that asshole was here."

"He showed up, unannounced! It's not like I invited him."

He grabs my hand, leads me across the room, and situates me on the couch. I hold my breath when he falls next to me and then drags me into his chest. I relax against him, and my heart calms when he starts massaging my neck.

"Why does it seem like the world's against us?" I whisper.

"It's not." He places a kiss on my neck. "People go through trials and tribulations, but we'll be okay. We can get through this because we have each other to lean on. It fucking killed me for you to think I blamed you for losing our baby. I was hurt. Upset. Expressing my emotions isn't something I excel at." He chuckles. "Those words came from Lauren, not me."

"That makes two of us."

I drop my head back on his shoulder to see him, and my body relaxes when he kisses away the tears hitting my cheeks.

"How about we start the night over?" he asks. "Let's act like your douche bag of an ex with bangs longer than yours didn't come here."

I reach up to circle my hand around his neck and bring him down for a kiss. "You have no idea how great that sounds."

I planned on telling him we needed to stick to being friends tonight, but that's all changed. Brett slapped some reality into me. I could turn my back on Dallas and have to deal with more men like Brett because I'm too scared to get close to someone capable of love, or I could spend my time with a man who has a heart.

Things might not work out with us.

Things might go wrong.

But being with him feels much better than being alone.

We stay on the couch and talk about everything that's happened since we last saw each other. Maven is feeling better and is back to her usual self. She's been asking hundreds of questions about where I am.

.

Dallas tucks me into bed and turns around to leave.

"Are you not staying the night?" I ask, disappointed.

He smiles. "Hell yes, I am. But I need to get rid of those ugly-ass flowers first."

I can't help but laugh. I needed that.

He comes back with an even brighter smile on his face, and I arch my brows in question.

"You baked me cookies," he states.

"Tried to." I frown. "They're a little burned."

"You do like me."

We spend the rest of the night eating burned cookies in bed.

"MAVEN MISSES YOU," he whispers in my ear.

It's morning, and the faint ray of sunlight peeks through the windows as we lie in bed. My hand is in his. My legs are a wild mess across his. It feels good to have him back here.

I shut my eyes. "I miss her. Tell her I'll be seeing her soon." His hand tightens around mine, and I sigh. "So, this is what grief feels like."

No wonder Dallas was so miserable when Lucy died. This pain is what he was feeling. This void in my heart is what he was going through.

"Losing someone isn't fun." His breathing slows. "I just wish we could've met him even if it was for only a minute."

His eyes are on me when I shift to rest my chin on his warm chest and smile up at him. I sag against his body when his arms wrap around my back, and he settles me next to him, his fingers tracing my spine.

"Him?" I ask.

He chuckles. "Is it bad I was convinced we were having a boy?"

I can feel his thick breathing when I stroke his chest. "I was so convinced we were having a girl, I had a name picked out."

"Is it Daphne?" he asks, and I can feel his laughter through his chest. "She can hang out with Scooby, and they'll chase ghosts together."

An even bigger roar of laughter comes from his chest when I pinch his nipple. "No!" I follow his lead, feeling it coming from the bottom of my stomach, and damn, does it feel good for something other than pain to consume me. "Can I ask you for a favor though?"

He nods.

"Let's wait until we have the baby before choosing a name. I don't want to get my hopes up and then have something happen."

His arm tightens around me. "Nothing will happen."

I reach up and run my fingers over the stubble on his cheeks. "Just in case."

"We'll wait. And, when you have our baby and it's a girl, we'll go with the name you choose. If it's a boy, we'll go with mine."

I smile. "I like that idea."

"Now, can I ask you a favor? You don't have to answer right away. Think about it and get back with me when you decide."

Damn it. Him and his favors.

"What?"

Sincerity takes over his features. "Consider moving in with me. I'll do anything to make you comfortable there. Sleep on the couch. Crash in the basement. Sleep in my truck if I have to."

"It didn't end well the last time I was at your house. I feel like too much of an outsider."

"I'll make things right. Make you happy there. Give me a chance."

I slowly nod. "I'll think about it."

"And ..." he draws out. "Just one more serious question."

"What more can you want?" I ask, faking annoyance.

"Why did you name your cat Scooby? Letting you name our child worries me."

"My grandfather had a cat named Scooby. No one understood why, and he never told us." I narrow my eyes at him with a smile. "So, consider yourself lucky to hear my reason."

"And what would that be?"

"Because my grandfather named his Scooby."

He nods. "Let's keep the cartoon names to our animals."

CHAPTER THIRTY-NINE

Dallas

I REMEMBER the day I told Maven that Lucy had died.

I sat her down and broke the news, and she didn't take it well. For weeks, she cried and lashed out. Trying to explain death to a six-year-old isn't easy. All I could tell her was that Mommy had gone to heaven, but she took that as Mommy had left because she was mad at her. We went to counseling with our preacher. I stayed at home for days, built pillow forts, and had tea parties with stuffed animals.

Telling her about losing one of the babies terrified me, thinking that she'd revert to that sadness. We'd lost too many people. Gone through too much hell. Maven had started suggesting names from her favorite books. Everyone we passed on the street, at the grocery store, at her preschool had heard her boast and brag about how she was going to be a big sister.

I took advice from my family and set her down last night. As badly as I wanted Willow at my side, she'd been through enough. Maven cried but is more understanding of death now. She said her mommy was taking care of the baby in heaven.

It's been a week since I asked Willow to move in. She hasn't brought it up again, and I know what I need to do before she does. And today of all days is when I decide I have to do something that will hurt me.

I didn't want to get out of bed today, but I had to pull my shit together and do it.

Today is a day I used to celebrate. Now, it's a day of darkness. My mom offered to watch Maven before I even told her my plans.

I take the drive I haven't made in a few weeks. I haven't told her the news, I've been afraid to tell her, but I can't be anymore.

I sit down in front of her gravestone and place the pink tulips, her favorite flower, in front of it.

"Hey, Lucy-Pie," I whisper. "Happy birthday." I chuckle, sitting back. "Big thirty-two."

I sigh. "I know I haven't been here in a while. I'm sorry. And I know you like me to be honest, so that's what I'm going to give you. I've been consumed with guilt, feeling like a trader, a bad husband, like you'd be disappointed in me. It was a dumbass thought because I know your heart. You'd probably want to slap me right now and tell me to get it together. You'd lead the way for me when I didn't know which way to turn. Tough love is what you called it."

My eyes water. "I'm having a baby. We were supposed to have two, but we lost one. It was like going through hell again. Maven wants you to watch over her baby brother or sister. Can you do that for us?"

The sun beats down on me, and a tear falls down my cheek. "I lost the baby like I lost you, and I was so mad. So damn mad. I felt sorry for myself. I was pissed at everyone … at everything. But my anger and fear is only going to make me keep losing people."

I sigh and slip my wedding ring off my finger. I stare at it one last time before digging a small hole in the dirt with my fingers. My hands shake while I bury it next to the tulips. "I realize now why you made me promise. I had no problem promising to be a good father, and that's what I'll do to both of my children. I reluctantly promised to find love again, and I hope you'll be proud of me when I say I have." I tell her about Willow, about our babies, about how excited Maven is to become a big sister.

I wipe my nose. "And, while you're up there, will you give our baby a hug for us?"

I won't forget about Lucy.

I won't try to replace her.

But I will let myself move on.

CHAPTER FORTY

Dallas

IT'S BEEN a month since we lost the baby.

A long and gruesome month.

There hasn't been a day that's gone by that I haven't gone over the things I should've done differently to stop the miscarriage from happening. I've read article after article and talked to Aidan about it at every appointment.

So, I've been doing everything I can to take it easy, attempting to stay on bed rest, like the doctor suggested, but I'm going stir-crazy.

The uncertainty of another miscarriage has been the only thing on my mind.

Dallas hasn't brought up his offer for me to move in with him. I don't know if it's been retracted or if he's scared of the rejection.

Stella insisted I do most of my work from home, and when I do visit her on set, she practically caters to me like I'm her boss. Lauren stops by before every shift. Rory and my mom regularly check in with me, and Dallas and Maven are here nearly every day.

Lauren is right. Having a good support system helps.

I sit on the couch and stare at the doorway to the nursery.

Something I do every day. I haven't been back in it since I lost the baby. Dallas keeps asking if he can put the crib together or start painting, but I can't bring myself to say yes.

It's not that I don't want this baby to have a nice nursery.

It's that I'm terrified I might lose this baby, too.

The front door opens, and Maven comes running into the living room. Dallas is behind her with a bag of takeout.

Her smile beams when it lands on me. "Can I ask her now, Daddy? Can I *pleeease* ask her now? I can't wait any longer!"

I tried to stop it, Dallas mouths to me.

She plops down next to me on the couch, and I play with her hair.

"Ask me what?"

"Um …" She opens her mouth but chickens out and slams it shut.

Well, that's new.

She whips around to look at Dallas. "Will you do it for me, Daddy? You say it much better."

He slowly nods, and I know what he's about to ask isn't going to be easy on me.

"Maven will be starting kindergarten soon. Tomorrow is Parents' Night."

"Will you please come with me?" Maven chimes in. Her spunk is back. "Pretty, pretty please? It'll be *so, so* much fun. They'll have snacks, and you get to meet my teacher! I'm going to big-kid school!"

I don't know if Maven told him she'd asked me to be her new mommy, but he hasn't mentioned it. And I don't plan to tell him. That's a secret between the two of us.

Dallas leans back against the wall and fights a smile on his lips. "There was no way I was going to stop her from asking you. You know she doesn't take no for an answer very well. Plus, I could use the company."

"Please," Maven continues to plead. "Everyone else is going to have their mommy there."

The air leaves the room.

"Maven," Dallas says, his voice almost sounding shaky, "you know Willow isn't your mom."

"I know, *but* she'd be a good second mommy." She closes her eyes in sadness. "She doesn't even have to be my new mommy. I just want her there, so I won't feel left out."

Dallas rubs his hands over his face. "I'm sorry. I wasn't expecting all that."

I wave off his answer, seeing the hurt on Maven's face, recognition hitting me. I was the girl without a father at everything. I understand her hurt, the pain she's going through.

"Maven, I'd love to go," I answer, shocking myself and Dallas.

She springs off the couch. "I told you she'd say yes, Daddy!" She wraps her short arms around me and jumps up and down.

My heart warms. I'm doing the right thing. Going to her Parents' Night will help me just as much as her.

WE DEVOURED OUR DINNER, and Maven fell asleep on the couch while watching cartoons.

"Want to talk?" Dallas asks.

I'm not reluctant this time. I'm not going to blow him off. I lead him to the kitchen.

He blurts out his apology as soon as we sit down. "I don't know where the hell the mommy thing came from. I'll break the news to Maven and tell her you had something come up."

"I'm going," is all I reply, but so much is said in those words.

"You don't have to do it if you don't feel comfortable. You looked like she'd asked for a kidney."

"It surprised me, is all. I want to go. I know what the need feels like to have two parents at functions because I was the little girl whose father never showed up. It was heartbreaking, and if me doing something as small as showing up makes that little girl feel better, I'll be there."

He leans forward and presses his lips to mine. "Thank you. You have no idea how much this means to me."

"YOU'RE GOING to love my school!" Maven squeals when we pull into the parking lot of the elementary school.

I run a hand down my stomach. No more hiding the baby bump. No more hiding my affection for Dallas and his little girl.

Maven's class is small, and we take a table in the back. Parents fill the room, greeting each other and spewing off question after question.

Everyone knows everybody.

Except for me.

But that doesn't mean they don't know *of* me.

"Oh, you're that actress girl's friend, right?"

"So, Dallas, this is the woman you've been spending all your time with?"

"I heard about what happened at the birthday party. That sounds so tragic to have the news come out like that."

If they're not asking ridiculous questions, they're staring.

There are a few exceptions though. Not everyone is nosy and rude. A few have introduced themselves without fishing for gossip, and they seemed genuine.

Dallas took Maven up to select her cubby, and my body tenses when someone sits down next to me.

"I was hoping you'd come," Beth says in a soft voice. "My daughter and Maven are in the same class this year. They're going to have a blast together." She smiles. "This is the first time I've seen you since you picked her up from preschool, so I haven't had the chance to congratulate you on the baby, and give my condolences on your miscarriage."

I flinch.

"I hope you don't mind that Maven told me, but I promise, your business is not mine to tell."

"Thank you," I whisper.

"How far along are you?"

This isn't an interrogation. She's not asking me this question out of spite. There is not a doubt in my mind that she's truly happy I'm having this baby.

"About five months," I answer, giving her a smile back.

"I remember the anticipation as the date gets closer. You're nervous the baby is going to come anytime."

I smile and nod. *I'm more nervous of losing my baby.*

Our attention is caught at the sound of Maven laughing. Dallas is down on one knee, helping her decorate her cubby with stickers and stuffed animals.

Beth tilts her head toward them. "He's a good man. A broken one, yes, but still a good one."

"He's been a good friend to me."

"Just a friend?"

I shrug. "Our situation is … complicated."

She pats my shoulder. "I hope I'm not overstepping my boundaries here, but there's something I want to give you." She opens her purse, and I notice the water in her eyes as she places a folded piece of paper in my hand. "My sister wrote this before she passed and asked me to give it to the woman Dallas fell in love with." She closes her hand around mine as a tear passes down her cheek.

I jerk it back to her. "You're mistaken. Dallas isn't in love with me."

"Read it. It'll help you understand how he loves you."

I DON'T MENTION the letter to Dallas.

I keep it tucked in my pocket and constantly check to make sure it hasn't fallen out all evening. The meeting doesn't last much longer after Beth leaves, and Dallas and Maven convince me to go out for dessert before going home.

Other than doctor's appointments, which Aidan started sneaking us through the back door for, this is my first time stepping out with Dallas since the miscarriage. I've been so terrified of getting judged, of people staring, of hearing vicious things coming out of their mouths, but I'm done with that now.

Tonight has made me feel comfortable.

Tonight hasn't made me feel like such an outsider.

Maven doesn't hesitate in unbuckling her seat belt when Dallas pulls up to my apartment. They've been here more than their house lately. She heads straight to the couch and drags out the crayons and coloring books I leave for her in the coffee table drawer. Her tongue sticks out as she colors, and Dallas makes each of us a cup of tea.

We watch a movie until she falls asleep with a crayon still in her hand. He kisses me good-bye, and they leave. I'm picking up the mess when I remember the letter. I take a deep breath, not knowing what I'm getting myself into, and lie back on the couch before opening it.

To the lucky woman who reads this.

Hello,

My name is Lucy. I'm sure you've heard about me. Possibly seen my pictures, my belongings, traces of me in the home we shared. You might've even known me.

I was Dallas's wife. And, since you're reading this, I'm no longer here.

Dallas is a difficult man. Always has been. He'll be even more difficult after my death, but please don't give up on him. If he's opened up his heart enough for you to receive this letter, you have something extraordinary. Receiving this letter means he's in love with you. I'm sure he's fighting it because he wouldn't be a Barnes boy if he didn't fight the reality that's right in front of him.

Watch his actions. Those are what speak his love. He's not the best at words, but the more you let him in, the more he opens up for you.

Don't be afraid. We've all had other loves. Don't think he can only have one because you've proven that wrong.

Please don't give up on him because he won't give up on you. When you make your way into his heart, he'll fight to keep you there. He's the strongest man I've ever known.

Thank you for loving my family and give Maven a kiss for me.

Lucy

I'm in tears when I finish, and I hold the letter to my heart.

CHAPTER FORTY-ONE

Dallas

WILLOW: **We need to talk.**

Her text isn't the only thing that worries me. She sent it at three this morning. The early hours of the morning are when your brain is working the hardest, going over important choices, the shit you want to forget but can't.

Is this a good or bad we need to talk?

Should I be heading to the airport?

After I drop Maven off at school, I call Hudson and let him know I'll be late today, and then I drive straight to Willow's apartment. Fingers crossed it's not empty when I get there.

I take the stairs three at a time and find her sitting on the couch. My chest gets heavy when I notice the moving boxes scattered everywhere. Some flat, some put together, some taped up with scribbled words on them.

She nervously glances back at me while I trudge across the room. I don't take my eyes off her–like it's the last time I'll get to see her. Her naturally plump lips that fit perfectly around my cock are puckered as she watches me. The hair I love twirling my fingers around is down in loose curls. The woman I've fallen in love with is going to walk away with the remaining pieces of what's left of me.

"Hey," she says. "You never texted me back. I wasn't sure if you got my message."

Why? Was she trying to get out of here before I showed up?

I snatch a half-filled box and dump out the contents. I need physical evidence that my life is going to change. That I'll be going back to the miserable asshole I was before she took me over.

"What the hell?" Willow screams, sliding off the couch in frustration.

I scowl at the items on the floor. Clothes. Shoes. My eyes zero in on the shoes she left at my house that night. Her gaze goes to me, then to the pile on the floor, and back to me.

Where did this sudden change come from?

We spend all of our free time together, and from what I believe, we've been enjoying it. No arguments have occurred. Every prenatal appointment has gone well.

What happened? Where did it go wrong?

"You going somewhere?" I ask.

Her brows scrunch together. "The moving boxes give it away?"

"Sure did." I struggle to keep my voice calm.

Stress is bad for the baby. We can't risk another miscarriage. I won't argue. Won't fight it. She's calling the shots. I'll move if that's what she wants, get a job bussing tables in LA if I have to, turn my life upside down to keep her.

Her head cocks to the side. "I thought this was what you wanted?"

I grit my teeth. "That's never what I wanted. Not once have I told you to pack up and ditch us. Just so you know, what you're doing is going to leave my daughter and me broken. Do you understand? You're not supposed to turn your back on us because we fell in love with you. I fell in love with you." I shake my head, my voice breaking. "And we don't want another person we love to leave us."

She blows out a breath and smiles.

The fuck?

"Did you bump your head? These boxes are for me to move in *with you*."

Her answer melts the burden off my chest. "What did you say?"

"I said, I've been packing my stuff because I'm accepting the offer of moving in with you, dipshit."

Damn, does my girl have a mouth on her.

Stupidity rails through me. So much time has passed since I asked her to move in, I figured it wasn't an option.

She's staying. Halle-fucking-lujah.

I crack a smile while she blankly stares at me.

"So, now that you know I'm not leaving your ass, promise me you won't do that anymore," she says, her tone turning emotionless. "If you want me to move in with you, you can't go around, saying things you don't mean."

I cock my head and stare at her in confusion. "What don't I mean?"

"That you love me." She throws her hands down to her sides. "We get along great, the baby will have two parents, but don't get my hopes up. I've made my mind up to move in, so you don't have to lie to me."

Oh, shit.

The L-word hasn't left my mouth again since we lost the baby. In fear of her running away, I've stopped myself every time. Now, my dumbass has blurted it out and ruined any chance of her moving in with me.

I draw nearer before she kicks me out, and I walk her back until her back hits a wall. I press a hand to her cheek, and hers wrap around my neck, massaging the built-up tension. I look down, searching for eye contact, but she's not giving it.

"Look at me," I whisper. My voice turns raw. Raspy. My breathing falters when she does. "I'd be lying if I said I didn't love you."

I didn't bring her home with me that night, expecting to fall in love. I never thought that having surprise babies, going on road trips, getting stranded, and then surviving a miscarriage would bring so many emotions out of me. That it would warm my cold heart. That'd it bring me closer to her.

She's managed to do that.

She makes me want to be a better man.

A man who believes in love again because he's in love with her.

She's a strong woman with a heart of gold, who brought a flashlight in my darkness to show me the way to happiness when I was fighting not to find an exit.

I won't lose her.

"Tell me you feel it, too," I say.

Worry is evident on her face. The hesitation tells me she's insecure about getting hurt again if she says it. My pulse quickens. The same feeling is driving through her. She wouldn't have agreed to move in if it wasn't.

"I'm scared of feeling it," she finally replies. "I'm scared that loving you is reaching for something that'll never be mine. A lifeline I can't reach because you're in love with someone else."

I look down at her, unblinking. "I'll always be your lifeline. You'll always be able to reach me because you have my heart. No matter what you're going through, I'll be at your side, helping you hold on."

Tears fill her eyes. "You can't love me like you loved her."

"You're right. The way I love you is different than the way I loved her. I've fallen in love with you in different ways, for different reasons, than I did with Lucy. I've fallen in love with finding love, learning your tics, how to make you smile, hearing your fears, and getting to know the deepest parts of your soul. I loved Lucy. I'll never stop loving the memory of her, but I can love you right along with it."

I grew up with Lucy. I loved her for as long as I can remember, but I don't remember *falling* in love with her because

I knew everything about her. This is something new to me. A different love but still love. You don't love the same every time.

I squeeze Willow's hips and hope my next question isn't pushing the limit. "You ready to admit you love me yet?"

She shakes her head.

"Then, why are you crying?"

"Hormones," she croaks out. "Fucking hormones."

"You can blame it on that for now." My mouth finds hers, giving her a long kiss, before pulling away and pecking the tip of her nose. "But I'll be asking again later."

"What are you doing?" she asks when I move across the room and pick up a box.

"Helping you pack your shit. You can keep the apartment for as long as you want, but I'm going to take as much time with you under my roof as I can get."

CHAPTER FORTY-TWO

Willow

DALLAS AND HUDSON are moving the few boxes I packed for my trial run at Dallas's.

I'm doing this.

Really doing this.

I stop on the porch before walking through the front door. I jumped down these stairs, barefoot, with tears running down my face. I stare at the door, remembering my last look of Dallas that day. *Let's hope history doesn't repeat itself.*

I haven't been back in the house since Maven was sick. Maybe I should've taken a tour, made sure I was emotionally stable to handle more than three hours here.

I'm going to walk in there, be strong, and do what's right for my heart.

For my baby. For *us.*

The excitement of spending more time with him and Maven is what keeps me walking. I love spending time with them. I'd go to bed, wishing Dallas were there to hold me, to kiss me, to share the moment when the baby kicked.

Dallas is still a man who struggles, but that only makes me fall more in love with him. Lucy's note sparked something inside me, an insight I never thought about when I shut myself down after considering a future with him. Dallas might be a little broken, but he knows what love is. He sacrifices for love, for his family—something Brett never did with me.

I'd rather have a broken man who knows how to love than a man with no scars who's never loved anyone but himself.

Dallas squeezes my elbow when I walk through the front door. "If you're not cool with this, let me know, okay? I'll call a realtor, and we can look for another property."

I stare at him, unblinking. "Are you talking about buying a new house?"

He practically built this house with his own two hands. He loves this home.

"If that's what makes you comfortable." He slides in closer and gently pushes a fallen strand of hair from my ponytail out of my eyes. His hands then rest on my hips. "This is your home now, do you hear me? *Our* home. I want you to be able to relax, to be able to touch me, to feel okay with having sex with me here." He chuckles. "Because we know that's going to be happening a lot as soon as our little one is born."

I smile. "You have no idea how much I've missed that." Especially with him. It's hard to go from having sex with fuck boys to Dallas and then being told you're on bed rest and that you need to refrain from sex. It's like tasting an expensive cupcake for the first time after years of eating cheap candy, and then it gets taken away from you.

His hand moves down to brush between my legs. "I might not be able to fuck you yet, but I promise I'll do something for you tonight."

I rest my hand on his chest. "I have something to look forward to."

"You most certainly do."

"All right, kids, take it to the bedroom," Hudson says, walking in. "And, speaking of bedroom, is that where you want me to put this stuff?"

I take my time while Dallas waits for an answer. "Yeah," I stutter out. "Sure."

I follow them down the hallway and into the bedroom, not sure if I'm truly ready for this. I take in a heavy breath and wait for the blow of bad memories and heartache to hit me, but nothing does when I walk in.

The furniture and bedding is new. I try not to make it too obvious that I'm searching for the signs of Lucy I saw last time I was in here, but they are now missing. The perfume bottle, the pictures, the clothes—it's all gone.

Hudson sets the box down on the floor and leaves the room.

"You got rid of her stuff?" I ask Dallas, guilt seeping through me. Forcing his hand to do this wasn't what I wanted. "I swear, my intentions weren't for you to erase her."

"I didn't erase her."

He holds his hand to his heart while mine pounds. He's no longer wearing his wedding ring. Hasn't been for a few weeks, but I haven't questioned him about it. I wasn't sure if he did it to make me happy, or because he wanted to for himself.

Now I know it's because he wanted to.

"No matter what, Lucy will always have a spot in my heart," he goes on.

I nod. I don't want him to lose that either.

"It was time I did it. I can't keep living in the past, especially when it was destroying my happy future. It was hell, don't get me wrong, pushing myself to do something I should've done months ago. I waited until I was ready, so thank you for giving me time to do that. I went through everything with Maven. She chose the stuff she wanted to keep, and then Lucy's family came over for their own keepsakes."

I sit down on the bed and trace my fingers over the new white bedspread. "Just don't kick me out of this bed, okay?"

He smirks. "Sweetheart, the only reason I'd kick you out of this bed is to fuck you on the floor."

I stand up to wrap my arms around his neck. He did all of

this for me. Opened his heart back up for me. He wants to make a home with me and have a family together because he loves me.

I love him.

I'm tired of running from it. Tired of fighting. I have to be strong and honest for our baby, for ourselves, for the six-year-old girl who made me a *Welcome Home* sign, which is displayed on the front door.

"I love you," I whisper into his mouth.

"There it is." He grins. "And I love you."

CHAPTER FORTY-THREE

Dallas

FOUR MONTHS LATER

THE EAR-BLASTING cry is music to my ears.

A sound I was afraid I wouldn't hear. I put the sadness that there should be two in the back of my mind. I won't let that loss interfere with the bliss of this moment.

No surprise to me, Willow was a fucking trooper. She spent ten hours in labor and didn't complain once. All that was on her mind was the excitement of meeting our baby mixed with worry that it might not happen. I stayed by her side the entire time, not moving once, because I didn't want to miss a thing. She needed to know I was with her on this all the way.

Our life has turned into a whirlwind of changes. Willow has moved in, but nothing has changed in the Barnes' household. It feels like she's been there forever. I was anxious at the beginning, given our history there, but losing our baby has taught us to cherish every moment.

Fuck the petty shit.

Fuck running.

Fuck being afraid.

His wails calm when Aidan hands him, wrapped in his blanket, to Willow. My breathing halts when she situates him in her arms, already comfortable with how he likes to be cradled, and she plays with his tiny hand while whispering to him.

I stare at them with compassion. With happiness. With love.

As much as I want to have my turn, I wait until she's ready. She deserves this.

My heart thrashes against my chest when she stares up at me with wet eyes. She moves her arm, shifting toward me, and I waste no time in scooping him up. He's perfect—from his full head of dark hair to his button nose—and he's squirming like a fish out of water.

I'm ready to take him home. To show him the nursery we've been working on for months. To give him love every day.

Aidan heard a heartbeat during every ultrasound, but the thought of losing our baby still hung over our heads daily.

The chance of another miscarriage was high. There could have been problems at birth.

Those burdens have fallen off me. That worry is gone. He's here, healthy, and staring up at me with sleepy, dark eyes that resemble Maven's.

He owns my heart already.

It's been a rough journey, but like our road trips, we've seemed to make them enjoyable, memorable, crazy. Our turns and detours made us stronger, made us love deeper, made us appreciate each day.

We name him Samuel.

After my grandfather.

Willow and Maven love his name just as much as I do.

Samuel Logan Barnes.

Eight pounds and four ounces of fucking adorableness.

My son. My new sidekick. More happiness brought into a life I thought was over.

I didn't know what I was going to get when we walked into the hospital this morning. My heart surged with fear with every step I took. Bad news had been a constant for me here. I'd experienced so many losses within these walls.

That ended today.

This place will no longer be a reminder of loss.

I lost people I loved here.

And I've gained someone I love just as much.

CHAPTER FORTY-FOUR

Willow

I AM A MOTHER.

I whisper those words to myself again. *I am a mother.*

This job, this role, means more to me than any I've ever had.

I tried to stay positive before Samuel was born, but it was hard because the doctor telling me there was a chance I'd never be able to hold him was a constant worry.

"Jesus, someone had better give me some Tylenol to cure this baby fever," Stella says while rocking Samuel back and forth, cooing.

Our friends and family have piled into the room, all of their attention on Samuel.

Samuel. I've only known him a few hours, but he already has my heart gripped in his tiny fingers.

My mom flew in a few days ago and has been staying in my apartment along with Scooby. She's fallen in love with Dallas and Maven, and we're already in talks of her moving here. I've caught the Blue Beech initiation bug.

Samuel has taken his first selfie and had his first diaper changed by me, and people rock-paper-scissored over who got to hold him first.

Hudson throws his hands up. "I'm all for making a baby. Tell me when and where, babe." He slaps Dallas on the back. "Congrats, big brother. You might be one ugly dude, but you make some cute kids."

Dallas laughs and punches him in the arm.

That gorgeous smile hasn't left his face since I handed him Samuel for the first time. Stella gives Samuel back to him as the baby-holding circle starts again from the top.

Dallas cradles him and rocks from side to side. "That's my boy."

Maven tugs at his shirt. "And my little brother!" she announces. "I'm a big sister now!"

We've had to nearly pry Samuel from her arms every time she's held him. She made a list of requests, and the top one was him sleeping in her bed. There's some explaining to do when we get home. Samuel can't be thrown into strollers and tossed on the floor after changing his diapers, like she does with her toy babies.

I'm exhausted by the time the room clears out, and Dallas is sitting on the edge of my bed. He gently climbs in next to me and laces our fingers together.

I close my eyes and sigh when his lips hit mine.

"We did it," he says. "We made a healthy baby."

I lean up for another kiss, making it last longer, and hold my hand against his cheek. "We did it." I stretch my legs out and drum my fingers along his skin. "A year ago, this is so not where I thought I'd be."

He chuckles. "Oh, sweetheart, it's a hell of a lot better than where I imagined I'd be." He situates himself to look at me better. "You saved me, Willow. You saved my daughter. And not only did you save us, but you also gave us Samuel as a bonus. I've been lifted from fires I never thought I'd escape because of you." He disconnects our hands to circle his around my wrist. "And, someday, you're going to let me put a ring on this finger." His lips graze my ring finger.

"Oh, man, did we go backward on that one," I tease. "First does not always come marriage."

"We do our own thing at our own pace."

"That we do."

EPILOGUE

Willow

TWO MONTHS LATER

I STRETCH out in the sheets and yawn when Dallas comes walking back into the bedroom with Samuel in his arms. I watch the silhouette of him with the help of the sunrise creeping into the morning sky. He's shirtless, wearing only a pair of loose gym shorts, and I lick my lips when he climbs back into bed.

"Dirty diaper," he explains with a grin. He pokes Samuel's belly. "You know our little man can't handle a dirty diaper."

Dallas is the only man … hell, the only person I know who enjoys changing diapers.

"Thank you," I whisper.

We agreed to take turns in getting up with him at night, but that hasn't happened. Dallas is a lighter sleeper and never wakes me up when it's my turn. He does whatever Samuel needs and comes back to bed without uttering one complaint.

Moving in with him was the right decision. My initial worry that it'd hurt our relationship is gone. It's only fueled more attraction and love between us.

Our bond is tighter, our love stronger.

"Daddy?"

Maven's voice catches me off guard. She's standing in the doorway with her blankie. Dallas or Samuel must've woken her up. She rubs her eyes and sluggishly stomps into the room. I scoot over and pat the space between Dallas and me, and she climbs right in. I smile when her head rests on my shoulder, and she snuggles into my body.

The cartoons come on.

We eat breakfast in bed.

This is my family.

One night changed my life.

One night gave me life.

KEEP UP WITH THE BLUE BEECH SERIES

All books can be read as standalones

Just A Fling
(Hudson and Stella's story)
Just One Night
(Dallas and Willow's story)
Just Exes
(Gage and Lauren's story)
Just Neighbors
(Kyle and Chloe's story)
Just Roommates
(Maliki and Sierra's story)
Just Friends
(Rex and Carolina's story)

Blue Beech Second Generation
Only Rivals
Only Coworkers

OTHER BOOKS BY CHARITY

BLUE BEECH SERIES

(each book can be read as a standalone)

Just A Fling

Just One Night

Just Exes

Just Neighbors

Just Roommates

Just Friends

TWISTED FOX SERIES

Stirred

Shaken

Straight Up

Chaser

Last Round

STANDALONES

Bad For You

Beneath Our Faults

Pop Rock

Pretty and Reckless

Revive Me

Wild Thoughts

RISKY DUET

Risky

Worth The Risk

ACKNOWLEDGMENTS

Writing can make you look selfish at times. It can make you feel selfish at times. When you're caught up in your story, it leaves only a small amount of time to spend with family and friends. Thank you to those who understand this. Thank you to those who don't get angry at me for this.

My Other Half, this is where I usually say something along the lines of, *"thank you for understanding when I don't cook dinner and we order pizza or get takeout,"* but who am I kidding? Writing or not, we both know my ass still wouldn't be in the kitchen making dinner. You get me, and there's no better feeling in the world to be around someone who gets you.

Jovana Shirley, thank you for helping me create a stronger story for Dallas and Willow.

Bloggers, thank you times a million. You do so much for so little. You are our biggest cheerleaders. Every post , every shout out, every picture is so much appreciated.

Readers, I wish I could give all of you a giant thank you hug. There are millions of books out there, and you chose to read mine. You have no idea how incredibly grateful I am for each and every one of you. *xoxo, Charity*

ABOUT THE AUTHOR

Charity Ferrell is a Wall Street Journal and USA Today bestselling author. She resides in Indianapolis, Indiana with her boyfriend and two fur babies. Her passion is writing about broken people finding love while adding a dash of humor and heartbreak. Angst is her happy place.

When she's not writing, she's on a Starbucks run, shopping online, or spending time with her family.

www.charityferrell.com